MAHiA
NOVOTNA

MIKE SCHIRN

First Published in Great Britain in 2024

Copyright © 2024 Mike Schirn

978-1-7385752-0-6 (hardback)
978-1-7385752-1-3 (paperback)
978-1-7385752-2-0 (epub)

Cover Design by Creative Covers
Typesetting by Book Polishers

FOR HANNAH

For your patience

For your forgiveness

God loves you far more than you will ever know.

Other works by the author.

Maria Novotna. Novel

The Body Language of Cars. Novel

An American in Paradise. Play

Where Love has Gone. Play

The King and Me. Play

Why I'm Late. Short stories and monologues.

The proceeds of this book, are to be used for the benefit of Ukrainian charities in aid of war victims.

This publication has been founded for the purpose of providing a small voice on behalf of those often overlooked in the complex and success driven culture of our age. To examine what makes the unexceptional exceptional and to entertain.

ON MY WAY TO
SOMEWHERE ELSE

It was while I was on my way to somewhere else that I missed you.
Were you the one whose hand I was meant to squeeze and hug for
joy and confess my most intimate thoughts, tease and say where you
have been.

On my day to somewhere else I thought I caught a glimpse of you
listening to me singing loudly while playing the fool, and praying
that you loved me. But I looked again and you were gone. Down
the long corridor where the echoes of time and children were now
forlorn hope. Never to say come play with me and take me to
discover the sea, and tumble on the blissful downs to unwind
beneath the summer sky.

It was while I was on my way to somewhere else distracted by the
rootless path that filled my head and robbed my heart that I missed
the road on which you stood. Waiting in that space no other could,
to capture the fragments of my incomplete self and make it whole,
and so make sense of the sun, and sense of my soul.

So shine and shine in my summer once more and wave and dance as
if we met on loves green shore. For, as long as memory lives. Hope
not realised never forgives, and like a child I ask god once more to
explain. How can a heart so unfulfilled remain.

'By conventional standards she wasn't beautiful.
But then she wasn't conventional.
She considered her mouth too big,
and her height made her feel self conscious,
and what went on behind the eyes was a voyage of discovery
enlivened by an intelligent and interesting polemic.'

1.

It was hardly fair to audition for a competition in which she would automatically win, but her mother assured her it was a minor irritation. The organisers were seeking musically gifted children in her home town of Kyiv, and Maria appeared uniquely qualified. She was eight years old, and exalted by friends and family alike. She had even performed a Chopin Etude for a local radio broadcast. The performance itself lasted a little over two minutes, but with her flair for composition, and engaging manner, her mother declared she was Ukraine's answer to Clara Schumann, who Maria assumed to be a distant aunt.

On the day of the audition, Maria felt supremely confident in her new cotton dress, as she joined a multitude of mini-maestros and pre-pubescent pianists, busily discussing tips to win the judges approval.

'While you are playing, hold your head in the air, as if you smell rotten eggs. It gives the impression you're a seasoned professional,' advised one candidate.

Another said,

'If you make a mistake, smile for all your worth. It demonstrates confidence!'

Maria had been practising for weeks, and her teacher assured her she would make a great impression, and that the experience would add to her growing list of achievements. Even so, well over an hour passed, and still not one candidate had been invited to play. The girl in front monotonously hummed, the person behind kicked the bottom of her chair, and the boy beside her placed his bow-tie in his mouth, and began chewing it. When the contestants were eventually invited to perform, a name was announced, and the candidate led away to a large hall. Shortly after, another name was called, then another. In all, over a dozen hopefuls came and went, yet no one who had auditioned returned looking triumphant. One reported they had been told to stop playing, whilst another was asked if he could play something else…

'Instead of the Nocturne?' enquired the parent.

'Instead of the piano!' sobbed the candidate.

The criticism of each performer appeared to get progressively worse, emerging from their ordeal either confused or tearful, and seeking the consoling words of a loved one. As a result, tension in the room mounted, and Maria's confidence plummeted. Her legs now felt like jelly, and the minor imperfections in her playing had now grown into self doubt the size of a Colossus that threatened to devour her. She had even begun to forget the music itself. Feeling unwell, she pleaded to return home, but her mother counselled,

'Just pretend you are entertaining friends at a Christmas party, and remember to smile!'

Suddenly, Maria's name was called, and she nervously made her way towards the hall. As she entered, a lone voice boomed from behind a dimly lit table at the back, and ordered her to climb several steps onto a vast platform, and make her way to the grand piano. The piano itself was bathed in a light that shone from a spotlight so bright, she could hardly see the music, as she placed it on the rack. After adjusting the seat, she was ordered to begin, and placed her hands just above the keys. Unnerved, her hands began to shake, along with the rest of her, and her fingers felt as if they had been encased in cement. Her heart beat furiously, and she began to panic. Again, she was commanded to begin, but all she could do was stare helplessly down at the unplayed octaves, within striking distance, terrified and unable to move.

Following a long, embarrassed silence, the adjudicator unexpectedly applauded.

'Bravo!, Ms Novotna, on your performance. It has given me a well-earned rest, and allowed me to contemplate Brahms' Lullaby and the lyrical playfulness of Mozart, without the inconvenience of having to hear you play them. No doubt your continued silence on the keyboard will be celebrated by music lovers the world over. Now, perhaps you would be so good as to delight me with an encore, and depart with the same flair for lethargy and indifference to the art of the pianoforte for which you are undoubtedly a virtuoso.'

His words had the effect of overriding her reserve, and ignited a determination and strength she never knew she possessed. Looking into the distance, she nodded her thanks for his advice, then straightening her back, and sticking out her chest, sat upright, and summoning all the courage she could muster, pointed her nose upwards, smiled as broadly as she knew how, and with the consummate skill of a professional, rewarded the adjudicator with the most rhapsodic and lyrically playful rendition of 'Jingle Bells' he was ever likely to hear.

This early episode of rebellion overcoming fear came to mind, as Maria entered the academy, on her way to Popov's studio, eager to discover if she had been selected as a soloist for the annual gala. She hadn't got very far, when the sound of a familiar piano sonata brought her steps to a premature halt. Its very familiarity, newly minted by exceptional insight and sensitivity. Heading towards the source of this musical revelation, she stood outside the room, and listened until the final bars had faded, before hurrying towards Popov's studio. On arrival, she contended the delay was entirely due to the pursuit of her musical education.

'Would you use that excuse attending a rehearsal with the Vienna Philharmonic?' Popov fumed. 'Obliging the maestro and a hundred and twenty musicians to sit around and debate the fat content of strudel, whilst awaiting your illustrious presence. Do you think your disrespect and ill-discipline would endear them to you? Or, more likely provoke them to educate your journey to the keyboard with a kick up the rear!'

'I heard Haydn's E Minor Sonata coming from the rehearsal studio,' said Maria, 'as joyous as a jig, and as light as soufflé.'

'That would be Dimitrov, who I hasten to add, is never late.'

'Then it's all your fault. If you hadn't taught him so well. I would never have bothered to listen.'

Popov's anger rarely lasted longer than a lesson, and could often be calmed by an exquisite passage of music. His serious musical mind was often in contrast to the liveliness of his humour, even though her indiscretion and unpredictability often brought them into conflict. In the final year of her studies, Maria had only a limited amount of time before she left the academy, and appearing as a soloist in the Gala could advance her chances of finding an agent. However, it wasn't the day to persuade Popov she was a cultured pearl rather than an uncut diamond. His was a mind that wasn't easily convinced by anything less than the raw energy of talent, solid technique, and an insight that persistently searched for meaning.

Like a ball of contained fire, he had an energy that through sheer force of personality imposed a formidable scrutiny of both the score and the person communicating the music. Originally from Zaporizhzhia, he was once a soloist with a growing reputation, but his career suffered from his opposition to Soviet rule. As a result, he had a reputation as an outsider, and many in the party condemned him as disloyal. Maria, on occasions, would glimpse the regret of someone who had been undervalued. His humour, though, would often undermine his ferocity, and the warmth and kindness in his eyes twinkled at the prospect of a prodigious instinct that could be instructed towards musical salvation. He also possessed hands capable of stretching an octave and a half effortlessly, and despite their size had an amazingly sensitive touch. His seniority also dictated the provision of a very large chair, universally referred to as the 'throne' by students. Positioned to observe, but not intimidate, a player, he would often demonstrate a section or phrase as a suggestion, but never an order.

He had lived in Odesa for more than thirty-five years, and had adopted it as his home. Located on the shores of the Black Sea, Odesa was one of the largest economic and cultural centres in Ukraine. For a start, its climate was kind, and its winters less severe than further West, and in spring its apricot trees, jacinth and lilacs brightened the city. Its beaches added to its popularity, and its Rococo Opera house, Philharmonic Hall and Museum of Modern Art gave it a European sensibility. The city was both economically and artistically vibrant. Even its Post Office and Railway Station were works of art. However, Ukraine's independence was hard fought, and the annexation of Crimea by Russia was an attempt to add a de-stabilising effect to Ukraine's sovereignty.

For now, Maria felt at peace with her surroundings, even though Popov had yet to declare he considered her ready to become a soloist. He had witnessed several exceptional talents emerge from the academy, and take their place on the world stage. She longed to join them. In the final analysis, diplomas were no substitute for experience, and she knew performing in public was the only real test. Her mind wandered back to the Haydn Sonata, and the revelation she had encountered that morning. More precisely, the extraordinary technique of Dimitrov. Often described as the 'prodigal peasant'. She discovered he had little formal education, and was raised on a farm outside Lviv. Popov had coached him from a young age, and he had entered the conservatoire as a teenager. Yet to Maria, he remained a mystery: tall, blond and androgynous. But most fascinating of all, wholly unsociable. A quality few possessed. Most in her year were either precocious, or had developed petty rivalries. The most enduring friendships often being forged between members of quartets, since they were collectively required to either shine or disband. Maria had formed a quartet of her own, and the collaboration had allowed her to thrive socially. The same could not be said of her solo efforts. She had played in several concerts, and auditioned for various agents, but slender, with auburn hair, and above-average height, that emphasised her legs, she attracted attention for all the wrong reasons. To gain more experience, she had secured a job at weekends, playing a selection of popular melodies and tedious 'hits' for an upmarket hotel close to Primorsky Boulevard. Unlike string players, who could secure employment with established orchestras, a classical pianist was required to build a reputation, before being entrusted with works that attracted a more discerning audience. Becoming a 'rising star' also required increasing engagements, and the odds so far did not appear favourable. Whenever she felt disheartened, she often headed for the refectory, and consulted Moiseiwitsch, a fellow student, whose unorthodox opinion and knowledge of the gossip grapevine she often sought.

'Become a Ukrainian Liberace' he suggested. 'Wear outrageous costumes, and decorate your ears with diamond candelabras. Then between a Chopin Waltz and 'chopsticks', be sure to mention your mother.'

'That would only appeal to people who hate music.'

'Insincere flattery is the sincerest form of insult to great art. In fact, it's an art in itself. So, ignore art, and concentrate on bad taste. It will always remain in fashion.'

Moiseiwitsch was fondly known as the 'Gypsy Jew' on account of his repertoire and playing agility, he was wafer thin, slightly built, and possessed the longest fingers she had ever seen on a violinist. What she appreciated most of all though was his candour.

'Tell me about Dimitrov,' Maria demanded.

'He has been hand reared by Popov and therefore still tender. A child of interminable parts. None of them ready to be consumed yet. So, not your type.'

'I heard him play the Haydn Sonata in E flat quite exquisitely.'

'Unfortunately, no one has managed to dig down far enough to discover the personality beneath his fingertips.'

'All the more reason for me to be intrigued then,' Maria insisted.

'My dear Maria. You are inexplicably drawn to incompatible companions. If you really want to know he very often uses an empty practice room after hours. However, if you feel tempted by adoption, I think you should know I have impeccable bedroom manners, and only snore during lectures on counterpoint.'

Maria was rarely tempted by flattery. By conventional standards she wasn't beautiful. But then she wasn't conventional. She considered her mouth too big, and her height made her feel self-conscious, her long auburn hair drew attention, and fell over her face in such a way she often had to part it like drapes. What went on behind the eyes was a voyage of discovery, enlivened by an intelligent and interesting polemic. Fond of exploiting an idea, rather than just accepting orthodox opinion, her playing was marked by clarity, each note precise, that gave it a distinctive quality, and her stage presence self-contained, without any affectation. Her Chopin wasn't showy, nor her playing of Beethoven heavy, and in the case of Bach, it was as if she weaved an intricate pattern of different shapes and colours onto a large quilt, and invited you to inspect the wonder of its inner beauty. Socially, she relished the challenge of disagreement, and nothing seemed to faze her, but underneath she felt insecure, and played host to a mass of contradictions. It was her intensity that made her distinct, however, it simmered just under the surface, waiting to be released, seeking a key that would unlock the creativity within. Her interest in Dimitrov, she told herself, was strictly musical. What she desired was to learn from a fellow musician with a refined instinct, that shone above the academic bar of the majority. Someone who knew how to unlock a deeper understanding of the technical and emotional content of the music. The thing that wasn't obvious. On more than one occasion, Popov had told her,

'If all you want to achieve is a mere rendering of the composition, you might as well study cookery. At least you'll eat. Technique simply allows you to play the piece. It's the insight and imagination that you add to the interpretation that makes you a true musician. And for the gifted few, a bringer of light.'

Was Dimitrov a 'bringer of light?' she wondered.

One morning, Maria arrived unusually early, and heard a series of bells coming from a nearby practice room. Drawing closer, she looked through the observation window, and recognised the slight figure with the shock of blond hair, sitting with his back to her. He was playing Liebestraum, rehearsing the same twenty or so bars of music. Sometimes playing with the right hand, using a light touch, sometimes simply playing the bass clef. At other times, playing the piece with syncopation, at others adding rubato. At one stage, he transformed it into a jazz number, taking the whole piece at break-neck speed, like Oscar Peterson jazzing up one of the classics. Maria had never heard anyone deconstruct a piece in the same way before. It was as if he threw everything into the air, caught all the pieces, and then re-assembled them. He simply did not practise like everyone else. Almost everyone else behaved as if they were playing for their tutor. Pausing over technical imperfections and polishing more difficult passages, to mirror a shiny example of how they understood the music. But Dimitrov took the music apart like a watchmaker of the old school, opening the back of a timepiece, to expose the wonder of the moving parts. As if to say,

'Look, can you see this part? Can you hear that? It's there for a reason. And that part, you think you know. You don't. See! What did I tell you. There it is. Listen again!'

For several weeks, whenever she wasn't studying herself, Maria sat outside the practice room, and listened to Dimitrov play. People that passed thought she was waiting to use the room. But all she did was sit outside and listen. One day the music stopped. Then the door opened.

'If you insist on sitting outside listening to me every time I rehearse, I suggest you apply for a season ticket!' he declared.

Maria stood up and looked acutely embarrassed.

'I'm sorry. I heard you practising a few weeks ago, and was interested in your approach to study.'

'Exactly what do you mean?'

'You don't as much rehearse a piece, as carry out an autopsy.'

Dimitrov smiled, and invited Maria into the room.

'And what is your approach?' he asked.

'I polish the parts I know well, and concentrate my technique and interpretive skills on pieces that present me with the greatest challenge.'

'Then you've missed several steps,' said Dimitrov.

'So, I'm beginning to realise.'

'Can you play?' he asked.

'Of course,' Maria said, smarting at his audacity.

'Then let me hear you play 'La Campanella',' he said with an air of amusement.

At first Maria was taken aback, and then regained her composure. After weeks of spying on his rehearsals, she could hardly refuse.

'Excellent choice,' she said bravely.

Dimitrov looked rather pleased with himself, as Maria sat nervously, hands outstretched, hovering over the keys. 'La Campanella' was one of the most difficult pieces in the repertoire, and required great technical agility and shade of tone. It also wasn't a piece you played by sight. You either could play the piece from memory, or you couldn't. Maria knew full well what lay behind Dimitrov's challenge, but refused to be deterred. She began slowly at first, and then picked up the tempo considerably, as she gained confidence.

Dimitrov turned his back, looked out of the window for a few minutes, then walked back towards the piano. Sitting beside her, he took over the keyboard from the più mosso, and then, slowing down, invited Maria to join him. Instinctively, she started to play the right hand part, and then began using both hands, dovetailing seamlessly with his playing, until eventually they became like musical sparring partners, each demonstrating their technical prowess, and ending the solo as a fiery duet. When they had finished, Dimitrov turned and looked at her gravely.

'You are good. Very good. You don't need me.'

'I need somebody to tell me that.'

'What does Popov tell you?'

'Popov wants me to shine like the sun, and glow like the moon. I suffer from a partial eclipse.'

'How good do you want to be?' asked Dimitrov.

He held up his finger and thumb, and demonstrated a barely perceptible gap between the two, before holding his hands wide apart.

'Because that much improvement requires this amount of work. The gap is what divides the accomplished from the Gods!' he declared. 'So. Which one of these options do you intend to pursue?'

'I'm not sure,' said Maria.

'Then don't waste my time!' he admonished. 'The most you'll ever amount to is a professional mediocrity.'

'Is that what you really think?'

'I know so!' Dimitrov announced bluntly.

Maria ran from the studio, tears streaming from her eyes,

and left the building. Everything she had heard about him was true. He was antisocial and arrogant. Even narcissistic. Rather than accept her admiration, he had delivered a back-handed compliment, and wounded her with an ungracious remark, calculated to make her feel inferior. Maria was furious. Once again, she consulted Moiseiwitsch, who advised she consider the altercation an opening move in a broader strategy.

'Leading to what?' she enquired.

'To more intrigue!' he replied. 'If you want revenge, you'll have to grow two skins. One for taking a shower, and the other for dealing with disappointment.'

'That still wouldn't make me a great pianist,' observed Maria.

'I disagree. Apart from anything else. It makes you a survivor. And that, in the long run could prove far more useful.'

'Thanks. You've just given me a delightful idea for revenge,' she said.

As the date for the gala drew closer, everyone knew it would only feature the most outstanding students of their year. There was hot competition among the violinists, less so, the brass, but more particularly, the pianists. Those more inclined to become répétiteurs, accompanied the vocalists in song or Lieder, whilst the most prestigious solos were given to the more favoured students. Apart from family and members of the public, by far the most exciting aspect of the showcase was that agents were invited to discover 'rising talent'. This always added an extra dimension of scrutiny and pressure to the occasion. Accordingly, the rivalry to take part was intense. The teachers knew this full well, and took advantage. It wasn't just the personal honour of a performer at stake, but the academy's prestige.

A month before, the building became a hive of activity. The programme was organised to highlight the skills of individual students. But no one knew who would be given solos, and who would be confined to the orchestra, until the tutors decided.

The slang for not being a soloist was 'the pits', a phrase now used as unsparingly as ketchup on chips. Popov was tight-lipped about who he had chosen to perform, but hinted at the type of repertoire the students might like to study, before the official announcement. Unable to remain patient any longer, Maria challenged Popov, whilst tackling a Beethoven Sonata.

'Is this what I'm playing for the gala?'

'No,' replied Popov. 'In fact you won't be playing a solo at all.'

Maria's heart sunk, and leaning forward, she placed her forehead on the keyboard, as if all the air had been extracted from her lungs, while Popov sat silently in his favourite chair, looking bemused.

'Is that all you want?' he asked, 'to be able to play your favourite Bach or Beethoven lollipop, and look like Venus? What I want is to challenge you.'

'How?' asked Maria.

'I want you to accompany Streich in two songs from 'Winterreise'.'

Jacek Streich was a six-foot-four bass baritone of immense power and charisma. At twenty four years of age, he was almost the finished article. Capable of tackling both opera and Lieder, and already being touted as a next generation 'Hans Hotter'.

'And my fate is to be his mousey accompanist,' she said.

Popov arose from his chair, and faced Maria directly. His face was bright red, and he deliberated in a cold precise manner, that projected his anger far more effectively than a dozen drill sergeants.

'Is that what you think accompaniment is? To register tempo, and fill in the gaps between the vocal line? Well! If you can't take disappointment, a musical career isn't for you.'

Popov did not waste his time with anyone unprepared to be guided by his principles, or his understanding of music.

'An outstanding accompanist is one of the highest musical achievements any musician can attain. You are not there merely for decoration, but to paint a landscape in which the vocalist can flourish. It's a skill that demands nuance, sympathy, energy, balance, colour and life. Sometimes, with unassuming subtlety. Sometimes, like a large orchestra. You complement the composition as an individual, but serve alongside another artiste, to satisfy the vision of the composer. Not just the lyric!' he admonished.

Maria was stunned. Popov had succinctly made it clear that Maria enjoyed the glamour of the grand showpieces, yet lacked the humility to appreciate what musical collaboration involved. She quickly apologised, as Popov retreated back to his armchair, and sat in silence. It was the silence of disappointment. Popov could abruptly end a lesson whenever a disagreement arose, even if a pupil were midway through a composition. Suddenly, sensing that their tutor had no further interest in teaching, a pupil would remain seated, expecting further instruction, when there was none. Eventually, they left the room with their tail between their legs. Maria understood completely, and gathered up her music.

'*Who* is Dimitrov accompanying?' she enquired, before her premature departure.

Maria had no choice but to grow the second skin recommended by Moiseiwitsch. On reflection, she was to learn a great deal from her encounter with Jacek Streich. For a start, he was well inside the music and character of the piece. Secondly, he knew a great deal about the history and performance of the work. She, on the other hand, knew very little about Lieder, and very quickly had to study both the music and historical recordings, to gain more insight. Streich, for his part, was temperamentally astute, and felt he held a significant advantage, due to her lack of knowledge. In rehearsal he expressed dissatisfaction with her playing, and exploited her inexperience.

'Do you really believe that the horse I am riding is pawing the ground beneath his feet?' he asked whilst rehearsing Abschied, 'or more likely than not, lame?'

'I'm sorry I'm unable provide the rendition of Gerald Moore,' said Maria. 'If you look carefully you'll observe that I have a pair of breasts. My stallion is more likely to be a filly. And by the way, apart from being no Hans Hotter, you're no Fischer-Dieskau either. Would you like to take it from the top again, or hire someone to shoot the mare?'

For once, Streich was at a loss for words, and begrudgingly accorded Maria more respect. But she had lost the opportunity to compete with Dimitrov on equal terms, and although the foray into Lieder had brought her unexpected musical dividends, she also felt distinctly subordinate.

In the following weeks, she purposely avoided Dimitrov, whenever he was anywhere in her vicinity, or she passed him on the stairs. If he happened to open the door to the studio where she was practising, she would ignore him, and if he did glance in her direction, then she would pretend he didn't exist. Not that he did. In fact she was certain, he didn't even care if she existed at all. Her revenge, she decided, would be aimed at the most sensitive part of his body, his ego!

On the day of the gala, the students performing were allowed to occupy the front row. Maria artfully claimed a seat directly facing whoever was seated at the piano. The order of the programme meant that she was to appear with Streich in the first half, while Dimitrov was allocated a prime spot in the second. When the time came for Dimitrov to perform, he began with a Schubert Impromptu, then acquitted himself to great acclaim with a masterful rendering of Chopin's Ballade in G Minor. He began the Ballade, as if he was thinking about what notes to play, before making the piano dance a waltz, then a pirouette, taking the listener through another door of discovery.

Who can invent such music? Maria wondered. Who

can conjure so exactly and forcefully that most intoxicating combination. Don't play so beautifully, she mentally begged, or capture the heart so completely. Please play a wrong note, or fluff a scherzo passage. But instead, Dimitrov transported the listener in one precious moment in time to another world.

Maria slumped in her seat, throughout his performance, with her arms folded and her legs crossed, as though completely disinterested in his playing. She yawned several times, and tilted her head back, staring upwards, as though something far more interesting was happening on the ceiling. This distracted various audience members, curious to know what she was looking at. In all, she gave a convincing performance of someone completely bored, and complemented her torment with a pained expression, as if being asked to listen to a five-year-old's first attempt at playing with two hands. Dimitrov pretended he didn't notice, and when it came time to acknowledge the enthusiastic reception of the audience, made a special point of looking straight at Maria, and bowing graciously towards her, as if she were the guest of honour. Everyone looked in her direction, and much to her embarrassment began to applaud her as well. Believing she had somehow contributed to his triumph.

At the reception afterwards, the domineering frame of Streich loomed large as he wandered among the guests seeking approval, but Dimitrov was noticeably absent. Nonetheless, she heard Dimitrov's name being mentioned several times, and watched as Streich was congratulated for his rendition of the Schubert. Maria, on the other hand, was told politely that people had 'enjoyed' her accompaniment. For his part, Popov congratulated Maria on doing a splendid job of reducing six-foot-four to four-feet-six inches.

'I had total confidence in you,' he confided.

It was, as Maria suspected, less about widening the breadth of her experience, and more about cutting Streich down to size. When she pointed out none of this was hardly likely to advance her career prospects as a soloist, Popov advised her to specialise in Bach.

'Why not Rachmaninoff?' asked Maria

'What would you rather be,' enquired Popov. 'a Bach specialist or a Rachmaninoff hack?'

'I'd prefer to be a threat to both.' she said.

Popov laughed.

'Yes. That is just what you would be. Meanwhile, you have come to the attention of Dimitrov, who has suggested that you partner him in playing duets.'

'Why me?'

'He was impressed by the way you accompanied Streich. Apparently, he thinks you have potential.'

'I don't want to play with him. He's arrogant and too full of himself.'

'How do you know?'

'That's what I've heard.'

'Then let him prove you wrong.'

At the end of the lesson, there was a knock on the door of Popov's studio, and Dimitrov entered carrying a large folder of sheet music. He bowed to Maria, but didn't smile. Neither did she. In fact Maria felt embarrassed. She had been ambushed. A decision had been made without her consent, and she considered it perfectly reflected the secondary position she occupied in Popov's heart.

'This is Yevgeny Dimitrov,' said Popov.

'Yes. We met briefly,' said Maria. 'I wasn't expecting a repeat performance.'

'You are free to say 'no',' said Popov.

Maria, paused just long enough to savour the moment, and then said casually,

'Very well, then. No!'

She then strode purposely towards the door, and left Popov's studio. She didn't get very far, however, before coming to a halt.

She was determined to fulfil her own musical aims and objectives, and completely resented the manner in which both Popov and Dimitrov had made a decision on her behalf. Expecting her to accept what they considered to be their superior instinct and insight. Reducing her to the position of a subordinate. She was incensed. It caused her heart to race, and her blood to boil. Her artistic pride and talent were worth far more respect than she had been accorded. She was being treated like a student fit for nothing more than a career as a second-rate soloist destined for a suburban ballet class, or the crowded menagerie of urban piano teaching. Turning back towards Popov's studio, she fully intended to reassert her authority, and declare she was no longer prepared to be humiliated. Just as she was about to make a grand entrance and formulate the words that would justify her anger, she heard the opening bars to Schubert's Fantasia in F Minor and stopped in her tracks. She had forgotten that Popov had once been a highly regarded soloist, and was now accompanying Dimitrov in the duet, both sympathetically and musically, reflecting the light and shade of Dimitrov's playing, and responding in equal measure to his virtuosity. Like two people sharing a delicious cake, eating their way through each layer, and savouring each morsel. Revelling in the journey, and indulging in the pure selfish enjoyment of a feast they had no intention of sharing. Maria waited until they had finished, and then entered the room. It was she who now felt humiliation.

Maria addressed Popov directly.

'I have changed my mind,' she said.

Popov retreated to his armchair, as Yevgeny placed the music back into his folder.

'Me, too,' Dimitrov said casually, and without acknowledging Maria, left the studio.

Maria was furious, and let out a shriek of frustration. This left Popov highly amused. He had never seen her look quite so perplexed.

'I'm glad you see how foolish you are,' said Popov.

Maria could have kicked herself. She had single-handedly sabotaged her own attempt to work with one of the most gifted musicians in the academy. She also grew more uncertain about her musical path. Perhaps, she considered, she should forget about being a soloist at all, and concentrate on finding a teaching post.

When she confided her dilemma to Moiseiwitsch, he suggested it had something to do with being an only child. The thought hadn't readily occurred to her, but it was true. By Ukrainian standards, she had been spoilt. Both her parents were doctors, and classified as professionals. But even with the advent of Perestroika, her parents had struggled financially, and had taken part time work in order to purchase a few extra luxuries. In Maria's case, this took the form of piano lessons and her education. She had been extremely fortunate, and demonstrated her thanks by becoming both serious in her studies, and on leaving the academy, determined to make a reputation for herself. Moiseiwitsch was sympathetic, but pointed out that during the period of economic and political instability, to which Ukraine had now become accustomed, her choices as a graduate fresh out of the academy would be severely limited.

'Who knows. In a few years, we may be part of the European Union. Then, all you will need to find work will be a passport and a smile on your face,' he said.

Maria considered her options. She wouldn't be the only pianist leaving the academy at the end of term, and considered two tutors were better than one. She therefore studied the Fantasia in F Minor, memorising both parts, and presented herself outside the studio where Yevgeny had gone one morning to practise. She stood in the doorway, looking suitably contrite.

'I am seeking another pair of hands,' said Maria.

'Is it only my hands that interest you?'

Maria bowed her head, and handed Yevgeny the music she was carrying.

'Please. Will you help me?' she asked.

Yevgeny's face broke into a smile. She knew that for him this was unusual, since he was often characterized as an antisocial loner, who didn't mix. Someone in a lofty tower, with only a piano for company. But for once, he let his guard down, and invited Maria to sit down and join him at the piano.

'Do you know it?' he asked

'Only from the outside,' Maria answered. 'Now I want to discover the interior.'

'Good,' said Yevgeny. 'Let us enter through the front door, and consider what we see, before discovering what is really happening. You see, it is not the notes themselves. It is what is happening around, in between, and what inspired them in the first place.'

Yevgeny started right at the beginning of the passage. He played it over and over, and then invited Maria to listen to the various types of rhythm he was able to introduce into the very first bars, and how it shaped the architecture of the whole passage. He then went on to demonstrate how even the smallest inflection, pause and rhythmic pattern could colour, and add additional layers of understanding and revelation to the composition, and how the composer purposely left room for both the performer and listener to embark on an adventure to discover the music within.

'It is,' he declared, 'always, the music within the music.'

At length, Yevgeny invited Maria to approach the music with a completely fresh mind. As they began to play, she suddenly felt free to absorb herself in the mystery of music making in a new and completely different way. As if someone had lifted years of routine practice and lethargy of repetition from her shoulders, and invited her to develop her own insight. Popov had invited her to think, analyse and emulate. But now, with Yevgeny, she heard something different in her playing. A new vibrancy, a new purpose, a new joy. The reward of not just playing well, but of putting her own stamp on the music. As if the music that had previously remained hidden bounced out of the score, and asked her to play.

'Hey listen. Hey look. Now it's a waltz, now it's a mazurka, how about a soft shoe shuffle?'

As they played on and on. Yevgeny shouted out a dance step, a march, a goose step, or painted a picture of a swirling dervish, a gypsy dance, a sunset, a stormy sea, a deserted beach. At each suggestion, the music took on a different type of magical existence. Like a kaleidoscope of altered patterns and colours, producing fascinating shapes and a new listening experience. The music left the bar lines, and roamed in the open expanse of imagination and discovery. It was no longer the piece she thought she knew. Or rendered for familiarity. But newly-minted from material that had something different and exciting to say.

They both agreed to repeat their joint practice session, and met twice a week, not for just duets, but also solo pieces, where Maria sought guidance. In many ways, she now listened to the advice of Yevgeny more than Popov. But something else had happened. She now felt a new sense of exhilaration and happiness. Popov noticed Yevgeny's influence, but did not discourage it.

'Do you mind,' Maria asked.

'My dear Maria,' Popov replied, 'when I was young, my idols were Horowitz, Richter, Lipatti, Schnabel and our own dear Gilels. What I wouldn't have given to have spent time picking their brains.'

'Do you think that Yevgeny is capable of reaching such heights?.'

'That remains to be seen,' said Popov. 'What I do know, is that your playing has blossomed. What other influence he may have asserted, to bring about this advance in your education, will no doubt prove less mysterious!'

One day when they met, Maria asked Yevgeny what he wanted to practise.

'Running!,' he announced.

Yevgeny took Maria by the hand, and led her from the academy to the top of the Potemkin Stairs. They ran down the steps together, and on reaching the bottom, Yevgeny led her in an impromptu waltz, before they headed in the direction of the beach.

For the first time Maria saw him. Not the meticulously prepared prodigy, but the awkward, socially inept, pasty peasant, that could move at once from musical sophistication to spontaneous amusement.

'You are full of surprises,' said Maria.

'Sometimes, I need to escape,' he said.

Yevgeny laughed, and then began pirouetting on the sand like a ballet dancer, before collapsing and landing flat on his back. Maria sat beside him, and amused herself by pouring tiny rivulets of sand onto his forehead as he made faces at her.

'I wonder what will become of us?' Maria asked.

'At present, we're applying for a passport.' he replied.

'I expect my destination will be more crowded than yours.'

'Then I'll ask God to make it bigger!'

'Do you believe in God?' asked Maria

'Of course, along with Bach and Beethoven!'

'You're beginning to sound like Popov.'

'What about you?'

'You mean do I believe in Bach and Beethoven.'

'No God?'

'I'm not sure.'

'That's scary.'

'Why?' asked Maria.

'Because you may need divine guidance. As well as luck!'

Maria gently brushed the sand off Yevgeny's forehead, and then found herself chasing errant grains that had lodged in his hair.

'What is it that scares *you*?' she asked.

Yevgeny's mood suddenly darkened, and Maria realised that the mere fact of asking the question had somehow disturbed the carefree abandonment he had displayed moments before. He then stood up, and abruptly announced.

'Playtime is over.'

'Have I done anything wrong?' said Maria.

'Of course not. It's just that I'm too easily distracted.'

It was a small but significant incident. For a moment, he had abandoned the unrelenting tunnel vision of practice, to enjoy a light-hearted moment of stupidity. But then felt ashamed. As if he harboured a secret guilt.

'Don't worry. I won't tell anyone you are capable of a mad moment,' said Maria.

'Then, I won't tell anyone that I entertain you with free music lessons,' Yevgeny replied.

Once again a door had closed, discouraging further discussion.

'Aren't you going to tell me?' said Maria.

Yevgeny sprinted towards the stairs, turning around every few moments, urging her to race him.

'Tell me!' she insisted.

'You scare me!' said Yevgeny. 'Haven't you noticed!'

2.

FOLLOWING UKRAINE'S INDEPENDENCE from Moscow, the academy in Odesa now hosted its own international piano competition. Whatever political quagmire the country faced, its musical life had blossomed. A new chamber orchestra had been founded, the Philharmonic was awarded federal status, and opera was flourishing, along with classical music, jazz, rock and arts festivals. Indeed the cities famous luminaries, including Gilels, Richter, David Oistrakh, and Shura Cherkassky among others, testified to its pre-eminence as fertile territory, in which world class musicians prospered.

'If we can't organise an international piano competition based on this stable of heavyweights, we must be mad!' Popov had argued, when the idea was first suggested.

The competition, held on alternative years to its established rival in Moscow and St Petersburg, attracted applicants worldwide, and every pianist who attended the academy longed for an invitation to compete. But the jury were independent of the academy, and all applicants underwent the same selection process. Entry was therefore not a foregone conclusion, and, until now, a matter that Popov refused to discuss with students until they were ready. Popov considered Yevgeny to be ready. And when Popov made up his mind, he was unlikely to change it.

'We have less than five months, and you already know much

of the repertoire they will demand. My job is to make sure you are up to the task,' he told him.

When Yevgeny first became a student, Popov had asked what composers he favoured least. Yevgeny had recited at least a half dozen, for whom he felt no affinity, whose melodic structure he declared was obscure, lacked drama, and failed in his view, to reward the listener.

'Good,' said Popov. 'We'll start with those!'

Yevgeny's first lesson had been to relinquish the notion of only studying those composers that displayed his virtuosity, and instead pursue those that required his talent to make others want to listen. It proved to be a valuable learning curve, and encouraged him to be more objective in his approach to both the music and the composer. Now, Popov considered him ready to face a new challenge, and invited Yevgeny to include Scriabin, Medtner, Ravel and Prokofiev in his repertoire, along with a range of contemporary composers. In addition, he arranged for him and a few hand picked students to undertake a series of concerts, in order to perform a varied repertoire, on unfamiliar pianos, and unusual acoustics in front of the public. Maria was invited to join this select group, and partner Yevgeny in the duets. Maria was happy with the arrangement, until it occurred to her that the choice to partner her with Yevgeny was in fact Popov's, and not Yevgeny's.

'Is it true?' Maria asked Yevgeny, during one of their rehearsals.

'I told him that you had been stalking me.'

'And what was Popov's response?'

'He said it confirmed why it would make you an ideal candidate.'

'Moiseiwitsch says it's because you have no desire to sleep with me.'

'Is that what he says?'

'Yes.'

'And what was your reply?'

'I told him that not wanting to sleep with me was the only reason I agreed.'

'Then, it has saved us both an unnecessary detour,' Yevgeny replied.

Maria agreed. Yevgeny lacked all the obvious attributes of masculinity, nor displayed any sign of outward romantic sensibility to anyone, except on that one short excursion they had made to the beach. 'What happened?' she wondered. What had happened to make him so protective? So private, so insular? What had happened to that deep unfathomable throbbing heart that could only communicate through his own remarkable pulse of musical expression. Where was his other life?

The answer to Maria's question, for the moment, remained unanswered. Popov was shortly to announce the four candidates he had chosen to compete in the competition. When the time came, he announced that Yevgeny, herself, and two other final year students, one from Korea and one from Poland, would take part. Popov had discussed the matter of their participation individually. Each one examined in depth about their strengths and weaknesses, and asked to challenge themselves more thoroughly than they had thus far been exposed. What he really intended was for them to enjoy their participation, and see the competition as a step towards the real world of performance. He also urged them to be excited by the love of performing, rather than cowed by the pressure of examination.

'It is about performing to the best of your ability' he declared. 'I want you to enjoy the fire, and not get burned!'

Popov quickly convinced Maria to display her acumen for Bach. She understood its lyrical complexity, and naturally identified more completely with its inner beauty. Popov also suggested Ravel, Grieg, Samuel Barber, and Shostakovitch. Maria agreed, even though she longed to display her virtuosity on the fiery pastures of Rachmaninoff and Beethoven.

'Steak isn't the only dish on the menu,' Popov joked.

'An occasional fillet mignon would be nice though', Maria declared.

Popov was highly amused.

'You are the only student who would know what that was!' he said, and began to laugh so much that Maria began laughing too.

Soon, neither could continue any sensible discussion. She therefore, gathered up her music and left Popov's studio, laughing uncontrollably, and deep down, strangely at peace with herself.

When it came to Yevgeny, Popov had to navigate an entirely different landscape. One tailored to his particular musical temperament. The early rounds would consist of solo pieces allowing free choice, plus a selection made by the judges. The final would consist of a major concerto with orchestral accompaniment. Popov had no doubt Yevgeny would be a finalist.

'I want you to play the Third,' ordered Popov.

'Why the Third?'

'Because everyone expects the Second'. said Popov. 'The Second gives them what they want. The Third gives them something more.'

Popov paced the room, occasionally glancing at Yevgeny, who remained deep in thought.

'You see, with the Third, there is no safety net. Here, he is a revolutionary. Here, his musical ideas have matured into something else. One is an eloquent romance. But this is triumph. This is about mastery. Now, you grow up. Now, you have nowhere to hide. Now, you face Goliath. With this, you don't face an audience. You face yourself.'

'Give me time to think it over,' said Yevgeny.

'I believe your feet are made to fill bigger shoes,' argued Popov.

Yevgeny remained silent. He had set his heart on the Second.

He had rehearsed it, and knew it so well. The Third was another matter entirely. It was as if Popov was hell-bent on proving a point at his expense.

'I will help you to take it apart, and conquer its complexity,' encouraged Popov. 'You will have to dissemble it, like a complicated piece of machinery, until you understand every grubby dot and moving part. After that, you will need to place yourself in the middle of the ring and wrestle with your own insecurity, until you have developed the arrogance to conquer it!'

To Yevgeny, the Third was the Holy Grail. A sacred piece to be approached with awe. Of course, he knew it, he could play it, but had yet to master its demanding landscape, and both Popov and he were aware of what sacrifices had to be made, to reproduce a piece of such demanding virtuosity.

'You have no other choice!' argued Popov. 'You must do it. For yourself!'

For the next month, Yevgeny could think of nothing else. He hid himself away, and Maria saw little of him. It was as if he had marooned himself on an island, and cut himself off from the transactions of everyday life. His singular purpose, to go beyond what Popov or anyone else could predict, and conquer his own Mount Olympus. To unearth the God of musical creation and overcome his fear in the process.

For her part, Maria found her mind floating in the exquisite creation of the Bach English Suites, the intimate quality of the Lyric Pieces of Grieg, and the incurable romance of Schumann. At the same time, Popov had sparked her interest in thinking about the orchestration.

'It can make or break a performance,' he declared, and played her various recordings of accompaniment by a variety of conductors.

'Listen to how he beats this. How he makes the orchestra sound urgent, builds the excitement and expectation. By the time the pianist enters, you want to stand up and applaud.'

It is what Yevgeny had advised also.

'Go and listen to the orchestral rehearsals,' he urged. 'Listen to the rank and file. Talk to the front bench. They will tell you what a conductor is like. How they respond and the energy of their playing. Turgenev, for example, is like a tired cow climbing a hill with a broken leg. He stops in rehearsals every few minutes, and the orchestra largely ignore him. Then he gets angry, and they play even worse. Toscanini for example used to rehearse each individual player as if they were a soloist. He was a martinet. No one dared to disrespect his authority. When you put it all together, however, the effect was amazing. Each orchestral detail came alive, and you noticed things in the music you never heard before. Popov is also marvellous. The orchestra love him. His conducting is very clear, his hands so expressive, and his facial expressions tell the orchestra exactly how he is feeling. As a result, they respond like his children. He wills them with the sheer force of his moment-by-moment involvement with each bar. Like a master chef would prepare a banquet filled with a variety of distinctive flavours. Allowing you to savour each one, as they contribute to an overall experience, leaving you wanting more. When he conducts, it is like you are in the driving seat, but underneath being propelled by a magnificent engine, allowing you to give your best performance.'

In fact, no one took very much notice of Popov as a pianist. He was largely only known for his somewhat unorthodox teaching. Yet, Yevgeny had noted, he was once a considerable musical personality. But now in his seventies, his life was about guiding others, and setting them free to roam in the pastures of the musical masters. In fact Popov went further. He considered that God himself spoke through the masterworks of the great composers.

'It's God speaking to us! Don't you know that! God! Where else do you think it comes from? An amoeba that popped up on the shores of the Zambezi ten million years ago?'

And Popov meant it. It was, he contested, the nearest thing we come to experiencing God.

'That is why you feel alive inside. That is why you are led to examine your soul. It's not just your accomplishment. It's your conversation with God!' he proclaimed.

Maria did not have the temerity to disagree, but asked,

'Can I converse with him through Schumann, or better still, Beethoven's Third?'

Popov laughed.

'Yes, the Schumann is for you. And the Beethoven has possibilities!'

When Maria relayed her conversation with Popov to Yevgeny, he laughed, and danced around the rehearsal room where they'd met.

'Two Thirds,' he shouted excitedly. 'We have two Thirds on our hands!' and began playing the central motif, where the piano enters.

Maria pirouetted around the room, as if she were a ballerina. 'Two thirds', they chimed, as if joining in a chorus of encouragement to some political dynasty. 'Give me two Thirds', they repeated, like two demented children demanding some luxurious confection to which, thus far, they had been denied. 'Two Thirds. Two Thirds Two Thirds. Make way for Two Thirds!' Everyone thought they were mad.

'Two thirds of what?' they were asked.

'Perfection!' they answered. 'Perfection!'

The first round of the contest brought all participants face to face. The academy held a reception to introduce them to their new surroundings, and the etiquette and rules concerning rehearsal space and practice. There were some language barriers, but these were largely overcome by the shared love of music. For the first four days, ten contestants a day would be heard, and the second-round participants announced on day five. Forty entrants would be reduced to twenty, and the twenty down to a final six. Each contestant made their opening bids before the jury, their contributions ranging from the divine to the complex, the romantic to the technically challenging. Each set out to display their consummate skill and confidence. Some of the less experienced became overwhelmed and were easily discounted, whilst others gave inspired or surprisingly good accounts of themselves.

In the first round, everyone was given their own choice of what to play, plus something from the programme selected by the judges, who quickly arrived at a decision on some, whilst others appeared to be subject to a more rigorous debate. The participants themselves were by and large philosophical, agreeing that the experience alone was invaluable, whilst a few took their disappointment badly.

Maria and Yevgeny compared notes, and agreed that they had reservations about one or two of the more 'assured' candidates, but thought the Koreans and Japanese possessed more humility. One of the more 'assured' contestants was a Chinese entrant, who at twenty-six was one of the oldest, and had considerable concert experience to his name. In addition, he was a pupil of one of the judges, Madame Petrova, who liked to advertise her services as belonging to the 'great Russian tradition', forgetting that the majority of the people she admired were in fact Ukrainian.

Popov counselled Yevgeny and Maria before each appearance, and advised them on what the judges would be looking for, and how to build their performance. What he mostly provided was confidence, and importantly, psychologically prepared them to perform to their best ability. Above all, he reminded them they must 'enjoy' every moment they were on stage.

Maria gave a good opening account of the Bach Partita in B Flat Major, whilst Yevgeny repeated his account of the Chopin Ballade in G Minor, and followed with Sonata Number 8 by Mozart, from the set programme, playing the opening Allegro with such a light and distinctive touch, it made the piano sound veritably joyous, each note appearing to bounce from the keys, and dance in the air. No leaden painting by the left hand, as was so often the case, but played as if it were a delicious soufflé. So good, you wanted to eat it. The tempo and brio combining to lift the heart of the listener beyond just another rendition to a shared experience. Music delivered in its purest form of joy, enchantment and freshness. As if no one had played it quite the same before, laying waste previous renditions, by finding something original to say inside and between the notes, and so disarming in its potency, that even the judges stopped writing and simply listened.

It came as no surprise that both Maria and Yevgeny were both elevated to round two. Least of all to Popov, who expected nothing less. Round two was more difficult, due to both the repertoire and the judging, that by necessity was more fastidious. The judges at this stage looked for something more unusual, with a high degree of technical difficulty and a surprise element in either the work or the performance. Preferably both.

Yevgeny played 'Le Tombeau de Couperin', making the prelude sound like a field of corn gently blowing in the breeze, drifting above the horizon, painting the colours of Ravel's musical portraits with such lightness and elegance of touch, that no one dared breathe. He continued with a performance of Prokofiev's Sonata No 7, that in the fourth movement blew everyone away, and left people standing up and cheering. It was nothing short of sensational.

'There are some things which are so self-evident, that dissent would be churlish', Popov proclaimed.

Maria opened her second round challenge with Beethoven's fourth Sonata, said to be dedicated to a woman with whom he was in love. She played the opening movement as if it were a conversation between two people, culminating in the increased beating of a heart, and the Largo as a deeper expression of introspection. Completing her contribution with Bach's English Suite, No 2, played with such flawless elegance, each bar singing and dancing in one continuous stream of inward conviction. Popov maintained no one could fail to recognise her mastery.

The debate among the jury for the second round was prolonged. They had departed to a separate room, and speculation among the contestants abounded. Understandably, no one wanted to leave. The Chinese competitor Liang Hua Zhang appeared especially confident, and with his entourage, sat separately from the other contestants, rather like a senior executive from a large corporation. He was a habitual smoker, and continually ignored requests not to smoke in the presence of other people. He had played the eighth Sonata by Beethoven, and produced a showy account of the Chopin Ballade in G Minor, which, by all accounts, he liked to include as an encore in his concert performances. Moiseiwitsch, who could always be relied on to comment with his usual precision and tact, said he thought Zhang mistook Chopin for 'chopping', and felt sorry for the tree he demolished during the final frenzied attack on the Ballade.

'But then again, I am only just fit enough to scratch the surface of a string. I couldn't possibly compete with someone skilled enough to attempt grievous bodily harm to a large block of hardwood,' he speculated.

Maria wished she could be a fly on the wall, and listen to the comments of the judging panel. She and others knew at least two of the judges had a history of antipathy towards Popov, who honourably excluded himself from the panel, believing his presence would make it difficult for him to remain impartial. He felt that no one who had a direct relationship with a contestant should be included. The judges were high profile teachers and musicians, so it was a matter of honour for each of them to be scrupulously impartial. At least, that was the theory.

In practice, Moiseiwitsch pointed out, 'If you owned a dog, and saw it being attacked by other dogs, you would naturally want to rescue it.'

Maria could see the wisdom of his remark, but believed professionals would always honour the performance of the music, above all other considerations.

'Then your naivety does you credit,' said Moiseiwitsch.

It was late the following afternoon, when the spokesman for the judging panel finally stood on the main stage of the academy, to announce the six finalists. He prefaced his remarks by exalting each contestant as a truly worthy professional, and praising each competitor as exceptional. It was, he assured everyone, a 'thankless task', to separate one competitor from another. But that, he confirmed, was the challenge the panel faced.

'Each one of you can hold their head up high, and be justly proud of your contribution', he continued. 'But let no one be in any doubt. This has been a gratifying experience for all of us. But ultimately, this year we have been searching for not just the new Gilels, the new Argerich, the new Pollini, or the new Richter, but a new light in the musical firmament, honoured by these illustrious predecessors!'

After a calculated pause, the names of each of the finalists were finally declared, during which the contestants sat holding their breath. The Korean was the first to be announced. He stood up, and was roundly applauded. After him a competitor from Poland, who excelled at Chopin, and had also given a memorable performance of the Mephisto Waltz No 1. Next to be named, was a Russian, Vaschenko, who championed Shostakovich, and played his five Preludes along with works by Scriabin. Another Russian was announced, this time a woman, Nataliya Kuznetsova, who was a pupil of Madame Petrova. She displayed a somewhat cold and remote temperament, with a repertoire to match, and according to Yevgeny had hidden behind the work, rather than exist within it. Later Popov would comment that her execution was like ice.

'Nothing melted, including a listening heart'.

By now, Maria knew for certain that her bid had failed, and felt her stomach churning, as the whispering of heightened speculation rippled through the audience, like bees trapped in a jar. The spokesman paused before announcing the final two choices, and then, giving a smile of satisfaction, announced the name of Liang Hua Zhang, whose entourage all stood up and cheered like a claque from La Scala, whilst everyone else applauded politely. Slowly, Zhang rose to his feet, and waved like visiting Royalty, as if he expected nothing less. Modesty was not an act of sacrifice he intended to make. He considered himself a kind of father figure, setting both the tone and standard to which he considered he owned the automatic copyright. The spokesman lingered over the last name to be announced, with enough delay to leave room for a drum roll.

Maria looked at Yevgeny, who displayed an outward expression of utter calm, although, she considered inwardly he must have been doing emotional cartwheels on a high-wire stretched to breaking point. Suddenly, his name was announced, and for several seconds it didn't register. He then stood up looking embarrassed, nodded to the spokesman, and abruptly sat down again. Maria immediately went to congratulate him. But rather than behaving victorious, he told her,

'You should have been selected for the final as well,' and looked deeply saddened.

'It's OK,' said Maria. 'I'm not ashamed of my performance. The rest is a matter of personal choice by others.'

'Nonsense,' said Yevgeny. 'You have a unique talent. It's not your fault the judging panel suffer from profound deafness.'

Maria later confided to Popov, it was the moment she saw Yevgeny for the first time.

'He was genuinely upset I wasn't selected for the final. Am I being stupid?'

Popov assured her that she had the makings of a very fine pianist, and there was no reason why she shouldn't have the possibility of a career.

'I had hoped to claim the honour of being a finalist before I left the academy, but will deal with the disappointment in my own way,' she told him.

'A career is about being very single-minded,' said Popov. 'Other matters often claim priority. You must always take that into account.'

The more urgent matter now was to prepare Yevgeny for the final. This also included rehearsing the orchestra, and was the point at which each finalist declared their selection. The pieces chosen, Beethoven's third Piano Concerto, Chopin's E Minor, the Prokofiev in C Major, the Schumann and Rachmaninoff, were all great showpieces. Unsurprisingly, Rachmaninoff's Second Concerto was the crowd-pleasing vehicle selected by Zhang, who boasted that it was his most requested piece. Popov was not unduly worried. He felt Zhang would invest it with enough superficiality to damage his chance of winning. He assured Yevgeny,

'Nothing matters now, except to do justice to the composer, and be true to yourself.'

Yevgeny's success meant a great deal to Popov. Yevgeny was the fruit of his labour, and Popov harboured great hopes that a major talent would emerge. He therefore saw victory in the competition as vindication of both his methods, and faith in nurturing the raw material of teenage promise to the threshold of a major performer.

The day before the performance, Yevgeny disappeared, and did not want to be seen. He withdrew completely into his own world, blocking everything else out. Thinking himself into the mind of the composer, and asking God for the courage to face the challenge. Maria had presented Popov with two cards, wishing them both luck and success. She could now only observe from the sideline and hope. On the card to Yevgeny, she wrote,

'You have already won. The rest is a formality.'

The final was to be presented in two halves. The afternoon session which began at 2pm, and the evening session, that commenced at 7.30pm. Yevgeny was allocated the evening session, and was to perform second. Zhang was accorded the honour of being last. Popov reminded Yevgeny he was performing amongst friends, 'because, everyone in the orchestra is already a fan'. In reply, Yevgeny said he would do his utmost to repay his debt to Rachmaninoff.

On the night, however, it was different. Waiting to perform, Yevgeny's normal self-control had begun to be undermined by the task ahead. He was no longer playing to his fellow students or well wishers, but a panel of judges, who would be only too aware of the giant peaks, structure and pitfalls that can open up and devour all but the most gladiatorial competitor.

Vaschenko had begun the Prokofiev, and Yevgeny could hear his competitor's artistic nerves being stretched. A minor fluff in the cadenza and a slight lack of the fluidity he had demonstrated in rehearsal. Then something worse, a memory lapse. The piano was now out of sync with the orchestra. Andropov the conductor was doing his best to rescue the situation, but to no avail. Vaschenko suddenly stopped playing, and agreed to start again from bar ninety three. This time, both pianist and orchestra were in accord, and Vaschenko continued with more technical conviction and renewed confidence. But it was clear to Yevgeny that the memory loss had cost Vaschenko dearly, and for the first time began to feel unsettled about his own performance, and recalled Popov's warning not to be influenced by anyone else.

As Yevgeny listened intently in the artistes' room a few metres away, he began to feel restless, and climbed the stairs to the rehearsal room. Closing the door behind him, he opened the lid of the piano, and placed his hands on the keyboard, but was unable to move his fingers. It was as if, by some disobedient trick of fate, they were warning of an impending rebellion, refusing to cooperate with the integrity of the will. 'What if what happened to Vaschenko happens to me?' Yevgeny thought. A small mistake that leads to a slight lack of confidence, and a slight lack of confidence leading to a lack of concentration, and a lack of concentration that results in humiliation. Yevgeny stood up, took a deep breath, and then walked towards the door. Suddenly, he noticed Szell, a fellow student, observing him through the small glass porthole, and as he opened the door, Szell stepped inside the room.

'I saw you sitting at the piano, looking worried', observed Szell. 'But I suppose even prodigies suffer.'

'No more than is good for me', answered Yevgeny.

'Anyone would be nervous, if they had to face Platonov and that witch Madame Petrova, apart from the fact that she's Russian, and he believes he can play better than anyone who has the temerity to perform in front of him. You see, we are all human, as Vaschenko has so admirably demonstrated.'

'That isn't going to happen to me,' said Yevgeny attempting to sound confident.

'The trick, my dear Dimitrov, is to create the right conditions in your head.'

'My answer is to create the right performance with these.'

Yevgeny held up his hands defiantly in front of Szell's face.

'No doubt, Vaschenko made himself the same promise.'

Szell sat down at the piano, and casually lit up a cigarette.

'Popov was concerned he couldn't find you. I said it was probably nerves. But don't worry, it can happen to anyone. It's just that sometimes we need a little help.'

'Popov says that if you're afraid to perform, you don't yet own the music,' Yevgeny replied.

'Popov has always been very skilled at encouraging others to climb peaks that he himself was unable to conquer. You're not the first to find the challenge irresistible.'

Szell extinguished his cigarette, closed the piano lid, and then stood face to face with Yevgeny. Then, after studying him for a few moments, he placed a small plastic sachet in Yevgeny's jacket pocket.

'What's that?' enquired Yevgeny.

'Just a little something to help with the performance. Don't worry, everyone uses it.'

Szell then left the room, closing the door behind him.

By the time Yevgeny reached the bottom of the stairs, Vaschenko had finished, and the judges were still deliberating in the short intermission before he was due to perform. There was no time to test the state of the instrument, or take one more dry run in preparation. Any hyperbole of his past performances, nor speculation of his future career prospects now mattered. Yevgeny knew that he could either rise like a lion, or fall like a stone on the barren desert of unfulfilled promise. All of a sudden, Popov appeared on the rostrum, baton in hand, and then Yevgeny heard his name being announced, followed by applause.

Stepping onto the stage, he adjusted the height of the piano stool and without acknowledging either the audience nor Popov, simply sat looking down at the piano keys, as if they were lining up to challenge him. He then turned his eyes towards the rostrum, and saw that Popov was waiting for a signal that he was ready to begin. Yevgeny took several deep breaths, his hands remaining on his lap, whilst the audience waited in hushed anticipation. He then nodded.

Popov began, his tempi like a heart beating with the expectation of impending excitement. Then Yevgeny commenced his momentous journey, with the familiar opening bars taken at a brisk walking pace, before the sudden burst of energy that propelled itself from the piano like an eruption. It was as if some supernatural force was surging up inside him, as he began to paint both bold and delicate colours, displaying the sheer beauty of its extraordinary musical landscape, rendering the familiar and incidental architecture of its genius anew, before heading towards the andante passage and onto the scherzo. And then, it was as if he began lighting new fires, making them dance to a staccato rhythm, and drawing in its themes like melting droplets before the cello's introduced gravitas, and the orchestra crescendoed to a melody, that required a response. The piano briefly decided to answer, and when it did, the notes weaved a magical thread in between the strings, and became an orchestra in its own right, continuing its journey like rays of sun dancing on the sea, that eventually floated to a delicate arpeggio, awaiting the return of the opening melody, that now led the way to something even more thrilling.

The woodwind and the piano were now calling to each other, responding to each other's ideas and building up to yet another climax, with the orchestra fighting the piano, until it concluded in a furious cacophony. They then began to tease each other momentarily, until the piano spoke again, this time like giant waves crashing against the rocks, signalling more excitement, before descending like molten silver, cascading down a musical waterfall, that voiced its dominance until the waves receded, to allow the flutes and French horns to calm the waters, whilst the piano dissolved into a cadenza, and invited the orchestra to eagerly reprise the opening bars, until at last the trumpets sounded, to announce the final coda of the opening movement. Then, there was a brief hush, before the orchestra painted a melancholy sunrise over a landscape of mountains and forests, after which the strings crescendoed and invited the piano to supply a thoughtful response. The cellos then intervened, to demand that the piano give voice to a new and vibrant romance. One that allowed us to hear the inner voice of the composer.

It was then that Yevgeny took flight once again, newly re-energised like never before, making the instrument sing and dance to a waltz and polka, until the woodwind called for reinforcements, and was joined by the strings, as the piano scaled new peaks, leading to a cantabile that became a unifying force, and produced a sound of melting scintillation, like tiny bells that diminuendo and crescendo, in contemplation of the finale. This milestone being announced by the bass clef of the piano, that again erupted with such power and majesty, that it overwhelmed the senses to engrave its memorable passages onto the heart. The final bars culminating in one last furious exchange between soloist and orchestra, in which Yevgeny struck the last chords with all the vigour of a pugilist, and in delivering the final triumph of its grand vision, threw out the idea of music being just an exercise of personal expression, but instead the means to transport the listener to a higher state of understanding. Not only of themselves, but the more complex question of life itself!

As the last notes faded, there was a stunned silence, and for one brief moment, it appeared that no one would respond. Then, a spontaneous burst of cheering erupted, like a firework, followed by applause, and then more cheering as people stood up, and began stamping their feet, and shouting 'Bravo!' The decibels becoming overwhelming, as if he were a reigning monarch who had just announced a national triumph.

Yevgeny looked across at Popov, who was mopping his brow. With every move of the baton and orchestral flourish, he had commanded and coaxed every nuance, colour, rhythmic subtlety and response from his players, who were now themselves responding enthusiastically. Yevgeny stood and slowly moved to the front of the stage, and signalled for Popov to join him. Popov stubbornly refused, instead preferring to acknowledge Yevgeny and his players from the podium. But the applause wouldn't yield, and with tears in his eyes, Popov finally turned towards the audience, and bowed his head slowly, before turning once again to Yevgeny and the orchestra, and lowered his head in supplication.

Exhausted, but ultimately victorious. the energy began to drain from Yevgeny's body, yet at that very moment, he felt neither elation nor even accomplishment. Instead, something he could neither have imagined, nor suspected. Humility! It was if he had invested not just the adrenaline of his talent, but something more. His performance had been driven by his whole life, haunted as it was at times by doubt and humiliation, but also blessed by something he was unable to define. Now, as he stood before an audience, at the very moment of justification, he realised something else. Fear. Fear and despondency.

'I will never be able to do it again,' said Yevgeny. 'Never. Never.'

Popov was bemused but confounded. To have witnessed such a performance by the very person who now resisted his own triumph.

'Why. Why? Why? Yevy!' begged Popov. 'Why?'

Maria had gone backstage to congratulate Yevgeny, and threw her arms around him in celebration. But Yevgeny sobbed uncontrollably. It was unfathomable. They accompanied him back to the waiting room, and Maria stayed with him, whilst Popov returned to the auditorium as the first bars of Rachmaninoff's Second Piano Concerto began to punctuate the air.

Maria too could not understand Yevgeny's state of mind. He had justly deserved his triumph, but somehow lived under an emotional volcano. The music he delivered, along with the alchemy of conviction, had seared itself into the heart, and had communicated something more intangible than mere objective performance. A higher state of musical baptism, that anointed the listener with new insight.

But in the end, it failed to penetrate the informed wisdom of the judges, who gave the First Prize to Liang Hua Zhang, whose performance was described by Popov as being fashioned with every fake crowd-pleasing gimmick known to man. The tossing back of the head, the exaggerated lifting of his hands to give the impression of technical brilliance, mopping his brow between movements, closing his eyes as if blessed by some spiritual immolation, and of course, his obscene, heavy-handed arrival at the main theme, which he played with all the subtlety of someone banging on the reinforced doors of a castle under siege. To round off his criticism Popov noted,

'The concerto was badly damaged, but fortunately, capable of surviving his vandalism.'

Nonetheless, Popov was profoundly disappointed. Not least because he considered it was a 'fix' between Petrova and Platonov, who often sat on the same judging panel on which their pupils were contestants. His anger and disappointment had been communicated to the judges in no uncertain terms. In response, he was told by an insider, that there had been no criticism of Yevgeny's performance. Indeed, there was universal agreement, he possessed prodigious talent. But Madame Petrova had maintained that Zhang, at twenty-six, was primed for an international career, whereas Yevgeny at nineteen years old, was far less experienced, and had plenty of time to win plaudits in other competitions. Platonov had supported her, by saying that winning would prove much more helpful at this stage of Zhang's career than it would to Yevgeny's, who he reminded them was 'unknown and had relatively little professional experience.'

'In other words, he was expendable!' Popov told his informant.

Yevgeny was honoured with second place, and was cheered far more vocally than Zhang, whose acceptance speech purposely failed to acknowledge either Yevgeny, or any of the other participants.

'Everybody knows who the real winner is,' Popov insisted. 'Anyone who understands music that is! And the reality of competitions, is that sometimes the winner has to lose!'

Yevgeny himself did not comment. There was he said, 'no point'. The music, he maintained, spoke for itself. His nobility dispelled what Maria initially mistook for arrogance, and in her eyes he had grown in stature. 'You can't dine out on the prestige of winning a competition forever,' Yevgeny reminded her. But Popov had taken the matter personally, and felt that he had somehow failed. He was, after all, not just any old teacher, but a professor whose pupils reflected his status by the very qualities he drew from their often-complex make-up. What made him different as a teacher was that he asked his pupils to lay bare their own fears and doubts when exploring their relationship with music, and to adapt their own emotional structure, by exposing what lay beneath the surface of the music itself. The purpose of technique, he insisted, was not only to serve what the composer had in mind, but to add an additional layer of spiritual insight. It was this he saw as the very essence of performance itself. 'If we take that away, then all we are left with is highly accomplished gymnastics for two hands'. Although some derided his methods as psychobabble, Popov felt that Yevgeny's unconventional route to his door was nothing less than an answer to prayer. For along with natural talent, Popov recognised something far more complex and sensitive in Yevgeny's soul.

The product of a doting mother and violent father, Yevgeny had been groomed from an early age to help run his father's farm. Except, he had no appetite to be a farmer, and instead displayed all the signs of growing ambivalence towards the future planned for him.

In response, his father made him perform menial tasks, and subjected him to beatings, in order to turn him into what he considered a 'man'. But rather than subdue Yevgeny's spirit, it resulted in a vicious circle, leading to rebellion.

'My father was an alcoholic. But it wasn't his fault. He, too, had been brutalised,' Yevgeny told Popov. 'As a result I kept running away. At first to my uncle's house, and then to a family in Lviv. As a result my schooling suffered badly. But then a miracle happened!'

One day, he was invited to the birthday party of a schoolfriend. He and a few others had been given tea, and played a few games, then later the mother, an accomplished singer and pianist, played the piano, and sang some songs to entertain them. Yevgeny was transfixed. Suddenly, he discovered a whole new world, that had so far been denied him.

Following this visit, he kept turning up at the house, and had to be continually taken home. It became an embarrassment, and resulted in more beating. But Yevgeny was besotted, and begged Madame Eshkol, his friend's mother, to teach him how to play. Music, he told Popov, 'was a luxury his parents simply didn't understand'. They lived barely above subsistence level. One night, Yevgeny's mother arrived at the door of the Eshkol's house, and begged them to take her son.

'It is not safe for him to remain at our home any longer,' she pleaded.

Yevgeny was nine years old, and when Madame Eshkol came to bathe him, found that his back and buttocks bore more than ample evidence of all the beatings he had taken. The remarkable thing to Popov was that Yevgeny's melancholia was not the result of all the beatings he had received. His sadness was due to knowing that his father couldn't help himself. And that his mother knew it too. To possess such insight, in someone so young, Popov found profoundly moving.

'My father kept telling me that wanting to be a musician was useless and effeminate,' Yevgeny told Popov. 'So, in the end, I agreed. That's when he beat me so brutally, my mother believed he would kill me.'

Madame Eshkol had later approached Popov, through someone aware of his reputation.

'You are unconventional, and so is Yevgeny,' she declared. 'In fact when he first came to live with us, I considered him to be a nuisance. I had given him some rudimentary music for beginners, and he mastered it in a matter of days. I thought it was a fluke, so gave him some grade two pieces, and then grades three and four. He became obsessed, and wouldn't go to school, so I consulted a psychologist, and in the end sent him to a teacher in Kyiv. Now, I am told, he needs to be placed in the hands of someone capable of developing his talent in order to realise his full potential.'

It didn't take very much convincing. Yevgeny already possessed the capability of independent musical thought, and the arrogant clarity of uncommon instinct.

'I can only add to what is already there,' said Popov.

In the aftermath of the competition, Popov was about to make another major decision.

'Come to my apartment for dinner,' said Popov. 'It's time we had a serious talk.'

His invitation to Yevgeny came as a complete surprise. As far as anybody knew, no one had ever been invited to Popov's apartment before.

'You could probably sell any photos you take of his apartment on the black market,' Maria told Yevgeny, 'or take me along to record the event for posterity'.

Yevgeny had no idea why Popov would invite him to dinner. Especially, since his performance hadn't elicited any interest from promoters whom Popov regarded as suitable. In fact he realised, once the fervour of the moment had passed, he would remain just another student. What he lived and breathed appeared as small pinnacles of momentary reflection in the lives of others. Maria disagreed. She assured Yevgeny that the performances of great artistes stayed long in the memory.

'You can't think otherwise,' she persisted. 'Why else would you perform?'

Popov had never mentioned his home life. It transpired he lived in a one-bed apartment close to the academy, situated in one of the back streets. The building was nondescript, and his apartment on the first floor was reached via a set of stone stairs. For once, Yevgeny was not carrying any music, and Maria suggested he take a bottle of wine to accompany the meal. Popov opened the door of his tiny apartment, and hugged Yevgeny like a favourite son. In fact, it occurred to Yevgeny that, in a way, is what he had become. Except that Popov had drawn a boundary between himself and his pupils, in order to retain the balance between teacher and taught. That was his privacy. Although, he emphasised, the power of his emotional insight, he himself only addressed in terms of music. Yevgeny was therefore, a rare visitor, and Popov received his gift of wine by reminding him that he didn't drink. Before he retreated to the kitchen to open the bottle and prepare the food, he led Yevgeny to his lounge. Looking around, it became apparent that Popov lived very frugally. A small dining table occupied the space by the window, and a vintage Blüthner took up most of the remaining space in the room. In between a threadbare carpet, and a large bookshelf, crammed with every type of publication and musical score, stood an armchair showing considerable age, and beside it a small table, that hosted an old radio and a portable record player. Piles of old vinyl recordings and sheet music occupied almost every inch of the remaining floorspace. Eventually, Popov entered, carrying a tray with a large bowl of goulash. He told Yevgeny that it was from a recipe given to him by a Slovakian conductor he had met at the Hotel Bristol some thirty-five years before, and was made special by red picadillo herbs, chilli, and, he emphasised, the best quality ground beef. He then poured Yevgeny a glass of wine and invited him to join him in a toast. Although, Popov's glass contained only water.

'What are we toasting?' Yevgeny asked.

'Your future,' said Popov.

It was clear that Popov had gone to a lot of trouble to prepare the meal, and before they began eating, Popov insisted on saying a prayer. In it, he thanked God for the blessing of Yevgeny's talent, and asked for protection and guidance for his future.'

'What future?' asked Yevgeny.

'Your future beyond the academic cloister,' declared Popov. 'To prepare and ensure the fruit of your gift is realised, not in just some academy teaching or earning a fee, but on the world stage. Someone who will be heard in all the best concert halls, influence choice, make recordings, and appeal to a whole new generation, just as Ashkenazy, Horowitz, Lipatti and Gilels. Great pianists captured at the very pinnacle of their power, who will be remembered. But a career doesn't happen by accident. It has to be planned. You have to be heard by the right people in the right places at the right time. Your career needs to be built by someone who knows what they are doing, and already has world-class contacts. In all my years at this institution, I have only recommended one pianist to this agent, and you will be the second. You are going to have to give up the life of a young man, and become totally absorbed and utterly single-minded. You will have to serve music before, after, and in between all other events that occupy your mind and your time. It is going to demand everything, and every ounce of your social tendencies will have to be sacrificed. But the rewards. The rewards, if you have the discipline, are beyond price. Nineteen! What I wouldn't give to be in your position. To enjoy the privilege of what these next years could bring. Between your fingers and your head is your heart. All three will be tested. A career in music is not for the faint-hearted. It demands everything, and then something more: character. However great your potential, it will be your character that determines your success, just as much as your skill. Your dedication will need to guard the flame of your gift, and your character will need to guard against all the temptation that gift creates. Do you understand what I'm saying? You are on the threshold. Now you enter the lions' den. Now you have to stand on your own two feet. To prove yourself. Not just to yourself, but to the world beyond. I want to know if you are ready for that to happen?'

'I'm not sure,' Yevgeny replied.

'Then that is my fault,' said Popov.

Yevgeny was taken by surprise, and completely unable to provide a comprehensive answer. He had only ever thought in terms of wanting to play. Not in the higher providence of having a career fashioned by a svengali.

'Where is this agent?' Yevgeny enquired.

'London,' said Popov. 'And well placed to ensure your development is taken at the right pace, and importantly, how to develop a lasting career. You could of course, stay here and play crowd-pleasing concertos. But ultimately, you would have to go abroad. There is no question about that. I would rather you went to London now, and make a name for yourself, rather than wait for General Putin to expand his empire, and march up the Potemkin Stairs, which in these uncertain times, he would dearly love to do!'

Yevgeny had given no serious consideration to life beyond the academy. Most musicians he knew were often unemployed or, if lucky, found work as rank-and-file-players with an orchestra or stage production. Nearly all became part-time teachers to supplement their income, performed short tours or worked seasonally. All lived precariously.

Popov was proposing that he move to a foreign country and place himself in the hands of someone who would effectively change his life. It was all so sudden. He explained to Popov,

'It's like swimming in the local pool one day, and then being asked to represent Ukraine at the Olympics the next.'

'Why not?' said Popov.

'Because your confidence in me, may be misplaced.'

Popov had strong convictions concerning the direction an artiste should take, and the experience to neutralise any determined opposition when the occasion demanded. He viewed Yevgeny's objections as being completely natural, under the circumstances, and urged him to trust his judgement.

'And what if I fail?' asked Yevgeny.

'Then don't come back,' said Popov. 'There will be no point.'

'It was as stark as that,' Yevgeny later told Maria. 'He simply presented me with the direction he believed my life should take, and then asked me what the alternative was? Except, I didn't have one.'

'What did you say?' asked Maria.

'I asked him for time to think it over. He gave me until the end of term.'

'But that's less than two months!'

'The way Popov proposed it, there is no choice.'

'But you can't speak English,' argued Maria. 'You'll be completely lost'

At her next tutorial, Maria confronted Popov about the ultimatum he had presented to Yevgeny. In reply, Popov acknowledged the difficulties, but emphasised the undeniable possibilities. He also gave examples of other child prodigies that had made the artistic leap from obscurity to international recognition, and reminded Maria they all had one thing in common.

'Any other life was unthinkable.'

Popov told Maria he had known the agent he recommended for over thirty years, initially as a soloist.

'He eats, lives and understands musicians for the unique individuals they are, yet he thinks like a businessman. He understands a career doesn't just arrive. It has to be constructed, nursed and given momentum. And for that, you need to know the right people. Yevgeny could stay here, receive good notices and rot. His early brilliance could then devolve into classical mediocrity, at which point he will resist challenge, and appear before less demanding audiences. Similar to ones you yourself will no doubt gravitate.'

Popov's observation took Maria's breath away.

'Why is Yevgeny's career so much more important than mine?' asked Maria, and added that she thought Yevgeny would be hopelessly lost in London, and unable to cope.

Popov was not in the least surprised by her response. It was often the method by which he could extricate an exceptional performance from a reluctant pupil. He therefore decided not to reply directly, but thought for a moment, and said,

'Well, if that's the way you feel, why don't you go with him?'

Maria was shocked at Popov's suggestion, and gasped.

'You are due to leave the academy at the end of term anyway.' he added. 'It also happens that London has some excellent musical institutions. You could always take a postgraduate performer's course. I would be happy to write a letter of recommendation.'

A thousand and one possibilities filled Maria's head. The

suggestion temporarily floored her, and she didn't know what to say. For a fleeting moment, the prospect filled her with excitement. Then she decided to ridicule the idea.

'It's totally out of the question,' she said.

'Think about it,' urged Popov.

When Maria relayed Popov's suggestion to Yevgeny, he didn't think the idea was so absurd. Whilst he couldn't speak English, Maria could, and although she would have to struggle as a student, he on the other hand could provide an income and take care of their accommodation. Apart from making sense financially,

'It might be interesting,' suggested Yevgeny.

The more she considered the idea, the more it appealed. As far as Yevgeny was concerned, her consent was vital.

'In fact, if you don't come with me, I won't go,' he insisted.

Whether he was serious or not, the darling buds of new opportunity began flowering with endless possibilities. They both would be leaving the academy with a clear direction. Yevgeny, to the experienced hands of someone capable of fostering a career, and Maria, to further explore her academic potential.

They were both grateful to Popov, and felt deeply in his debt. For his part, Popov had sound reasons for believing they would be better off in London. For years, Vladimir Putin had been using political unrest, insurgency and a series of crises as an excuse for military intervention, and had now annexed the Crimea. It was, concluded Popov, an ominous indication of a much larger ambition.

'At this point in our history, your future is better served elsewhere,' he warned. 'If you make a success of music, then the world is your oyster!'

3.

VIKTOR GORLINSKY WAS a promoter of considerable charisma and entrepreneurial flair. He represented a number of world class pianists, and had contacts with the managements of many famous orchestras worldwide. As Popov reminded Yevgeny, he could make or break a career.

He had sent Gorlinsky several recordings of Yevgeny with extensive notes on his background and repertoire. 'You must realise, however,' Popov wrote, 'that he is still very young and unworldly. I trust you will treat him like a beloved son, which is what he has become to me'. Yevgeny was unaware of Popov's deep affection. Popov rarely showed it. Yet his pupils were his children and Yevgeny was special. The piano had become an expression of his inner conflict, and his sensitivity led him to pursue something beyond the perfect reading of a score. That is what Gorlinsky had heard, and Maria also acknowledged.

'Are you jealous?' Popov had once asked her.

'Not jealous. But envious. Not of the work. That I could do. No. It's the prodigious gift of instinct. That is what I envy!' said Maria.

'Me too,' agreed Popov. 'Me too.'

Gorlinsky, on the recommendation of Popov, offered Yevgeny a contract. However, it wasn't for a duration of five years, as Popov had suggested, but one year, in which Yevgeny was to be paid a set salary, and perform in any number of concerts at venues, places, and at such time as 'contracted' by Gorlinsky. In other words, he would be on probation for a period of one year, during which time his potential would be assessed.

Popov told Yevgeny,

'Once the ceremonies are over and the paperwork completed. You are on your own.'

Popov cried on their departure, and presented Maria with a heart-shaped locket containing a few mustard seeds.

'It represents the faith I have in you!' he declared, and made them both promise they would report their progress on a regular basis.

Maria's parents had provided the means for her fees, plus a small allowance, and had taken the announcement of her move to London as more a matter of political expediency than higher education. Yevgeny, however, had remained estranged from his parents, but told Maria he planned to send them money, as soon as his income permitted. In the meantime, Gorlinsky had arranged temporary accommodation for their arrival in London, but during her first week at college, Maria found them a room each, sharing a house with three others. Pooling their resources, she felt confident they could survive perfectly well. But not everything had gone to plan. Maria had wanted to accompany Yevgeny to his first meeting with Gorlinsky, but the impresario who spoke seven languages including Ukrainian, told Yevgeny to leave his chaperone at home.

Rather than his office, Gorlinsky instructed Yevgeny to meet him at a rehearsal studio, and to bring a selection of works that he would like to hear. Among them Chopin, Bach, Rachmaninoff, Beethoven, Liszt, Scriabin, Ravel, Prokofiev, folk songs, jazz, at least two contemporary composers, and to include Gershwin and Broadway standards.

'I want to hear everything,' he told him.

Yevgeny proved that the recordings sent by Popov were no fluke, and he was up to the demands of performance. Afterwards,

Gorlinsky took him to lunch, and outlined how their association would proceed. He demanded solid application, sobriety, punctuality and an adherence to the professional standards that ensured continued confidence in his agency. He also told Yevgeny he would start him off with performances in smaller and more intimate venues, and enquired about his health and living conditions. He then told him that sleep and discipline were important factors for success, and arranged for him to practise at a studio close to the Wigmore Hall in London's West End. By the time they had finished dessert, there was hardly an aspect of Yevgeny's life that Gorlinsky was unfamiliar with. As a result, Yevgeny told Maria later, he left the restaurant feeling he had been 'branded like a prize bull.'

'Well. You are certainly full of it!' Maria said.

Yevgeny lowered his head, scraped his foot on the floor, and chased her through the house, threatening to toss her in the air. They then set off for Hyde Park, and resumed their initial discovery of London. It was a world away from the familiar compact centre of Odesa, and full of interesting and quirky diversions. But it also proved to be one of their last periods of freedom.

The very next week, Gorlinsky sent a schedule of engagements to Yevgeny, with instructions concerning the venue, programme, accommodation, travel arrangements and performance conditions. It was soon very clear Yevgeny, was going to be kept busy, something that somehow came as a shock. Maria had assumed they would be spending most of their spare time together. But often, when her study and lecture periods had finished, Yevgeny was about to perform. It was the 'realpolitik of a performer's life,' he maintained. A bargain they had both entered into as part of the journey. It inevitably meant they would be seeing much less of each other. The one exception were the days when they were both free to meet for lunch. On these occasions, they usually met in Kensington Gardens, and shared a home-made sandwich, or, if they felt in an extravagant mood, dined at the Victoria and Albert Museum, close to the college.

One day, they decided to have lunch in the ground floor restaurant of the museum, and occupied a table situated in the middle of the dining area. Yevgeny, who was feeling especially light-hearted, shared with Maria an amusing story Gorlinsky had told him concerning Popov. Apparently, Popov, in his prime, was a highly gifted pianist, and someone the party longed to welcome as a loyal member. Unfortunately for them, he was a virulent anti-communist, and knew that celebrity came at a price. Gilels himself, he noted, was being accompanied by the KGB on his tours! Popov's dissent therefore seriously hampered his career, and as a result, many less-talented pianists were rewarded with the kind of prestigious engagements he himself was denied.

One such celebrated advocate of the party machine was Sergei Babushkin, who arrived in Popov's home town one day, to perform Tchaikovsky's First Piano Concerto. Babushkin, a recipient of one of the State's highest honours, and a personal friend of Brezhnev, was labelled the 'Steinway Strangler' by Popov for his heavy-handed playing, and belief that interpretation was conditioned by ideology. The concert itself, held at the town hall, with a front row graced by party officials, was therefore ablaze with excitement, as the coat-tailed heavyweight took to the stage, and acknowledged the well-primed applause of the audience. Some acolytes even shouting 'Bravo', before he had even struck a stubby finger on any of the keys. In fact, according to Gorlinsky, Babushkin had taken several encores even before he had placed his well-rounded bottom on the piano stool.

The playing of the concerto was, therefore, to be a foregone party triumph, with the added 'frisson' that the concert was to be broadcast for posterity. Accordingly, the hall was hushed as the famous opening chords were blasted from the resonant Steinway, and the orchestra responded with the full vitality of a battalion about to invade Poland. The well-known melody now enjoying the expanse of its cavernous surroundings, as both soloist and orchestra set out to perform its public execution. After a short time, however, something began to catch Babushkin's eye. At first he ignored it. Then once more, he was distracted. He kept glancing at the conductor, employing the use of his eyebrows to signal something was wrong. The conductor however, refused to be diverted from driving the orchestra onwards, with the type of decibel count the party revered. All the while, Babushkin gallantly played on, attempting to attract the conductor's attention. Pssst… the inconsiderate interruption of a musical Philistine could be discerned… Pssst! Babushkin tried once again to get the attention of the maestro, his head nodding furiously towards the uninvited spectator. It proved pointless, however, as both orchestra and conductor refused to be distracted from their commitment to Tchaikovsky. Then Babushkin began to include a few wrong notes, to alert someone. But the conductor, believing that Babushkin was undergoing some kind of breakdown, attempted to cover up these mistakes by demanding the orchestra play twice as loud, whilst Babushkin's response was to play twice as fast. Both parties now engaged in a race to the finish, like two antagonistic egos locked in open combat, until Babushkin's playing accelerated at such an alarming rate, his hands skidded off the keyboard and he lost control, like a Formula One driver crashing through a barrier at the climax of a Grand Prix.

The conductor, now incandescent with rage, put down his baton and stared at Babushkin in disbelief, whilst Babushkin, his hands now shaking, pointed his finger towards the top of the piano, where inches away, a large hairy tarantula, complete with furry underbelly in matching ebony, stared at him menacingly from the grand tier of the music stand. Having been so rudely awoken by the opening chords, the tarantula had slowly emerged from under the open lid of the piano, and accompanied by the musical vibration of Tchaikovsky, made its eight-legged progression across the model D, and took up an attacking position opposite the terrified gaze of the concerto assassin. The beady eyes of the velvet arachnid, belonging to a friend of

Popov's, now staring at him, fangs open and ready to pounce on the hapless and perspiring Babushkin.

Those nearby now also began pointing to the toxic eight-legged intruder, and in a matter of minutes, the auditorium was ordered to be cleared, and the party officials promptly escorted to the exit. The whole building being vacated, as if a bomb was about to explode!

Popov himself, seated in the gallery, walked casually away with a smile on his face, and on enquiring about the reason for the sudden evacuation, was told it was because a poisonous spider had been found on the piano.

'Ah. That would be Babushkin then,' said Popov. 'No wonder everyone was in a hurry to leave!'

Yevgeny delivered the punchline with such libidinous energy, that both he and Maria burst into loud spontaneous laughter, that disturbed several people seated close to them. Maria put her finger to her lips and apologised, warning Yevgeny to behave himself. But it was apparent he was feeling especially mischievous, and for some reason, very pleased with himself.

'I never thought Popov could stoop so high!' said Maria, before Yevgeny leaned forward and said quietly, 'I think you have an admirer.'

He then indicated with his eyes for her to look towards a table in the far corner, occupied by a middle-aged man. Maria glanced around, and looked at someone appearing to be either writing or drawing on a small writing pad.

'Why me?' she asked. 'Why not you?'

'I somehow think he prefers redheads,' said Yevgeny.

'Oh really? Why not blondes?'

Maria turned around again, and this time looked directly at the man, and smiled in the same way she would as if someone had held a door open for her.

'He's probably English,' she remarked.

'How do you know?' asked Yevgeny.

'Because they always look embarrassed if you acknowledge them. It's a national characteristic.'

'Very well,' said Yevgeny, 'let us put your theory to the test. When we have finished, why don't you wave me goodbye, and head towards the ground floor galleries. If he remains in the restaurant, I owe you lunch. But if he follows you, the next time we dine, you'll be in my debt for the lofty sum of one vegetable lasagne plus a double espresso.'

'He'll be too embarrassed to follow me,' said Maria.

'In that case, let's make it smoked salmon instead!'

Shortly after, Maria stood up, and with outstretched arms, bid Yevgeny farewell. Then after leaving the restaurant, made her way to the ground floor gallery, that contained a large display of ancient sculptures. After some time, she glanced casually around, and in the distance, observed the man inspecting a statue of Neptune by Bernini. She then hid behind Sampson, circled David, and after looking thoughtfully at the Rodin, weaved her way through various exhibits, including Donatello and Michaelangelo, before heading towards the South East Asian section. He dutifully followed at a discreet distance, but obviously, had now realised that Maria was happily teasing him. Eventually, she arrived at the Japanese section, and paused at a cabinet displaying a collection of kimonos. The man entered the room, and hovered in the background, whilst Maria purposely remained stationary at a particularly striking exhibit. Observing him in the reflection of the glass, she could see he was hesitant to approach, so folded her arms and turned her head slightly, to signify she was fully aware of his presence. He tentatively arrived, and stood silently beside her. Then, without taking her eyes off the exhibit, she remarked,

'Now that you are in front of the object you came to see, what do you think?'

The man replied he thought it was 'a work of art'.

'And what about Rodin and the art of Southeast Asia?'

'I hardly noticed them,' the man answered.

She found his replies unexpectedly disarming, but her assumption was correct. He was English, and looked acutely embarrassed during their brief exchange.

'I think you should know your love of art has just cost me the most expensive thing on the lunchtime menu!' said Maria.

'I'm sorry,' said the man.

'Your tour of the ground floor gallery being the result of a bet!'

'I thought as much.'

'It's OK. In some countries, following people around is a full time occupation that includes a pension,' said Maria.

'Then you must be Russian!' the man exclaimed.

'Please don't say that so close to the armoury section. Especially to a Ukrainian.'

The man held out his hand, and introduced himself.

'I'm Stephen. A teacher at a loose end during the last days of the summer holiday.'

'What are you a teacher of?' asked Maria.

'English.'

'I thought so.'

'Really?'

'Yes. A science teacher would be more concerned with facts. Whereas you are more contemplative, like someone influenced by too many brooding poets.'

'Are you always like this?' he asked.

'Forgive me. I'm feeling in a light hearted mood today, just like Yev, the boy sitting with me at the table. Except his English is hopeless.'

'And yours surprisingly fluent.'

'Yes. My parents thought of everything, including the serious business of study, to which I must return,' said Maria.

'So soon?'

'We're like fleeting paths that crossed by accident,' said Maria. 'Thanks for accompanying me on my whirlwind tour of Asia.'

Maria shook his hand, and began to hurry towards the exit, with Stephen in pursuit.

'Wait!' he called out.

Maria came to a sudden stop.

'I don't even know your name,' he explained.

'Maria.'

'Maria who?' he persisted.

'Just Maria,' she said.

Stephen quickly reached into his pocket, pulled out a napkin, and wrote down his name and mobile number.

'Here is my number. Just in case your friend is interested in improving his English.'

Maria hesitated, and then, taking the napkin, said,

'Of course. He is the one with the great career prospects. I'm just a student!'

'Of what?' Stephen enquired.

Maria smiled at him, and did an amusing little dance with her fingers.

'I'm a pianist, and my friend Yevgeny is going to be very famous one day!'

Again, she apologised for her childish deception, and almost skipped through the door into the afternoon sun.

Their meeting had been amusing and refreshingly open, but like other middle-aged tutors, she had observed, he appeared jaded, and somehow in search of something he was unable to find. Like many others, a man of contemplation, that espoused an answer for others, he was unable to find for himself. He was, she concluded, somewhat educated but 'lost', and remembered he watched her intently, as she melted into the human traffic of South Kensington.

His name was Stephen Kline, and later Yevgeny kept referring to him as Maria's most devoted 'follower'.

This brief interlude of passing amusement was quickly forgotten with the announcement of Yevgeny's Wigmore Hall debut. Something for which he had eagerly awaited. It also gave him a valuable insight into the extent of Gorlinsky's immense ambition. On arriving at his office one day to discuss repertoire, Gorlinsky was in the middle of a phone conversation with a well known American soprano. He had apparently been trying in vain to persuade various major orchestras to invite a young Finnish musician on his books to be their 'guest conductor', and had discovered that the soprano was preparing to make a recording of the 'Four Last Songs' of Richard Strauss. Gorlinsky suggested she might like to use his protégé's services for her recording. She replied that it would be extremely difficult, because a conductor had already been selected, and that his client was not very well-known.

'That's perfectly true,' said Gorlinsky, 'but after he's made the recording with you, he will be.'

The soprano laughed, and said,

'Yes, on the back of my name,' to which Gorlinsky replied, 'Daarling, you owe me a favour… Time to pay up!'

That was it! Gorlinsky's client was engaged.

What hold, Yevgeny wondered, did Gorlinsky have over her?

He was later to learn the soprano was once well-known to the opera-going public, but no one else. Gorlinsky suggested that she turn her attention to Broadway, and make a recording of showstoppers, believing it would not only attract her own fans, but an army of people who had never set foot inside an opera house. In the event, the recording was very well reviewed, displaying a completely different side to her vocal and dramatic possibilities, and sold well. So much so, that Gorlinsky suggested that she turn the recording into a one woman show, with him as producer. As a result, 'Broadway Diva' became a hot ticket in the West End and on Broadway, and the soprano owed him big time. She must have known that one day Gorlinsky would be knocking on the door for what he termed his 'secret per cent'. Not all sopranos were as lucky though. A well respected 'name' once came to Gorlinsky, looking for representation. He listened to her, and reported she had one of the finest voices he had ever heard. Unfortunately, she looked like a frump, was overweight and middle-aged. So, in the end he said to her,

'May I be frank? You have one of the finest voices before the public today. But I have no idea what to do with you, other than getting you engagements wearing a large suit of armour with matching helmet, just in case Wotan has a tantrum, during the third Act of Götterdämmerung. But thank you for coming.'

On another occasion, he was rumoured to have suggested that Cleo Laine sing in a jazz version of 'Carmen', and positively drooled at the notion of her interpretation of the Habanera and Seguidilla. Her vocal range being used to twist and turn around all those delicious phrases, positively fed into his creative juices. In fact, he loved jazz and jazz musicians. Sadly, his idea never came to fruition, but he was always thinking out of the box.

'Why shouldn't a great jazz artiste also sing Bizet?' he asked.

In fact, at their first meeting, Gorlinsky ordered Yevgeny to play him a jazz version of 'Manhattan' by Gershwin, 'just for the hell of it!'

But now his first real test had arrived, one that could attract national reviews. Gorlinsky suggested the programme should be interesting, and contain a few surprises. One of them being to premiere a work by a young composer. The idea immediately found favour with Yevgeny, and he pleaded to know who the composer was.

'I have someone in mind,' said Gorlinsky. 'It's just they aren't aware of it yet.'

A week later, Felipe Vargas bounded up the steps of the rehearsal studio in the West End, and hugged Yevgeny, as if he was a long-lost brother, from whom he had been parted since birth. He reminded Yevgeny of a young Antonio Banderas, and thought his music was inspirational. A Mexican studying at the academy, he had written a set of tangos for piano that perfectly suited Yevgeny's infectious and spirited bravado. They required South American panache, and the kind of rhythmic exhibitionism, reminiscent of castanets glistening in the sun, as a couple enact the nearest thing to foreplay fully-clothed. They were so exuberant and infectiously youthful that Yevgeny exclaimed 'I love them! I love them!' in Ukrainian, as Felipe looked on highly amused, and feeling proud of himself, responded 'Bravo, Signor Yevy!' so loudly, their excitement could possibly be heard by shoppers a mile away. It was another of Gorlinsky's inspired ideas, welcomed by Yevgeny. The remainder of the programme consisted of Schumann, Bach, Ravel, Poulenc, and Ligeti, plus a Strauss waltz arranged by Liszt, and Yevgeny's own arrangement of 'La vie en Rose'. But the Tangos proved to be the highlight, and provided the encore, with Yevgeny discarding the piano stool, and standing up like Jerry Lee Lewis, repeating one of them at double speed, he dubbed 'Tango-boogie'.

Gorlinsky was delighted, and dubbed him 'Jerry La Paz'.

It wasn't the usual stiff upper lip classical debut, so beloved by agents promoting young artistes, but a separate calling card, that enabled Yevgeny to show his unique talent.

After the concert, he introduced Maria to Gorlinsky.

'You must hear Maria,' suggested Yevgeny. 'She is a fabulous pianist, and currently getting lots of offers!'

'From whom?' Gorlinsky enquired.

'From you!' answered Yevgeny, cheekily.

Gorlinsky appeared to mentally circle Maria, and then asked, 'What experience do you have?'

She replied that she had so far only undertaken concerts in Ukraine.

'At present, I have my hands full,' said Gorlinsky, 'and not looking to expand my representation.'

'Couldn't you loosen your belt, just a little?' implored Yevgeny.

'Unfortunately, that would leave me less time to go tango-hunting,' Gorlinsky replied.

The meeting was brief, and Maria found Gorlinsky curiously aloof.

'He is attracted to fame, said Yevgeny. 'After all, he has all those five finger flirters from China and Korea for beauty!'

Gorlinsky's idea of publicising the premiere of a new composition, had aroused the curiosity of some music critics. The result was Yevgeny received uniformly good reviews in three national newspapers, and commenting on the encore, one observed,

'Here was a pianist not afraid to live dangerously.'

It was to prove an ominous prediction. But right now, Yevgeny was enjoying the pianistic equivalent of an Indian summer. Busier than ever, he and Maria now only met briefly for breakfast on a Sunday morning, before he prepared to travel to his next schedule of engagements.

The meeting with Gorlinsky had not even yielded the offer of an audition, and now Yevgeny's workload was to separate them even further. As a result, Maria felt homesick. She missed her friends at the academy, especially the intimate indiscretion of Moiseiwitsch, the cafés in Derybasivska Street, Primorsky Boulevard, the monthly visit to her parents, and her beloved Kyiv. She began to feel the cold chill of exile, and spend more time at the college. There, she found plenty of opportunity for performance, and was working towards making her own auspicious debut. The competition was fierce. Pianists from China, South Korea, Japan, America, Asia, Europe and Scandinavia, some so young they required a chaperone, many precocious, some barely teenagers, all brilliantly and exceptionally talented.

'What is your selling point?' she was asked in one of the lectures on 'getting recognition.'

It seemed being an exceptional pianist was just the beginning. Success required identifying your niche, finding the 'right' agent, and the employment of such strategy, as finding favour with a well known musician. Endearment being as crucial as superior confidence, and the ability to simply play well… the road to nowhere. Survival as a musician being as much about business as about performance.

'Maybe, Liberace had something to teach us after all,' she announced amusingly.

The audience for her individually-tailored sensibility of the humorous kind did not always suit everyone's taste, and the pianists she knew mostly liked to talk shop. Earlier in life, she had taken up the violin, and often gravitated towards the string players. In the same year at college was a cellist named Edward. He had tousled hair, aquiline features and wrestled with tidiness like some people have a habit of wearing the wrong colours. Disorganised and rather shy, he reminded her of someone out of the nineteenth century. English, slightly nervous and eccentric in manner. He had played in several concerts, and she was taken by how he caressed the cello, as if making love, whilst in the act of producing a soothing mellow sound. She considered he had a uniquely sensuous relationship with his instrument, but most of all, was attracted by the passion he invested in music-making, and also appeared to be a 'loner'. One day, she spotted him having lunch on his own, and approached him.

'Excuse me for asking,' she said, 'but what's a 'complete arse'?'

The mere act of her presence seemed to arouse in him a mild panic.

'Why do you want to know?' he replied.

'I heard someone refer to it in conversation.'

'It defies translation,' he answered.

'That's why I'm asking,' said Maria, 'since we are *all* translators!'

Maria had provoked his interest, and was delighted to learn that he also played the piano. She asked him if he would be interested in helping her form a quartet.

'Otherwise, it's going to be a long winter,' she said.

By now, she had cultivated friendships with a small circle of like-minded people, and a quartet, she calculated, would allow her to spread her social wings. Although the people at her flat were all students, they had all made their own alliances, and largely met at the bathroom door. For most, it had become a cliché reserved for the participants of flat sharing. All, that is, except for Yevgeny, who occupied the tiny attic room at the top of the house that contained a single bed and, more enviously, a wash basin. This exclusivity cost him a higher proportion of the rent. But he was the only one earning a full-time income. The hours he kept meant that he was rarely seen, but could be heard sometimes climbing the stairs in the early hours, and was never awake early morning. Often, when Maria looked in his room, he was sleeping, and at night rarely at home. The 'realpolitik' of musical apprenticeship, she decided, came at a heavy price. Not that she was alone for very long, nor lacked admirers. One of the main attractions of Edward was that he wasn't predatory. He had tried to kiss her in the lift once, when they were on their way to a party. But she pulled away. He was dreadfully hurt, and she explained that there was someone back home, that prevented her from committing to any other relationship. It was a lie, but before she could add any further authenticity, he simply said,

'Please, there's no need to explain.'

No more was said, and the rejection was despatched with the efficiency that was to become the hallmark of all her potential conquests.

'What's wrong?' a friend at the academy had once asked.

'My father instilled in me the attraction of virginity,' Maria answered defensively.

'It's an attraction that one day could lack customers,' her friend advised.

Her frigidity was the consequence of an earlier incident. As a result, a psychiatrist had been consulted. But the facts had been disputed, and she carried the guilt of being branded both a 'troublemaker' and an 'unreliable witness'.

She was sixteen, and her father and mother, worried about her lack of menstruation, had sent her to a well-known gynaecologist for a routine examination. The doctor himself appeared youthful, was very charming, and possessed an extremely reassuring manner. He requested permission to examine her, and when they were alone, asked her to remove her pants, and lie down on a couch. He then told her that he just needed to 'take a look,' and asked her to 'relax'. All she could do was close her eyes, and attempt to remain emotionally detached. In a very short time, she instinctively felt something was wrong. He had inserted his finger into her vagina, and now began attempting to stimulate her clitoris. For several minutes, she remained pinned to the couch, frozen and unable to move, as he cynically and ruthlessly violated her innocence. Suddenly, she let out a scream of pain, and he instantly removed his hand. In less than five seconds, a nurse from the outer office entered, and the gynaecologist ordered Maria to get dressed. Instead of apologising, however, he removed his gloves, appeared agitated, and ignored her. On returning home, she told her parents what had happened.

'How do you know he wasn't just looking for evidence of menstruation?' her father asked.

'Do you think I don't know my own body. Besides, he asked me some odd questions before the exam. Like, if I had a boyfriend.'

Her parents were visibly shaken, and disturbed by the accusation. The question being examined though was not the culpability of the consultant, but of his position and prominence. More importantly to her parents, he worked at same hospital in Kyiv as they did.

'It would be highly embarrassing to bring an accusation of this nature,' her father stated.

'What about the other victims?' questioned Maria.

It was decided that Maria's mother should approach the consultant. She asked to see him privately, and reported verbatim Maria's accusation. The gynaecologist flatly denied any inappropriate behaviour, and told the mother that if the accusation was repeated, both she and her husband would face the full extent of legal action to defend his reputation.

'It's up to you,' her mother told Maria, 'but if we take this further and make a complaint, you cannot change your story.'

Like many other issues in her life, the incident was papered over in the name of expedience. Everyone was always trying to survive something. Therefore Edward was persuaded to keep his distance, whilst at the same time their friendship signalled to other predators she was 'taken'.

Apart from performing together, Edward introduced her to listening. They therefore took in as many diverse attractions as possible, including concerts at the South Bank, modern and classical ensembles, recitals at the Wigmore Hall, clubs, pubs, soul, jazz funk, blues, reggae, and the rhythms of Africa. Sounds that had, so far, never made her acquaintance. She wrote effusively to her parents and Popov, declaring that both she and Yevgeny were each in their own way 'hitting all the right notes'. But she was still nowhere nearer to a significant London debut, and Yevgeny, whenever she did manage to see him, was always exhausted.

One day, she and Edward were browsing in a bookshop, and he showed her a book of poetry he had begun to read, entitled 'Perhaps Love'. As usual, Maria made light of it.

'If that is a question for me,' she clarified, 'demand outstrips supply!'

Later on, when they were browsing in one of the department stores, she glanced at him, and saw him looking in deep despair.

'What's wrong?' she asked.

'I can't stand the torment any longer,' he answered, and looked at Maria in a way that left no room for doubt about his feelings.

Generally, Edward was a very private person, who displayed his emotions in the most subtle words and gestures. Especially through music. He normally absorbed hurt, and would avoid confrontation at all costs. But today was different. He told Maria that he had gained a great deal out of their music-making, conversations and disagreements about human rights, politics, ethics, music, art and the whole spectrum of the human race's absorption with themselves. But he couldn't, and was totally unable, to continue seeing her just as a 'friend'.

The only outcome he could accept would be a relationship, or nothing at all.

Maria was totally unprepared for Edward's uncompromising position. She had already made some tentative enquiries concerning future employment of the quartet, and had thought ahead to a Wigmore Hall debut. But whatever happened in the future, Edward would no longer be an active ingredient in the development of her life. She felt disappointed, and in many ways, angry. Although there had been no physical dimension to their relationship, she completely failed to understand how he could walk away from all the tangible and positively enduring aspects of their compatibility. The inter-personal undercurrent of understanding, exchange of ideas, humour, shared interest and affection.

'Do you think that has no value?' Maria asked.

'It's like believing the wrapping is of more value than the gift inside the box,' he said.

Edward's reply was given more in sorrow than spite, but nonetheless decisive.

'You are a very talented pianist,' he assured Maria. 'You'll have no trouble finding work.'

The compliment was like handing her a consolation prize she had no other choice than to accept gracefully. As a result, she turned her back on the idea of a quartet, and threw herself wholeheartedly into the pursuit of a solo career. For this she would require insane persistence, need to expand her repertoire, and utilize her engaging personality in the cause of networking. In exchange, her likely reward would be unpredictability of income, instability of work, and a delay in having children. The careers advisor did not defrost the icing when she presented the cake.

'You know there are immensely talented pianists out there still struggling for work?'

'Perhaps I should I take a plumbing course instead?' Maria commented.

But worse was to come.

On returning home one Friday evening, she was invited by her housemates for a 'chat'.

All three housemates looked very solemn, and there was an atmosphere of hostility in the room, that was unmistakeable. James, the eldest member, acted as their spokesman.

'Are you aware that Yevgeny has not paid the rent for the past six weeks?' he asked.

The suggestion caught Maria completely off-guard.

'He informed us that he was owed money from fees, and would bring your rent up to date by the end of the month. The end of the month was two weeks ago.'

'Yevgeny is scrupulously honest and financially responsible. If he hasn't been paid, then it's the fault of his agent,' said Maria.

'You don't know the half of it,' said James.

Maria was invited to follow him to Yevgeny's small attic room, at the top of the house. When they arrived outside the room, he told her to look inside,

'See for yourself,' he said.

Maria opened the door slowly. The room was dark, and the curtains were closed. She turned on the light, and was faced with Yevgeny's unmade bed, his clothes strewn across the floor, empty cups, tissues, wrappers, polystyrene containers, and scattered amongst the debris, the unmistakable evidence of personal decimation, used hypodermic needles.

'We came up earlier to deliver a notice to quit, and this is what we found,' James said.

Amongst the foul air of betrayal, all Maria could think about was the state of Yevgeny's mind, and that he must be urgently in need of help.

'Now we know where the money went,' said James. 'It's no longer simply a matter of money. It's a breach of the tenancy, and puts us all in danger of losing the roof over our heads.'

James began to recite at length the extent of Yevgeny's antisocial behaviour, with the full force of a prosecuting counsel's indignation, outlining a foolproof case, that ended with the ultimate sanction.

'But Yevgeny needs help,' stated Maria. 'It's help he needs, not rejection.'

'That's your problem, not ours,' insisted James.

He delivered their decision with the cold-cutting anger of the righteous, whilst the others offered no dissent, and insisted that there was no other course they could follow. It wasn't just a question of the money any longer. Yevgeny and Maria had to vacate their rooms by the following weekend.

'Naturally, we'll keep your deposit, but you both will still owe for several weeks!'

The atmosphere had now become so poisoned, there was no point in attempting to broker a resolution. Their position was non-negotiable. It wasn't that they didn't understand the issues involved. The problem was they did. But the rules were the rules.

Maria went to Yevgeny's room, and slammed the door. She wasn't mad at them, but angry and frustrated. Yevgeny rarely answered his phone, and it went straight to voicemail.

'Come home. Straight away,' she urged. 'We have to talk!'

Several hours later she heard him climb the stairs, and sat facing the door as he opened it.

She had now made his bed, tidied his room, and bagged up the remnants of his tardy occupation. All that is, except for a few items that she had wrapped in a tissue, now nestling in the palm of her hand. Yevgeny did not smile when he entered. He looked drawn and thinner than she remembered, and behind his eyes was a world weariness that perfectly reflected an inner conversation. He could do nothing else but sit beside her. He then placed his head in his hands and remained silent. Just as shouting can sometimes clear the air, to make an ugly point, so silence can lay claim to something more powerful.

'It's the unsaid that can ruin lives, not confession,' Popov once argued.

Maria now reminded Yevgeny of this, and then asked pointedly,

'What happened?'

'You know already,' he replied.

'I know the what. But not the why.'

Maria opened her hand, and exposed a few examples of the evidence she had picked up.

'How long?'

'Since before we left.'

'How bad?'

'You don't want to know.'

'So how do you occupy your time, now that you're no longer playing? Or can you play with an arm like a pin-cushion?'

'I'm trying to forget I ever did.'

'Well, you should know that your new love has now made us homeless. You need help, and you need it urgently.'

Maria left the room, without saying another word. Her mind silently assessing the unfathomable crisis for which she could supply no answers. Everything about the situation was too hazardous to contemplate. The one thing she did understand was that she now had no other choice than to become the breadwinner.

4.

THEY HAD WAITED outside the door for sometime without getting an answer. Then the buzzer sounded, and the catch was released allowing them to enter a hallway, leading to a large metal staircase, and then to a room the size of a small hall. The room was bare except for a long table and several chairs. Maria and Yevgeny sat down and waited. Fully ten minutes had passed, until a middle-aged lady hurriedly entered. She neither smiled, nor introduced herself, but instead took two forms from her folder, along with two pens, and placed them in front of Maria and Yevgeny.

'Apologies for the delay. We're short staffed. Before we begin, please could you fill in these forms.'

Maria briefly studied the forms and filled in the first line stating their names.

'We came here for some advice,' said Maria. 'We are from Ukraine, and Yevgeny here cannot speak English well. I will need to fill the form in for him.'

'Very well. What's your address?'

The woman took the forms and looked at their names.

'We are required to vacate our accommodation at the end of the week,' said Maria.

'We do not accommodate. We only treat, and our services at present are under severe pressure.'

'But Yevgeny needs help now,' said Maria. 'Next week or next month is no good. He is unable to work, and we are short of money.'

'What about you?' the woman asked. 'Are you seeking treatment as well?'

'No,' said Maria. 'I'm clean.'

'Our programme requires someone to make a commitment of several months. Possibly much longer. It will also require discipline and regular attendance. Is your partner able to make that commitment?'

'Anything.'

'We are also obliged to make an assessment. Plus, it would be enormously helpful if you had a settled address.'

'I understand,' said Maria. 'You don't want to help us!'

'On the contrary,' said the woman. 'I'm being far more helpful than you realise. It's not just a case of waving a magic wand. Many start the course, but not everyone has the discipline to finish. It's important you understand the level of commitment required. I suggest you go away and think about it. Then let me know what you decide.'

The interview was short but stark. Deliberately so, Maria suspected. As they walked away, she told him,

'You have no choice. The alternative is annihilation.'

Yevgeny confessed he had been summarily dismissed by Gorlinsky, two months before.

He had initially become addicted to the cocaine Szell had introduced to him at the competition.

At first it made him feel confident, energetic, and totally alive. But eventually, the highs were replaced by low energy, lack of concentration, sickness and memory loss. He had cleverly managed to cover this up at first, but gradually his performances had begun to suffer. He was the first to notice, of course. When a conductor took him aside and asked, 'Are you OK?', Yevgeny pretended he was recovering from a cold, and in later concerts, excused his erratic playing as being 'unwell'. By this time, his medication included heroin.

It was a performance of the Mozart C minor piano concerto

that brought matters to a head. He had negotiated the early movements confidently, but completely fell apart during the chromatic section leading to the finale, and exited the stage without acknowledging either the conductor or the audience. When he returned to his dressing room, Gorlinsky was waiting, and ordered Yevgeny to take off his jacket and roll up his sleeve.

'All your future engagements are cancelled,' Gorlinsky declared. 'My office will call you when I have the patience to formally dissolve our association!'

The first thing Yevgeny turned to in despair absorbed all his money. His plea bargain that he would seek help made no difference. After several weeks, he received through the post a letter, asking him to attend the office by appointment. He went with the intention of appealing for understanding and assistance. But to his complete shock and dismay, was not greeted by Gorlinsky himself, but by Popov. Yevgeny, was taken completely by surprise. Popov, he knew, rarely travelled anywhere, and was overwhelmed he had journeyed such a distance. Yevgeny expected he had been invited to act as a mediator, and use his influence in negotiating his future under Gorlinsky's management. But from the tone of his opening remarks, it became clear that Popov was not there to facilitate a reconciliation.

On the contrary, Popov had rarely been so angry, and immediately disarmed Yevgeny of the notion of any practical or emotional support. Rather, he felt he had been betrayed by Yevgeny. Popov's vituperation being delivered in a manner so precise and so bitter, it had the inescapable finality of an execution.

'What have you done?' Popov demanded.

Yevgeny remained silent. There was to be no appeal. The man who had taken him to his heart like a father, and groomed him for the most perfect of all idyllic prospects, was now holding up a mirror for Yevgeny to witness his own disgrace. Each word more wounding than the last.

'You have killed two things. Two things. Music and your soul,'

Popov declared.

'And that has rendered you useless. Useless! Are you so arrogant that you can turn your back on the truth. Do you know it any more? In a world flooded by the fake notion of equal worth, you above all people, could reveal the legacy of real genius. There is no such thing as equality! Is someone making the baying sounds that howl and scream, equal to the beauty of Beethoven and Mozart? No! But we live in a world where everyone must have equal worth. Where talentless morons are worshipped, and given the merit of equals. But we know the truth. We know it! That shrinking circle of people that can still tell the difference between feeding the soul and the ever growing pit of ignorance that compliments half-wits, and declares they have talent. And you threw it away! The thing that not only made you unique, but made you breathe. You've chosen destruction over joy, and want over triumph. You've fed yourself hate, and denied yourself the very essence that confirmed your existence. You are now dead. Dead to the world, dead to music and dead to yourself. You had one chance. One chance in a lifetime to reproduce that significant something that eludes most of mankind. And you wasted it. That unique gift, given by God to the chosen few, and you've thrown it away. I've come all the way here, to tell you this, face to face. You're finished. You're finished, because you have so little respect for music and for your own humanity. Above all you're finished because you've got no guts. You'd rather curse your veins, and allow the demons to control your thoughts and ruin your life. You've destroyed your God-given talent, destroyed your career and destroyed my respect. So die, if you insist. It's better that you finish it now. Go ahead. Stick a needle into your veins, and slaughter the very thing that gave you a reason to exist!'

Even as he spoke, the anger that Popov displayed could not conceal the heartbreaking disappointment he felt. It wasn't just Yevgeny who had been destroyed. It was now all too obvious it was Popov, too. That youthful leap into the rhapsody of such universal privilege enjoyed by the chosen few had been stolen, and now floundered on the thorns of such systemic and empty purpose, it amounted to a momentous act of self-destruction.

'Is that what you want?' Popov screamed.

Yevgeny could no longer look Popov in the eye, and faced with the full ferocity of his condemnation, hurried from Gorlinsky's office in tears. Popov shouted for him to come back, but, within less than a minute, Yevgeny had reached the street, and like Jonah hiding from God, joined the seething tide of humanity, to drown in the insecurity of his compulsion.

'We have no choice but to return home,' insisted Maria.

To her mind, the predicament that Yevgeny now found himself in would be impossible to resolve, without the involvement of outside agencies. And even then, it would not rescue his career.

'If you had wanted to execute your future, you could not have chosen a more perfect scaffold,' she told him.

Yevgeny pleaded for Maria to stay in London and continue her studies. But, he reasoned…

'To precisely what would *I* return? To my home town, to Popov! To any useful purpose? No. In Odesa, my disgrace would be a hundred times worse than what it is here. Here I can sink into the mire of obscurity. There I would need to go into hiding. If it's all the same to you, I'll disappear, and take my own chances. It's time I learnt to survive on my own terms, even though the terms are painful.'

Maria hoped that Yevgeny would change his mind. They had little money, and were required to vacate their rooms in a few days. Maria consulted the college, and went in search of work as a pianist. But the work she could find paid little, and wouldn't put a roof over their heads. Then she had an inspired idea. 'What if we got a live-in job at an hotel?' she suggested to Yevgeny. She had noticed during their short stay on their arrival, that the serving staff and chambermaids at the hotel were mostly foreign. 'I can offer myself as a cook, as well,' she suggested. But she warned Yevgeny, 'You must promise to get help. Otherwise, it's all a waste of time!'

Yevgeny, promised on his knees, and through tears of sincere contrition, that he would attend the course, and undergo all and every sacrifice that was demanded. But she must have known then, even if she didn't want to admit it to herself, it wouldn't be easy. Often, he would disappear, and his phone would be switched off. Sometimes he would appear to be alert, and at other times in what she described as 'the space between two spaces'. Like a photo that would go in and out of focus. She knew that until work started on his recovery, he would prove totally unreliable.

They went from hotel to hotel, seeking work. She started at the major West End hotels, and then remembered Bloomsbury, where they first stayed. The road led up from the north of Holborn to the Euston Road, and was lined with hotels of every description. They left early in the morning, and Maria stated that herself and Yevgeny were students, and would undertake any kind of work, as long as it included accommodation. Most hotels she was to discover had an arrangement with agencies abroad or in London, but even when a possibility presented itself, Yevgeny, whose English was poor, could not be considered for either bar work or waiting on tables.

'Can you read this?' he was asked by one Manager. 'We come as a package,' Maria insisted.

But Yevgeny was almost always preoccupied. In fact, it now occurred to her that more than a few objections were due to his air of indifference and non-involvement. He would walk into the dining room, or disappear into the toilet, and leave her to negotiate. In fact, Yevgeny was totally unsuitable for relating to guests, or undertaking any but the most mundane of tasks. But it seems, he was considered too indifferent to accomplish even that.

'He can wash up or make up a room,' stated Maria.

But although her appearance and personality were business-like, there were no takers. She could have found work on her own, but Yevgeny's behaviour proved an obstacle. Then she had what she believed was a piece of luck. Their verbal application at a small two star hotel had just been rejected for what seemed the hundredth time, when a man who had been sitting in the reception area followed them out of the hotel. He introduced himself as Georgi.

'I hope you don't mind me saying,' he told them, 'but you are going about finding a live-in position the wrong way. You need an agency that already has plenty of work, and can put a roof over your head.'

'Do you know any?' asked Maria.

'I can let you have the number of someone who employs people, without asking too many questions,' he replied.

'It has to be for both of us.'

'Of course,' he said.

Maria thanked Georgi, while he wrote down a name and mobile number on a scrap of paper.

'It isn't the Ritz,' said Georgi, 'but it's better than sleeping on the streets.'

'Right now, we'd be grateful for anything.'

Georgi was swarthy and dark, from Eastern Europe. He was stocky, and the stubble on his face reminded her of someone who kept short accounts when it came to sleeping. Despite that, he possessed a roguish charm, that Maria calculated could both attract and repel. He told them he worked at a local casino, and kept late hours.

'I am from Belarus,' he added. 'So we are cousins. I look after you. Right!'

Maria smiled, and spoke a few words in Russian to him. But Georgi did not respond.

He then handed her a piece of paper with a mobile number written on it, and said,

'Ask for Lily.'

'Is she from Belarus too?' asked Maria.

'Maybe she comes from somewhere else. What do you care!'

Maria glanced down at the number, thanked him, and walked away, still determined to find a hotel that would employ them.

But time was getting short, and the agencies she contacted the next day required a work visa and other paperwork she was unable to supply.

Maria grew increasingly desperate, and called the number scrawled on the piece of paper. A woman answered and simply said, 'Yes?' Maria explained that she had obtained her number from Georgi, and was seeking work for herself and Yevgeny.

'Only Yevgeny has a work visa,' said Maria. 'I'm a student.'

'That doesn't matter. We take care of it.'

'We both need study time,' said Maria.

'Where are you?' said the woman, then asked Maria to write down an address, and gave her directions. 'We're a little out of the centre, but don't worry about that. We will transport you everywhere you need to go.'

It was evening when they arrived outside a large store situated at the end of a long terrace of High Road shops in East London. Grandly named 'Kaz International Stores,' it occupied over half the parade in an area, surrounded by terraces of three-storey houses turned into flats, alongside council estates that housed a cosmopolitan population, that gave it a separate and more complex identity. As soon as they entered, they were spied by a man behind a long counter situated very close to the entrance. Behind him was a bank of screens that appeared to survey every inch of shelf space in its seemingly endless interior, crammed with aisles of grocery, fruit, vegetables and household goods. Whilst another man was busy stacking shelves, he was mentally taking stock of who was in the store. As Maria and Yevgeny approached the counter, he looked up, but neither smiled nor offered any greeting.

'We have an appointment with Lily,' said Maria.

The man remained expressionless, and tilted his head back in the manner of an aggressive doorman.

'Who is asking?' he enquired.

'Maria and Yevgeny,' replied Maria. 'I spoke to her earlier

today.'

The man picked up his mobile phone and spoke in what Maria immediately recognised as Russian.

'Wait here,' he ordered.

In a few minutes, a woman appeared, and asked them to follow her. She led them to a large storeroom at the back of the store, and from there into a small office situated in the far corner. Leaning forward on the desk, as they sat before her, she observed them for several moments, and then asked,

'Where are your belongings?'

'We have only packed some overnight things. The rest of our possessions are at Victoria station.'

'That's not a very good idea,' said Lily. 'Left-luggage offices are notorious for losing peoples possessions.'

'We're not familiar with London. Supposing we were robbed?'

'We will require both your passports.'

Maria handed Lily both her and Yevgeny's passport, who briefly glanced at them, before placing them in the drawer of her desk.

'We'll hold onto these for the moment.'

'Does that mean you are offering us a job?'

'Have either of you done domestic work before?'

'What's the pay?' enquired Maria.

'Six pounds fifty an hour. For a guaranteed payment of forty hours a week.'

'For both of us?' enquired Maria.

'Of course.'

'When can we start?'

'Tomorrow morning.'

'If you remember, we have nowhere to sleep,' Maria reminded her.

'You're lucky. A girl has recently left us to work in Birmingham.'

'Yevgeny doesn't speak very good English, but can wash up, clean and make beds.'

'I am sure we can make use of him,' said Lily. She then

produced two contracts from her desk drawer, and invited both Maria and Yevgeny to sign them.

'What are these?' Maria asked.

'These are contracts declaring that you are both independent contractors, who work on a self-employed temporary basis, and are responsible for your own outgoings, taxation and public liability.'

'Does that mean you don't employ us?'

'It means you are both independent operatives. You get to keep any money you earn. But of course, we will naturally ensure you are always kept fully employed.'

Maria glanced briefly at the two-page document, written in what appeared to be legal jargon that amounted to a release form.

'Is alright?' Yevgeny asked Maria.

'You mean we are both independent, but you will supply accommodation.'

'Of course,' replied Lily. 'Although, you must remember, it implies you are part of a family. And just as in any family, we naturally expect loyalty.'

Lily smiled at Maria approvingly, and obviously enjoyed the subtle improvisation that underlies a conversation that can occur between two women. Maria also detected something more. A cunning that represented a different kind of intelligence. Lily also spoke English with a Russian accent, but right now, Maria had no desire for controversy.

'What about the address?' quizzed Maria.

'Just sign,' said Lily. 'I'll complete the details later.'

Maria and Yevgeny followed Lily, as she led them back through the storeroom, and then exited through a side door to an alleyway, that led to a flight of steps, leading to the upper parts. From the outside, the building consisted of the shop, with flats occupying the two upper storeys. On the first and second landings, a door led to the entrance of the flats above the shop. However, on reaching the second landing, instead of entering one of the purpose built flats, Lily unlocked a large steel gate that led to a further staircase leading to the roof. Climbing this iron staircase, above the eyeline of the building, they found themselves on a large expanse of flat roof, where, hidden from view, were half a dozen small brick-built single storey buildings, rather like cabins. Each building was separated by a distance of about four metres, one at each end of the roof, and two on each side, facing each other. Each cabin front consisted of one door and one window. Lily unlocked the door of the nearest cabin, and invited Maria and Yevgeny to look inside. The accommodation consisted of a shower room with a basin and toilet, in the corner of a stark and cramped space, that housed two bunk beds and a small set of drawers on one side, and a crudely constructed built-in wardrobe, split into four sections on the wall opposite. The floor of the cabin was concrete, with only a slip mat between the bunks to offer any comfort from the cold, and a larger nylon mat occupied the remaining space between the beds and the wardrobe. The only window in the building was adjacent to the front door, and had curtains that were drawn, and the only fresh air that could enter the building was via a small opener at the top of the window, or an air vent in the shower-room. Lighting was courtesy of a lone bayonet fitting in the ceiling, and make-up, clothes and magazines filled almost every inch of unused space, and the whole place reeked of stale perfume.

'The room is in a mess,' commented Maria.

'That is because this is the girls' block,' declared Lily. 'You can occupy the top bunk in the corner. Yevgeny can share with Luca and Ivan.'

Maria and Yevgeny then followed Lily, as she led them past another cabin she referred to as 'the girls' other block', and to a building opposite she described as the 'canteen'.

'Everyone shares the canteen. It has a microwave, a fridge and cupboard space, together with a table and chairs. It also houses the only TV in case you get bored. Next to it is the laundry room. We advise people to arrange their own schedule. It avoids disagreements.'

'And what about the block at the very end,' enquired Maria.

'Who is that for?'

'That's the isolation block,' said Lily. 'Sometimes people get sick.'

'And what happens if someone needs to see a doctor?'

'We never entertain people who arrive needing a doctor. We're not a hospital.'

'And how safe are our belongings?'

'Most complaints arise from disputes between the girls, which is why we insist on keeping peoples' valuables in the office, along with their mobile phones. After all, you won't need them while you are working. Perhaps you could let me have yours before you start work tomorrow morning.'

Lily smiled, but Maria did not return the gesture nor respond. Then Lily asked,

'Are you hungry?'

'We haven't eaten since early morning,' said Maria.

Lily led them inside the canteen, and told them to help themselves to anything they could find.

'I'll return later, and introduce you to the girls,' she said.

Lily departed in the direction of the stairs, leaving Maria and Yevgeny to make coffee, and locate some soup they could microwave.

'I don't want to stay here,' said Yevgeny.

'Right now, we have no choice,' said Maria. 'Between us, we'll be earning five hundred and twenty pounds a week. If you can hang on for just a couple of weeks we'll have enough to get a place of our own and you can start your treatment. Can you do that? Can you hang on. Just until we get back on our feet again.'

'I might need to borrow some money,' said Yevgeny.

'I've only got the money left over from my allowance.'

'Couldn't you ask for more?'

'My parents have sacrificed enough already. It costs twice as much for a foreign student to study here. Apart from which, I won't be defeated.'

Yevgeny, remained silent, and clutched his chest.

'How much do you need?' asked Maria.

'Can you spare fifty?' he begged.

Suddenly, voices were heard coming from the direction of the stairs. It was the sound of female chattering, although not in English. Maria and Yevgeny exited the canteen, and after a few short steps, came face to face with a group of girls. They stopped momentarily, and looked apprehensive. Then the smallest in the group stepped forward.

'Who the hell are you?' she asked.

Before Maria could answer, Lily arrived and introduced Maria and Yevgeny.

'You will have to be on your best behaviour,' she warned. 'They're from Ukraine, and not used to how we work.'

'What does *he* do?' said the girl. 'Add variety?'

'This is Sukhon,' interrupted Lily. 'She's from Thailand, along with Hong and Noi. The rest are from Vietnam, all, that is, except for Bao, who doesn't belong anywhere.'

With the exception of Sukhon, the rest of the girls appeared subdued by the presence of Lily, who took the petite Thai aside, and whispered something in her ear, before departing.

'I've been ordered to take charge of you,' said Sukhon.

'Take charge?'

'You'll be sharing with me, Hong, and Noi. Your boyfriend will be sharing with Luca and Ivan.'

'He's not my boyfriend. We were fellow students.'

'Students of what?'

'Music.'

'Are you sure you're in the right place?' she enquired curiously.

Sukhon accompanied Maria into her new accommodation, and introduced her to the other girls. Some could only speak basic English, and Bao, who was Chinese, hardly any. It was clear that Sukhon was the spokesperson for the group. The other 'penthouse', as Sukhon referred to the breeze block cabins, was occupied by Kim, Mai, Apple and Bao.

'We call ours the 'Bangkok Hilton', and the other one, 'Saigon

International',' said Sukhon. 'Chopsticks are optional.'

With three other girls using the bathroom and changing, Maria realised the living accommodation would quickly become chaotic. She had been allocated an upper bunk, but immediately felt uncomfortable, and decided to return to the canteen. On leaving the cabin, she was confronted outside by the presence of Lily, and another man talking to Yevgeny.

'Yevgeny's English is far from perfect,' Maria reminded Lily, as she approached.

The man who had his back to her, turned around. He was about five feet ten in height, and built like a bull. The first thing Maria noticed was the width of his back. His torso reminded her of someone who lived on a diet of steroids, and when he was introduced, her suspicions were confirmed.

'This is Luca,' said Lily. 'He is the foreman of our little team. Yevgeny will be sharing with him and Ivan.'

Luca made no formal acknowledgement, but looked her up and down, like someone would assess a prize cow before an auction.

'Yevgeny needs sleep and is highly strung,' Maria informed Lily. 'Is it possible he could have a room on his own?'

'If you look very closely, the Ritz is just behind you on the right. Unfortunately, tonight, they are fully booked. But if it makes you feel any better, someone will leave a breakfast tray outside his suite tomorrow morning at seven am. Which is when I expect you both to be ready for work.'

The exchange was like a short sharp shock. Luca placed his hand around Yevgeny's neck, and then ran his hand down his back, as if assessing his likely stamina. He then smiled at Lily, and laughed, as if in answer to some private conversation they had both shared earlier, before leading him away in the direction of his new quarters. Later, Yevgeny told Maria he was feeling unwell.

'It won't be for very long,' she reassured him.

5.

It HAD BEEN a busy week. Both Maria and Yevgeny had been driven to separate hotels, and allocated duties by a 'supervisor', and then transported somewhere else by Ivan, who was effectively the junior partner of Luca. Ivan, in his mid-twenties, said very little, and seemed to be in mobile contact with either Lily or Luca, almost constantly. He told Maria he was Italian, but Sukhon told Maria he was Albanian, who had ideas above his rank.

'Is there a ranking system?' Maria asked.

'What do you think?'

'And what about Luca?'

'He's Chechen. so be careful,' warned Sukhon.

Maria rarely encountered her, or any of the other girls, in the places she was sent. When she mentioned this, Sukhon told her they worked 'different shifts'. For some reason, Maria was drawn to her. Mainly, she liked her resilience to authority. The other girls were mostly silent, and talked mainly about their mood, money and family. They somehow kept their distance. But Sukhon was different.

'Call me 'Scrawn',' she said. 'Everybody else does.'

'Why?' asked Maria.

'Because Luca finds it hard to pronounce anything with more than one syllable, so started calling me 'Scrawn', and the name stuck.'

Scrawn was the most open of the girls, and the only one in

whom Maria felt she could confide. Her main concern though, was for Yevgeny. On the rare occasions she did get to talk to him, he either seemed very tired or unwell.

'I want to leave here,' he told her. 'Let's go somewhere else.'

Inwardly, Maria was in emotional turmoil, but begged him to give it just one week.

Yevgeny was clearly out of his depth. He had been given various menial jobs, but was suffering withdrawal symptoms. He confided to Maria he had maintained his supply with help from Ivan and Luca.

'How long will it last?' Maria enquired.

'Drugs don't last,' replied Yevgeny. 'They only allow you to exist until the next fix.'

'As soon as we get paid, we're leaving,' Maria insisted. 'But I'm not spending the money on drugs. You're going straight to rehab.'

The week ended with a payout ritual, that took place in the canteen on Saturday, between noon and 1pm. This was to coincide with the early morning shift that returned around midday, and the afternoon shift, that began work at two o'clock. Lily was accompanied by a man Maria saw coming and going occasionally, named Max. He dispensed cash from a large metal cash box, and asked people to place their signature on a sheet under the heading, 'Casual Labour'. When it came to Maria's turn, she entered the canteen, and presented her own calculations in the form of an invoice.

'What's this?' asked Lily.

'It's the bill for the hours we've both worked. I am sure you'll find it's in order. I worked approximately seventy eight hours, including this morning, and Yevgeny who worked all week in Kensington, completed eighty.'

'You're an independent operative, so we wouldn't pay anyone else's money to you.'

Lily kept her eyes trained on Maria, and then asked Max.

'How much do we owe Ms Novotna, our famous pianist?'

Max looked down at the sheet in front of him, and then

reached into the cash box, and withdrew some twenty and ten pound notes plus several one pound coins.

'Eighty five pounds,' he announced.

Maria was stunned, and looked down at the money that had been placed before her on the table.

'According to my calculations, you owe me five hundred and seven pounds!'

'But we have only ever agreed to pay you for forty hours. Regardless of whether you work for thirty five or ninety.'

'In that case you owe me another one hundred and seventy five then!' said Maria.

'Which is what we have paid you. Minus, of course, twenty five pounds a night for food and accommodation. Where else in London do you think you could find such a bargain?'

Maria clenched her fist, and struck it down on the table so hard, the contents in the cash box momentarily jingled. Visibly shaken, Max grabbed the cash box, and holding it close to his chest, slid his chair back from the table, leaving Lily to confront the verbal onslaught Maria now launched.

'This is nothing more than slave labour, and you should be arrested. Do the hotels only pay you forty hours when I've worked for nearly eighty! And what about Yevgeny? Where is he?'

'Oh yes. I almost forgot to tell you. He hasn't been feeling well. In fact he hasn't been at all well since he arrived. You bought a very sick man into this community. Someone who it appears, has a one hundred pound a day habit.'

'I want to see him. Now!'

Maria hurried from the canteen and entered the 'boys" block, but found it empty. Lily had followed, and confronted her on leaving.

'He's in the isolation block,' announced Lily.

Maria pushed Lily aside and on reaching the isolation block, found the door locked. Demanding to be let inside, Lily unlocked the door, and when Maria entered was immediately confronted by the sight of Yevgeny, lying on the bed. He appeared to be asleep, and she began to shake him, and started tapping him lightly on the cheeks, begging him to respond. He opened his eyes briefly, but appeared to be sedated. Maria shook him once more, and asked him if he could hear what she was saying. She then attempted to lift him out of the bed. But he was too heavy for her to carry.

'It's no good. He's out of it. As you should know, since you've been helping him pay for his supply,' said Lily.

'We're going!' announced Maria. 'We're going right now. Pay him what you owe him, and we'll leave.'

'I'm afraid that's impossible,' said Lily. 'Apart from the fact that he's in no state to travel, he also owes us a great deal of money.'

'What for?' demanded Maria.

'For his drugs,' said Lily. 'What else do you think keeps him going?'

'What are you saying?' said Maria. 'That he's in your debt?'

'I'm afraid so. He's a heroin addict, and he's been one for a very long time. You haven't therefore, done yourselves any favours.'

'We're going right now. Otherwise, I'm calling an ambulance and the police.'

'And tell them what? That you're both here working illegally, and your boyfriend is a drug addict, unable to pay his dealer. We'll end up looking like the Sisters of Mercy for helping two struggling students.'

Maria slapped Lily hard across the face, and took off in the direction of the staircase leading to the street. She raced down two flights leading to the second landing, but on reaching the large metal gate, found it locked. Attempting to gain a foothold she slowly began to climb the solid metal frame. On the other side, there was a seven foot drop, and the spikes on top of the framework offered her no other choice but to grab hold of one of the spikes, and vault over the top. Momentarily, she lost her balance, and landed awkwardly, the throbbing in her leg confirming she was suffering a bruise to the knee. However, no sooner had she attempted to stand up straight, than the door of the flat leading off the landing flew open, and she fell backwards from a crack to the jaw. Her elbow took the full force of the landing this time, and she suddenly felt both sick and dazed. Then before she knew it, Luca was carrying her into the bedroom of the flat itself. Maria was too shocked to say anything, as Luca placed her on the bed and then stood guard watching over her. Shortly afterwards, Lily entered and instructed Luca to make some tea.

'If you are attempting to keep me a prisoner, you are in deep trouble,' said Maria.

Lily approached Maria, and sat on the bed beside her.

'I don't need to keep anyone a prisoner. Everyone here is a willing volunteer.'

Lily examined Maria's jaw.

'Be thankful. Your pride has been more injured than your jawbone. If Luca had used any real force, you would have been out cold until tomorrow morning!'

'I'm still leaving with Yevgeny.'

'At present, he owes our organisation over a thousand pounds. Ivan has been running his errands, just to help him function. Frankly, we'd be only too happy to see the back of him. All you need to do is settle his bill.'

'Don't worry. I'll find your stinking money. Right now, he needs to go to rehab.'

'Let's just say, at present, you owe eleven hundred pounds on his behalf. Not including his considerable upkeep.'

'Take it out of the free overtime we both supplied.'

Luca entered the room carrying two cups of tea. One, he gives to Lily, and the other he places on the bedside table next to Maria.

'You know you could wipe your boyfriends slate clean within a week,' said Lily.

'It would amount to nothing more than a few hours work.'

'A few hours work?'

'You're an intelligent girl. You mean to tell me that you don't know the score. For such a serious student, you appear to lack a fundamental education.'

'If I ever did decide to become a whore, it wouldn't be to assist the Russian obsession for slavery.'

'Just think of it as an occupational hazard,' said Lily.

'You have quite a nice little operation. It would be a pity to throw it all away on two hapless students. Think of it as a hazard you should avoid yourself.'

Lily got up and began to pace the room. At the same time, Luca closed the bedroom door, and stood menacingly in front of it.

'You know, I think you are absolutely right,' said Lily. 'You are hapless. Especially Yevgeny. Luca here will willingly testify how easy it is for someone with a serious heroin addiction to overdose.'

Luca leaned against the door and began smiling broadly.

'Yes. It's amazingly common. Just an absent-minded injection. It could happen at any time, any place. Not necessarily here. It could happen for instance on the way home from work, in a hotel bedroom, or in the street.'

'I think we should keep a very close eye on him,' said Lily. 'He needs protecting from himself.'

'Two homeless students. One who is a drug addict, and the other a nun,' said Luca.

'But of course, if one is a user, very often the nun is liable to break her vows.'

'Luca is, I'm afraid, far more pessimistic than me. He often gets angry, and blows a fuse. I do everything I can to calm him. But sometimes, he believes there is no alternative to brute force. I really do hope you are going to co-operate. I like you. When I first saw you I said to myself, here is someone who can earn a great deal of money. In fact I'm so confident, that I'm going to make you an offer I have never made to anyone else. Ever.'

Lily sat on the bed, and, drawing close to Maria, took her by the hand, and began to rub it gently, as if she were consoling a friend.

'I am going to guarantee you a thousand pounds a week. Cash. No deductions. I'll also ensure Yevgeny has all he needs. In fact, he won't even need to skivvy in a hotel kitchen. All you have to do is agree to work the next few weeks for us in some of the most exclusive hotels in London. You'll work where we want, when we want, and for as long as we want. In return, you'll eat in some of the most sumptuous restaurants, wear fashionable clothes, and entertain some very wealthy clients. It won't even seem like work at all. More like taking one long holiday, and getting well paid at the same time.'

Luca agreed.

'You've landed on your feet. If someone offered me a thousand pounds a week, just to lay around, and expend no energy, in five star luxury, I would say, when can I start?'

He stared coldly at Maria, then said,

'You don't seem very grateful'

Maria's pulse was racing and her mind was in turmoil. She felt trapped and needed time to think.

'Now Luca,' said Lily, 'Let's give our latest recruit a little time to get her breath back. I am sure she'll see the absolute sense of our offer. Very soon.'

'I do hope so,' said Luca. 'In fact, I guarantee it.'

Lily squeezed Maria's hand, and then examined the bruise on her knee and elbow.

'Let's get you cleaned up,' said Lily 'In fact, while you're here, why not take a hot bath?'

Lily led Maria to the bathroom, and started running the bath, whilst Luca stood observing from a distance.

'We'll also see about getting you some new clothes,' said Lily. 'I would say you were about a size eight, possibly ten.'

Maria didn't answer. Entering the bathroom, she closed the door, and dropped to her knees. She now realised the full horror of her predicament, and the ransom demanded. Her first instinct was to alert the police, but for that, she needed contact with the outside world, and her first priority was to ensure no further harm came to Yevgeny. Both Lily and Luca were unpredictable, and more than capable of carrying out their threats. It was clear they also enjoyed a history uncomplicated by mercy. She had yet to gauge the extent of their criminality, but was in no doubt their disregard for justice made them ruthless adversaries. Blood had now formed a crust on her knee, and as she sunk down in the bath, she began to construct in her mind a strategy for escape. She had often heard the girls describe both the 'inside' and the 'outside', when talking among themselves. Now Lily had revealed the real purpose behind her organisation's domestic service, she knew escape came at a price. The girls spoke mainly in Thai, and she had purposely been paired with someone who hardly spoke any English on the shifts she had been allocated. Each day, Ivan and Luca had dropped the girls off at different hotels, in an anonymous white van, accompanied by a small menacing man named Pavel, who they referred to as a 'supervisor'. Pavel would collect a list from the Duty Manager, and give instructions concerning the preparation and cleanliness of the rooms, periodically checking the work they were doing. His main task, she now realised, was to ensure the girls stayed 'on site', as prisoners of both domestic and sexual slavery, controlled by Lily and Luca, and were kept apart from the outside world. She wasn't sure how far their network extended, but realised Lily now considered she was a flight risk, and needed to buy time, in order to rescue Yevgeny. She also decided it might be useful to make a friend of 'Scrawn'.

After her bath, she got dressed, and found Lily waiting for her in the kitchen. 'I've made you a sandwich,' said Lily, and invited Maria to sit at the opposite end of a small table.

'I think you should relax for the next few hours. Later you can try on a new outfit, and then we will treat you to a nice meal in the West End. How does that sound?'

Maria was escorted back to what the girls laughingly referred to as the 'penthouse', and the gate was again secured. By this time, Scrawn and the rest of the girls had departed.

Luca unlocked the isolation room, and signalled for Maria to enter. Yevgeny was still asleep. His emaciated body looked like a feather wrapped in a blanket. His hair had grown longer, and his skin looked haggard and pale. She took his painfully thin hands, and began to feel the strength in his fingers. They now felt brittle and lifeless. He couldn't work, even if he wanted to. He had purposely been sedated. By what means, she didn't know. But since he had functioned the previous week, it was obvious this was meant as a warning.

'Bang on the door when you're ready to leave,' said Luca, before departing.

Maria knelt down next to Yevgeny, and began to stroke his hair, and talk to him softly, as if comforting a child, reassuring him that he would get well again. Suddenly, the tension in his face began to fade.

'It's all my fault,' she whispered. 'All mine.'

Some time later, Maria banged on the reinforced door, and shortly after, heard the lock being turned. Luca took Maria by the arm, and escorted her back downstairs to Lily's apartment, and led her to the bedroom. Laid out on the bed in front of her were two dresses. One black and one blue. One was a Balenciaga, and the other, a Chanel black one-piece. 'Try them on,' said Lily, then exited, and closed the door behind her. Maria couldn't move, and stared down at the dresses for some time, before Lily re-entered. Picking up the blue Balenciaga dress, she held it up against the slim frame of Maria.

'I think this is more suitable for a first date.'

She then left the room, and returned five minutes later, to find Maria staring into the dressing room mirror, looking dejected.

'You look a million dollars,' she said. 'You'll find some half-decent make-up on the table. Go easy on the rouge though, and use the most suitable flesh tone, especially around the jawline. You need you to look your best for tonight!'

Later that evening, a Mercedes S class pulled up outside a five star Hotel in Park Lane, with Ivan acting as the chauffeur. After dutifully opening the rear passenger door, Maria, accompanied by Luca and Lily, made their way to the reception area, and took the lift to the restaurant that occupied the top floor. They were shown to a window table, with spectacular views over London, and while Lily browsed the cocktail list and the 'à la carte' menu, Luca observed Maria, who looked ill at ease.

'Feel like a cocktail?' enquired Lily.

'No,' Maria answered.

'You might as well. It's one of the perks of the job.'

'The job?' questioned Maria.

'Entertaining.'

'Is that what you think you are both engaged in.'

'Sure. Sex is entertainment. Not Tolstoy, of course, but it passes the time.'

The waiter approached, and Lily ordered a cocktail for herself and Luca, followed by fish, and a steak.

'I don't have to ask what Luca wants. He always has the same. What about you?'

'I don't feel like anything,' said Maria.

'She'll have the Dover sole, legumes, and Provence truffle,' Lily ordered.

While they waited for the cocktails to arrive, Lily outlined Maria's assignment.

'After our meal, you are going to have the honour of meeting a Saudi prince.'

'Really?' said Maria.

'He's very rich and very generous. Especially if he likes you.'

'And what about me. Do I have a say?'

'Do you pick an audience when you play the piano? No. You play for whoever buys a ticket. This is exactly the same. It's just that, instead of playing an instrument, you become the commodity. Sex is a commodity, just like everything else. Some people trade in shares, some people sell insurance, and some people sell pleasure. It's a business, just like everything else.

Somebody has something to sell, and another person wants to buy it. Your high-minded virginity has already been breached, so why not use it for financial gain? Anyway, apart from being very charming, the prince is an extravagant tipper.'

'Some girls would be only too willing to pay us for the introduction,' said Luca.

'You have a choice,' said Lily. 'You can make this evening a pleasurable experience, or cause your boyfriend a great deal of pain. Heroin withdrawal without medication can be an agonizing ordeal. And you are being asked to do so little.'

'He's lucky to have you,' agreed Luca. 'Extremely fortunate.'

Following the meal, Lily made a call, and they took a lift to one of the lower floors.

On alighting from the lift, they entered a dimly lit corridor, and Lily instructed Maria to knock on the door of a suite, some five metres away.

'We won't be far away,' she assured Maria. 'Do everything he asks you!'

Maria knocked on the door very softly, hoping that it wouldn't open. When it did, an obese man of Middle-Eastern appearance answered, in a dressing gown that remained partially open, to reveal a white vest and a pair of brown pants, and invited her inside. There were no introductions. He already had a drink in his hand, and approached the minibar.

'What are you drinking?' he asked.

'Water,' responded Maria.

'You can't drink that,' said the man. 'Have a whisky instead.'

'No, thank you,' said Maria.

'Very well, have an orange juice.'

The man beckoned Maria to sit on the sofa, whilst he removed the top from a small bottle, and poured the contents into large glass. He sat opposite, in order to get a good look at her, his eyes surveying her body, as if he was about to unwrap a gift that came in the post. Mmm!... he drooled,

'What's your name?'

'Is it important?' Maria replied apprehensively.

He was unshaven, and his greasy hair remained uncombed. There were dark circles under his eyes, from either a long flight or partying, and when he sat down his large belly protruded between the parting of his dressing gown. He looked in his late forties, and appeared to be suffering the effects of alcohol.

'You look a nice girl,' he said, 'different from the others.'

'Different?' queried Maria.

'Yes,' he said.

Then, in the very next breath, he ordered her to strip.

'You mean take everything off?' said Maria.

'Of course. Take everything off,'

He spoke as if speaking to someone who had come to turn down the bed, before leaning back in his chair, and placing his hand inside his pants. Maria felt disgusted, both by him, and with herself. Even the look and smell of him made her feel sick.

'Didn't you hear me?' he said.

'I can't,' said Maria.

The man took his hand out of his pants, reached for an open bottle of whisky on the table beside him, and topped up her glass.

'Your boss says this is your first time. So I'll be patient.'

'Thanks for being so understanding,' Maria replied contemptuously.

'The thing I'm not prepared to do is be deprived of something I've paid for in advance.'

The man stared at her, as if expecting an apology. Maria shifted uncomfortably on the sofa.

She had never given any real thought to prostitution. It had always seemed a transaction involving little emotion by the sex worker, and presented as illicit behaviour, instead of consensual abuse.

The man then leaned forward, and lowered his voice,

'First time, eh? Well, the honeymoon period is now over. You know what that is, don't you? It's the period between 'I do' and 'you'd better'!'

He delivered his implied threat looking both hurt and intimidating, and then pointed to the bulge in his pants.

'I'm feeling frustrated after a long journey,' he said, 'and I especially like your lips.'

He then opened his mouth, and circled his lips with his tongue.

'Is that all I am to you, a fleshy interior?' asked Maria.

'I know how to reward obedience. So why don't you make a start, by helping me relax?'

He fixed his gaze on Maria, then leaned back in anticipation.

'You'll find I'm very generous to people who please me,' he said.

Maria looked pensive, then got up from the sofa, and nervously stood before him.

'If you don't know what to do, I'll teach you,' said the man, and closed his eyes.

'I don't think that will be necessary,' said Maria.

A smile flashed across the man's lips, and then he said, 'Make it wet.'

'Very well,' said Maria.

Without uttering another word, Maria emptied the liquid from her glass, complete with several cubes of ice, and poured it directly onto the man's groin, and left the room.

She hadn't got very far, when Lily approached.

'Well?' she asked. 'That was quick. What happened?'

'We had a drink, then he became aroused, and sprung a leak. That's all.'

'Are you sure?' queried Lily.

The next moment Lily's phone rang, and she looked at Maria. Lily then began apologising profusely.

'Don't worry. We'll send someone else. Absolutely. Of course! This time, we'll make sure you're not disappointed...'

Almost at once, Luca appeared, and taking Maria firmly by the arm, forced her bodily into the lift, before they made their way to the ground floor.

'You have made a very big mistake,' Lily warned.

'I have a heavy period,' said Maria.

On reaching the ground floor, Lily grabbed Maria by the arm, marched her into the women's restroom, and ordered her into one of the cubicles. 'Prove it!' she demanded, and waited while Maria put her hand under her dress, and in a few moments, produced a blood-stained sanitary towel. When Ivan finally pulled up to collect them, Luca practically threw Maria into the back seat of the car.

'Your luxury vacation is now at an end,' he promised.

Lily said nothing further to Maria, and instead, escorted her back to the 'penthouse' in silence.

When they arrived, Maria demanded to see Yevgeny, and banged on the door of the isolation block. The door was locked, and she turned to see Luca standing behind her.

'He's not in there,' he said.

'I don't believe you,' Maria replied.

Luca unlocked the door, and allowed Maria to go inside. All she found was the empty bed that Yevgeny had occupied, and all traces of his occupation erased.

'What have you done with him?' Maria demanded.

'He's staying with friends,' said Luca.

'Do what you like with me, but please take him to a hospital,' Maria begged.

Luca leaned against the door, and began to crack the knuckles of his fingers.

'If I wanted to, I could throw you off this roof right now. 'Broken hearted student jumps from roof, after learning of boyfriend's death from an overdose. Witnesses testify she was distraught.' Tell me, how would you prefer to leave the building?'

Lily, who in nearly all matters of conflict, positioned herself immediately behind the anabolic shoulders of Luca, attempted to pacify him.

'Now Luca, I think our student of music has some serious thinking to do, concerning her next performance.'

Lily escorted Maria back to 'Bangkok', and locked the door behind her. For a moment, Maria regretted her hasty act, and wished she had handled the matter differently.

'That's what I would have done,' said Scrawn, after Maria had confided her ordeal.

'Premature ejaculation is one of the perks of the industry. Although, if it was me, I would have provided a few extras, to ensure he increased the gratuity!'

Maria's heroic gesture, although emotionally satisfying, now appeared a hollow victory.

'Where would they have taken Yevgeny?' enquired Maria.

'This is just the tip of the iceberg,' said Scrawn. 'They have places everywhere. They're into employment agencies, security, building contractors, mini-markets, transport. You name it. They even own the dry-cleaning shop at the end of the parade. If ever there's a police raid, we've been ordered to run across the roof, and hide in their attic. He could be anywhere.'

'Why not escape?' Maria asked.

'Where to?' challenged Scrawn. 'If I walked into the nearest police station tomorrow, what would I say? 'Please Mr Policeman, make me a useful member of society. I speak English, Thai, German and dirty, have had the pox twice, STDs are a working hazard, and I come complete with a cocaine habit.' How much would someone pay for all that experience, do you think? Even if they rescued me by lunchtime, they'd be wishing I'd disappear before they had afternoon tea. It's not that they don't care. It's just that there's too many of us. And even if they sent us all home tomorrow, within a week, I would be chasing German tourists in Ko Samui screaming, 'Massage!' As it is, I do some 'overtime', and get to send enough home, to keep my family alive. I have a son. But he's not going through what I've been through. He's going to have an education. See, the point is not so much about being trafficked. It's about making sure the alternative is a lot better.'

Scrawn's voice began to break, and for a brief moment, her scatty and often resilient guard slipped. Maria put her arms around her, and they embraced each other.

'How much do you owe?' asked Scrawn.

'They told me I owe eleven hundred.'

'Then you'd better find yourself a rich boyfriend.'

'There is someone I could call. But there's only a remote possibility he could help.'

'A remote possibility is okay. It's the remote impossibilities you should avoid.'

'He's an Englishman. But I hardly know him.'

'Right now, you don't have a choice.'

'All I have is a phone number. And that's currently not a lot of use.'

'Don't be so sure.'

Scrawn asked the other girls if they minded Maria using her 'hidden asset'. The other girls nodded, and Scrawn reached deep down inside her pants, and produced a mobile phone wrapped in thin plastic, in the same way a nurse might coax a baby's head from the womb.

'Let's just say I have my own private 'love child',' said Scrawn.

She removed the phone from its plastic cover, pressed the power key, and handed it to Maria.

'Go ahead, make the call,' she said.

Maria's pulse began to race, and her hands began to sweat. Her mind filled with the endless possibilities that her action could unleash. But along with it, the knowledge that the gang were in a position to impose the ultimate sanction against Yevgeny's life. For a moment, she hesitated and looked at Scrawn.

'I know what you're thinking, but the law doesn't give you justice, only procedure,' said Scrawn. 'Be smart, and plan an escape route.'

Maria then searched her small notebook, and found the number that Stephen Kline had scribbled on a napkin at the V & A many months before.

'Where are we tomorrow?' Maria asked.

'On a Sunday, it's either Whitefield Street or the Argyle!'

'Where's that?'

'Near Kings Cross.'

Maria hesitated, wondering what to say. As she did so, Scrawn took her by the hand, and looked at her solemnly.

'Whatever you intend to do, make it quick. These people take rebellion seriously!'

Maria nervously pressed the eleven digits that would determine her fate…

'I don't know if you remember me…,' she began, and then explained she needed some urgent advice, and asked Stephen Kline if he would be willing to meet her.

It was clear that Maria's call had come out of the blue, and he had likely forgotten who she was. There followed an embarrassed silence, then he asked,

'What advice?'

'It's complicated, but I don't know who else to ask,' pleaded Maria. 'Can you meet me tomorrow?'

'Tomorrow?'

'At Kings Cross.'

'Tell him Kings Place,' Scrawn advised. 'It's easier to find.'

Maria confirmed the place, and told him 3pm. There was another embarrassed silence, then he said apologetically,

'I'm not sure I can help you.'

'Nor am I,' said Maria. 'But I'm hoping you'll at least hear me out.'

Maria handed back the phone, and told Scrawn she hardly knew Stephen Kline, and had no realistic expectation he would keep their appointment.

'You should have phoned your mother instead,' declared Scrawn. 'They always know what to do!'

The other girls agreed, and Scrawn entertained them by pretending to call her own mother…

'*Hi Mum. Yes… working hard as usual, … of course, … well, they treat me like a queen, with my own luxurious apartment on the fifth floor of the palace. In fact, life is just one long holiday. Only yesterday, I had an invitation to dine out on a microwave dinner for one, in a rooftop restaurant. Yes… I know… so romantic… Well,… my escort's very muscular, with a short temper… white knuckles… and spoils me rotten… The boss? Oh, she's a real lady! Always apologising after she robs me blind, and the men insist on spraying themselves with cologne, every time they rape me. In fact, they all have such lovely manners, it makes it quite impossible for me to leave.'*

Hong and Noi joined in the joke, and walked around the tiny space between the two beds like fashion models on a catwalk, bumping into each other, and making various comments about the English weather, high-class hotels, and the lack of civility from Ivan the chauffeur. It was a rare moment of levity between the tiredness and boredom of incarceration and the precariousness of their lives. The only contact they were allowed to have with the outside world was a portable television propped up in the corner of the canteen. It chattered away mindlessly, as they retreated into an endless consumption of noodles, baked beans, soup and rations of cocaine.

Scrawn and the girls were all young. But already the ravages of ill-treatment and drugs were beginning to take their toll. As Scrawn observed,

'Time is only kind if you're the one choosing where to spend it.'

Petite, with very long hair, she reminded Maria of a care-worn child, somewhere in her mid-twenties. Her education however, was home grown, from the university of streetwise, and although Noi was taller and the prettier of the two, she didn't possess the chutzpah of her friend, who, although she lacked any formal education, was capable of profound philosophy.

'They may own your body,' Scrawn observed, 'but never allow them to take up residence in your head.'

Before Maria set off the next morning, Scrawn advised Maria on the layout of the hotels and the location of Kings Place.

'Don't leave it too long. Until then, your period had better be long and messy.'

Fortunately, Maria was assigned to the Argyle, which was closer to Kings Cross, and busy, and at about 2.30pm, Maria feigned illness, and asked Pavel to send for a doctor. Bao, who was assigned to work with her, backed up her story, and told Pavel that Maria had been sick.

'Make do with an aspirin,' said Pavel. 'You're nothing but an actress!'

'You'll soon find out,' exclaimed Maria, and produced an empty paracetamol bottle.

'She took lot in hand,' said Bao.

'You stupid cow!' said Pavel. And began shaking Maria violently.

Maria collapsed, and Pavel threw her onto the bed, and ordered Bao to make a strong black coffee. Maria refused to drink it, so he ordered Bao to assist him to take Maria into the bathroom, and run a cold shower.

'If you think your ticket out of here is in a hospital, you had better think again.'

Pavel held Maria's head under the cold shower for several minutes, and then thrust her head down the toilet, and ordered her to be sick. But Maria did not oblige, and could hardly stand. Instead she clung to Bao, who began to walk Maria slowly around the room, and began talking to her in Mandarin.

'She need air,' pleaded Bao.

'Keep her walking up and down the back stairs,' ordered Pavel, 'and don't let her out of your sight!'

Bao nodded, and they exited slowly, down the back stairs. Once they reached the ground floor, Maria pushed the bar of the emergency exit, and told Bao to wait until she returned, and tapped on the door.

Her hair was still wet by the time Maria reached Kings Place, and spotted Stephen Kline.

As she approached him, he seemed visibly shaken by her appearance. The carefree youthfulness of the previous summer had now been replaced by someone far more sober and disconcerting. Dark circles now appeared under her eyes, betraying a weariness and sorrow, that curiously contrasted with the spontaneous and upbeat nature of their previous encounter. Insisting she didn't have very much time, they went and sat by the canal.

'You said you needed some advice?' asked Stephen suspiciously.

'I didn't know who else to ask,' said Maria. 'That day at the V&A, I somehow felt I could trust you.'

'I suppose I should feel flattered,' Stephen replied, unenthusiastically.

'Yevgeny has become very ill, and is unable to work, and I have given up my studies to take care of him,' said Maria. 'We are looking for someone to sponsor our return home.'

'It's not so much advice you need then. More a banker?'

'It's a matter of life and death,' pleaded Maria.

'Or perhaps just another one of your bets!'

'Yes, and one that Yevgeny and I both lost!'

Stephen took Maria by both hands, and searched her wrist and arms for signs of needle marks. It was clear he believed she and Yevgeny were addicts seeking money to feed their habit. She assisted him by rolling up her sleeves.

'I'm not interested,' he said.

'As usual, I gambled and made the wrong choice,' said Maria. 'Please accept my apologies!'

'How do I know you're telling me the truth?' he demanded.

'Because the truth would shock you even more than my poor excuse for a lie. So please, go home to your genteel English castle, on its rolling hill, where the sun never sets. Yes, we are broke, and desperate to go home, but you're right, I haven't told you everything.'

'I don't think for one moment you have.'

'Except the truth will take you out of your vacuum-sealed bubble, and disturb your cosy idea of all the things that make you feel secure.'

'You don't know the first thing about me!' said Stephen.

'OK, I'm not going to put any layers of honey on this for you. There is no point. If you must know, Yevgeny is a heroin addict and has become unemployable. In our desperation to find work, we have ended up in the hands of people traffickers. At present they are holding him against his will, and demanding the repayment of a drug debt, in order to force me into prostitution!'

Stephen looked visibly shocked, and told Maria that as sympathetic as he was, she should go to the police.

'Have you ever asked yourself why websites selling sex expand daily, and drugs are more available than a haemorrhoid preparation?' she argued. 'They're only hidden if you don't look.'

'Then I'll go to the police for you!' said Stephen.

'If they were raided tomorrow, the girls would be too frightened to talk, and by lunchtime the next day, they'd re-open for business. Besides, I don't even know where Yevgeny has been taken.'

Stephen looked perplexed and lost for words. In the course of a few minutes, Maria had presented him with a set of circumstances he had never before been confronted. Matters which, for the most part, belonged to an underworld he had never come into contact with. He knew about drug dealers, gangs and street violence from a distance, but had never soiled his hands on the people that caused the problem. This wasn't what he had expected, and Maria knew it full well.

'I wish I could help,' he said apologetically, 'it's just I'm the wrong person to ask!'

'I need a driver. Someone to take him to rehab. It won't be a pleasure trip. It will also involve you in truths you would rather not know,' Maria persisted.

'I own a vintage Jag, not a Ferrari. You'd be taking a far bigger risk using me than the police!'

'These people are very clever. Very dangerous and very clever. They think they have thought of everything.'

'Then why is it you believe you can do something experienced police officers can't?'

'Because I know them,' said Maria. 'And I know how they think. I have a plan, but it's going to fail, unless you absolutely trust me. If you don't trust me, then Yevgeny and I could lose everything. Including our lives.'

'What plan?' asked Stephen. 'You started off by asking for money. Now you want to involve me in some kind of plan to save your lives!'

'I haven't quite worked out the details,' admitted Maria.

'Then my advice is to call the police.'

Stephen stood up to leave, as if he was the victim of a hoax. He had only taken a few steps, however, when Maria confronted him.

'I apologise for wasting the peace and quiet of a Sunday afternoon on the insignificant lives of a couple of foreigners,' she stated.

Maria hoped against hope that, underneath the rhetoric of denial, Stephen harboured enough curiosity to consider she could be telling the truth. After all, her story must have seemed too bizarre to be true. Yet, too far-fetched not to be.

'Now, you're trying to make me feel guilty,' he said.

'I'm also appealing to your conscience, not your over-used common sense!'

Maria's eyes displayed an urgency that left Stephen no room for doubt.

'Give me a couple of days to think it over,' he said.

'We don't have that much time,' replied Maria.

'Are you being serious?' asked Stephen.

'Right now, you're the only person who can help us!'

Stephen's face not only betrayed discomfort, but also profound confusion. Maria pulled up his sleeve, and wrote the number of Scrawn's secret mobile on his wrist.

'I'm sorry I don't have any spare napkins,' said Maria.

Stephen didn't say goodbye, and disappeared quickly into the afternoon crowd, as if eager to escape. When she reached the Argyle, Maria tapped on the exit door, and Bao let her in.

'I told Pavel, you in toilet being sick. Now I think you better recover fast!' said Bao.

When Maria returned to 'Bangkok', she reported her meeting with Stephen to Scrawn, and pondered the fact she might never hear from him again.

'Since you defied them, and upset a valuable client, they'll turn you into a crack addict, and teach you to perform tricks all day for a rock.' Scrawn warned.

'Why do they try so hard to break our spirit?' asked Maria.

'Because we are the ones who still hope,' Scrawn answered.

In the early hours, Stephen sent a text message.

I'll drive you to rehab. Nothing else!'

6.

FOR THE NEXT few nights, the doors were locked earlier than normal, and the atmosphere more tense. Maria was convinced it was something to do with her. She wondered if Pavel had become suspicious of her charade at the Argyle, or if Bao had said something. She had taken a big risk by meeting Stephen, but now had no other choice than to hope, and pray he would follow through on his reluctant promise to trust the plan of someone he hardly knew.

So far, faith had played little part in Maria's survival. Or so she thought. But it now took on more significance. Not so much for the privilege she once enjoyed, as the misery she now witnessed. Each night on the pillow on which her thoughts wrestled, she said a silent prayer for the girls. It had nothing to do with any holiness she could legitimately claim for herself, but instead asked God to end what she regarded as the casual and inexcusable exercise of humiliation, that poisons the soul, and leads to the wanton destruction of hope.

There was also speculation concerning the increased security, which not only inhibited movement between 'Bangkok' and 'Saigon', but also limited use of the kitchen. However, what it mostly did was psychologically undermine the trust between the girls and their captors. It was intentional, but no one was sure why?

Scrawn's earlier advice had also unnerved Maria. She knew

the visible members of the gang, but not who controlled the whole organisation. Maria suggested it could be Max, since he controlled the money.

'No,' said Scrawn. 'He's only the bookkeeper. In fact, unlike the others, he's not the least bit interested in sex, and lives a quiet family life in suburbia.'

Scrawn also told her one of the websites the gang used to promote the girls was called 'Dangerous Liaisons'. Not only that, but the business was growing so fast, they had even bought their own hotel, and used part of it as a full time brothel.

'I've worked there,' exclaimed Scrawn. 'It's like them. Low class!'

'Would they have taken Yevgeny there?' Maria asked.

'Who knows, they're like an octopus. They have suckers everywhere.'

The next day, when Maria was alone with Ivan, she told him that very soon it would be Yevgeny's birthday, and demanded to see him, if only for a few minutes. Ivan stroked Maria's cheek, and then placed his hand on her breast, and smiled.

'According to Luca, you're the type who is treated to a luxurious meal, and then throws it back in their face.'

'I'm also a fast learner.'

'So tell me fast learner. Where is it?'

'What?'

'The mobile, of course!'

'I don't have one.'

'Someone does.'

There had always been a routine search of the girls returning from a shift. They were searched for drugs, and anything that allowed them to communicate outside the supervised 'call time' carried a severe penalty. A small amount of cocaine was permissible, but they didn't want the girls on heroin. It was too expensive, and the girls could become unmanageable. They liked them compliant with a coke habit, and understood the economics of the percentage. They were allowed just enough money to keep their families alive, and enough coke to keep them in-line, along with a few luxuries. Extra rations were earned in return for sexual favours, and they occasionally became minor dealers amongst themselves, with money changing hands for a 'hit'. But the sum total of their existence was fear, administered with a precise cynical insight into the upside benefit of psychological control.

That night when the girls returned, Maria told Scrawn about her conversation with Ivan.

'They often search the place when we're out,' admitted Scrawn. 'They were just pressing a button hoping to find radio canary.'

That night, the door was locked as usual, and Maria asked Scrawn if she could have access to the 'love child'. She called Stephen Kline, and gave him precise details to follow. She told him she wasn't very confident that the plan would work, but asked him to trust her. After Maria handed back the phone, Scrawn revealed she had a 'secret boyfriend', and tonight, they had agreed to talk. Feeling exuberant, she crawled under the blanket, curled herself up into a foetal position, and began a conversation in half concealed whispers, interspersed with occasional giggling.

Their conversation hadn't lasted very long, however, when footsteps were heard coming towards their block, and suddenly a key was heard being turned in the lock. Scrawn tore off the bedclothes, and, terminating the call, quickly inserted the phone into the privacy of her vagina, barely a split second before Lily, Luca and Ivan entered.

Lily ordered the girls into the shower room, whilst Luca and Ivan turned the room upside down, first by stripping the blankets and sheets off the bed, then turning over the mattresses, inspecting the pillows and ransacking the drawers, ensuring every lining and pocket was searched, and anything capable of concealing an object the size of a mobile phone broken open. Unable to find anything, they then began treating every item of clothing like rags, occasionally ripping the fabric, and ensuring any memento, photograph, or keepsake was dashed against the hard concrete floor, before emptying the contents of their handbags and make-up unceremoniously in the middle of the room, including their pathetically small suitcases. They were then herded into the living area, and made to stand semi-naked in front of their belongings, now resembling a discarded pile of debris.

Lily, Luca and Ivan then entered the shower-room, and the girls listened as objects were being moved on the shelf, thrown down or broken and heard the lid of the cistern being removed. There followed the sound of a hushed conversation, before Lily, followed by Luca and Ivan, left the bathroom to confront them.

'Satisfied?' said Scrawn.

'Strip,' demanded Lily.

Scrawn stepped forward defiantly, and folded her arms.

'There's hardly anything left to degrade.'

'Oh, I wouldn't say that,' responded Lily.

Maria wore a pair of pyjamas, and Noi and Hong were in their bras and pants, whilst Scrawn wore a pair of grey track bottoms and a pink cotton top, with the image of a panda and two strategically placed paw prints, with the words, '*In need of protection*' printed underneath.

'You are either having problems with your eyesight, or in the market for underwear models,' declared Scrawn.

'What do *you* think?' said Lily.

Ivan who had been silent until now, confronted Scrawn.

'She doesn't think,' he said, then began patting her down like a police suspect, starting from her rear end and the inside of her legs, and after demanding she raise her arms, ran his fingers up and down her back and sides, before invading the inside of her cotton top.

Scrawn didn't move a muscle, but all the while looked him in the eye with contempt, as his hands came to rest on her breasts.

'Feel anything you are grown-up enough to handle?' she asked.

Ivan repeated the exercise with Maria, but as his hands moved towards the inside of her thighs, the memory of her ordeal at the hands of the gynaecologist years before, ignited her instinct of defence. Suddenly, his eyes opened wide, and he jumped back with a sudden jolt of pain, that almost knocked Lily off balance. Then after recovering sufficiently enough, he retaliated, by slapping Maria hard across the face.

'Happy now?' said Scrawn, addressing Ivan as if he were a schoolboy.

'Shut up, you slut!' he shouted.

Lily put her hand up, to restrain Ivan from any further assault, and after studying the girls for a few moments, signalled for her companions to leave. The transparent failure of their inept mission, allowing the girls a rare moment of triumph, and for Scrawn, the intoxication of striking a blow on behalf of her own subversive freedom. She then blew a defiant kiss towards Ivan, as if he were a departing punter, whilst Luca and Lily appeared somewhat subdued, as they prepared to depart like a small defeated army.

Scrawn beamed victoriously, and was unable to resist one last parting shot of bravura, as they turned to go.

'We were rather hoping that, once you've cleaned up the mess, you wouldn't mind spraying the room to get rid of the smell,' she said.

The girls' morale soared, and they nodded in agreement at Scrawn's final anarchic flourish. But no sooner had their relief begun to turn to celebration, than the muffled sound of a vibration began to pulsate from the direction of Scrawn's pelvic floor.

It could have only have been a negligible portion of a second before the trio departed, and the door once again came to rest in its reinforced frame, but just before the door could close, Lily's head turned around, and she looked in the immediate vicinity of the girls. Her eyes on stalks, and with the instinct of a bloodhound, she stared in gleeful satisfaction towards the torso of Scrawn, that now betrayed its hidden treasure in her most erogenous zone. Scrawn's face quickly turned from the triumphal glow of a few moments before into one of overwhelming culpability, as the forbidden contraband illicitly bleated between her thighs.

Lily walked towards Scrawn, with a look of haughty superiority, and, accompanied by Luca and Ivan, held out an upward palm, demanding delivery of the device, busily pulsating in the deepest reaches of her tiny frame. Scrawn, ignominiously, retrieved the object with the injured sensibility of a small child, and handed it to Lily.

'Some people call at the most inconvenient times, don't they?' said Lily.

The phone had ceased vibrating, and the agents of repression now sought to regain domination of the territory they had lost. Ivan stood alongside Lily, gloating, whilst Scrawn, knowing that pleading a defence was useless, had no other choice than to wait like a subordinate, for her fate to be decided.

'Did you imagine we didn't know?' Lily asked Scrawn.

'Why should she need to hide something everyone else takes for granted?' said Maria.

'You, like everyone else, are in no position to ask anything,' Lily replied.

A silence fell on the room, as if a foreign power had invaded, and rounded up hostages.

Hong and Noi got dressed, and sat on the corner of their beds, with their heads bowed, whilst Scrawn remained at attention in her track bottoms and girlish T-shirt, like a defendant at a court martial, with Maria beside her. After an interminable period of unbearable silence, Luca briefly departed, and returned with a baseball bat, that he began to lightly tap on the fingers of one hand.

'Perhaps you would be so good as to accompany Luca,' Lily said to Scrawn.

'What if she refuses?' asked Maria.

'Then you'll both enjoy the same punishment,' replied Lily.

Scrawn began to visibly shake, and clasped her hands around her upper arms. Then Luca placed his hand on her shoulder, and led her away. Not long after, Lily and Ivan departed, locking the door behind them, leaving Maria, Hong and Noi, standing among the forlorn remnants of the girls' material possessions. They looked at each other, deeply troubled, and then proceeded to the small window by the front door, and opened its restricted access to the night air. They were not able to see as far as the isolation block, but heard the door opening, and then a short time later, the sound of Scrawn's cries, as a series of blows, at the sadistic hands of Luca, landed on her fragile body. Then, following a brief period of silence, the voices of Lily and Ivan could be heard, as they withdrew into the men's block, like cowards, afraid to witness the result of their complicity.

At this point Maria and the girls hoped that Scrawn would be returned to their care, and listened out for some sign she would be released. But instead, the haunting sound of her begging for mercy rang out from the bare surroundings of her incarceration, as the punishment resumed. This time with far greater relish. Each blow that connected with her body sounding like a rag doll being attacked with an iron bar. The pitiful baying of a once merciful child, now bearing witness to the sorrowful reminder of an unenviable journey of betrayal and lost innocence.

Maria banged on the locked door of their block in protest, and shouted for the punishment to stop, and was joined by Noi and Hong, who shouted their support in Thai. The girls in the next block also demonstrated their solidarity, by hammering on their own door, and shouted defiantly. The commotion reaching such a pitch, they were hoping that someone in the street or a nearby resident would call for help. But no one responded, and no alarm was raised. Then suddenly, the banging ceased, and nothing remained, except an atmosphere of brutalisation, that hung in the night air, like energy being sapped from the lungs of its impotent witnesses, who had no other option than to stand helplessly by, as the sorrowful whimpering of their streetwise, amusing and artful companion grew more faint.

There followed a long, dark silence, as if the moon had evaporated into a black hole, and the passing traffic had been re-directed into a subterranean car park, as the inhabitants of the 'Bangkok Hilton' and 'Saigon International' waited in anticipation. Suddenly, they heard the door of the isolation block open, and Luca exit in violent intoxication.

'See what you made me do!' he shouted. 'You hear me? You did this! You chose to defy me. She brought this on herself. She knew the rules. You know them. But you won't listen!'

Luca's voice trembled, betraying something unexpected in his self-justification. A trace of remorse, almost self-pity, like a stain he attempted to explain away. Maria almost caught a glimpse of him staggering, as he moved about outside. They then heard Lily's voice attempting to calm him down, before she led him back inside the isolation block, and closed the door.

Maria shut the window.

'Come, let us pray,' she said.

Maria led Noi and Hong back to the sleeping area, where they stood with their heads bowed.

'I'm praying to Christ. Is that okay?'

'It's okay,' said Hong, while Noi nodded in agreement.

'Oh Lord, we pray for our sister Sukhon, who we know you love. We pray for your unlimited mercy, healing power, and for her to be delivered from the pain and sorrow of her situation. We pray that you give her the strength to survive. Lord would you open the cell door, like you did for St Peter, and allow her to walk free.'

The girls remained silent for several minutes, and then Noi said to Maria, 'We'll pray to the Lord Buddha as well,' and then searched in the pile, until a damaged statue of Buddha was found, and after placing it on a table by the bed, lit a candle, and kneeled before it. Outside, there appeared to be no movement, and after Noi and Hong had said a prayer, they began clearing up the mess that served as a sharp reminder of their own privation, until eventually, all three collapsed on their bed, hoping Scrawn's defiant nature would allow her to survive. A few hours later, Maria detected some barely audible movement, and heard the steel gate at the bottom of the stairs open and close.

The next day brought no answers concerning the fate of Scrawn. The mood was both subdued and tight-lipped among Ivan and Pavel, and neither Lily nor Luca were anywhere to be seen. On the way to work that morning, Maria confronted Ivan.

'What has happened to Scrawn? Where is she?' Maria demanded.

'She's been transferred,' said Ivan.

'To where?'

'Never you mind.'

It was the first time that Maria had seen Ivan display embarrassment, his demeanour and body language betraying the evasive cunning of guilt.

'Liar!' she exclaimed.

'Take it as a warning,' he replied.

Later, there was speculation among the girls that either Scrawn had been beaten unconscious, or that her wounds had proved fatal. The consensus favoured the latter, and the resulting restlessness sunk into the community, like a stench poisoning the atmosphere, spreading fear, and for the very first time, talk of anarchy. The threat of this impending rebellion reaching the ears of Lily, she decided to act, and later that night addressed the occupants of both blocks.

'I am well aware everyone is concerned about the events of last night. It was of course regrettable, but, I'm afraid, necessary. There's a reason why mobile phones are forbidden out of hours. It's for the benefit of all, and to ensure our business interests remain secure. Our friend Sukhon knew that full well, but chose instead to defy the rules. That's why she had to be punished.'

'Don't you mean executed?' challenged Maria.

'You, of all people, should be aware of the consequences of rebellion,' replied Lily. 'After all, someone else is already paying the price for your failure to co-operate.'

No one raised any further objections, and Lily departed with her dubious authority intact. Her words carried no reassurance of closure, but simply the menace of retaliation. The girls' reaction was one of resignation. They hoped against hope that Scrawn was alive. But in their hearts, no one believed it. Destabilisation and division were the liquidity on which their captors relied. However, the girls had lost an insolent stone in the shoe of their oppressors, and they knew it. As a result, they held an ad hoc memorial in the canteen, and Maria shared a memory of Scrawn listening to a recording of the 'Love Duet' from 'Madame Butterfly' on her MP3 player.

'Why do you only like posh music?' Scrawn had asked Maria.

'Music isn't posh. It's just music,' Maria replied.

'But you have to be educated to understand it.'

'You tell me?' Maria said, and handed Scrawn the device.

'What's it about then?' Scrawn had asked, listening intently.

'It's a man telling a woman he loves her,' answered Maria.

Scrawn listened with tears in her eyes, and at the end of the duet she removed the headphones and handed them back.

'I can't listen any more,' she said. 'It's beautiful, but I don't understand it!'

The ceremony, like the life of their dear friend, was pitifully brief. Maimed at the start, and assigned a fate of surrender to the worst of humanity. She was a fatality of the economically unviable, whose brief life was now being toasted with tea.

Her voice breaking, Maria attempted to add a note of nobility to the proceedings, while the rest of the girls looked deeply saddened.

'Your tiny, funny, indiscreet and spunky frame paid too high a price. I toast you, and ask God to allow you the light of a braver day,' she prayed.

Suddenly, Hong demanded,

'Where is your God? Does he cry for us, or has he gone missing?'

The girls dutifully disbanded, amid an air of hopelessness. The isolation block was now empty, and both Luca, Lily and Ivan avoided it. It had become spiritually out of bounds, and whenever the girls glanced in its direction their eyes were downcast. But other matters now took precedence in Maria's mind, and timing was crucial.

The incident had created deep distrust between the girls and their captors, especially Luca. The idle chit-chat between them having all but ceased, and the girls employing a strategy of silent revolt, whereby orders were either ignored, disobeyed or undertaken without enthusiasm, there was now a marked division between the two. Polite insolence, which as Hong pointed out, was a particularly Southeast Asian sign of disrespect.

'When they attacked Scrawn, they attacked all of us,' she proclaimed.

Maria decided she now had to make her move, and requested a face to face meeting with Lily.

'Have you come as a spokesman for the girls?' Lily enquired.

'Partly,' confirmed Maria. 'To begin with, they demand more freedom and access to the internet, and more time to phone their families. One hour on a Saturday is no longer acceptable. They also want some freedom to go out and shop, buy their own make-up, and visit the hairdressers. And for the doors not to be locked at night.'

Lily looked at Maria ruefully with a half-smile. As if an employee had come seeking a raise.

'You don't know how anything works, do you? With your college education and a privileged background. You probably think that life should be fair. Is that what you think? That it's like a carpet rolled out, to protect you from all the dirt under your feet. That you are entitled to a soil-free existence. It doesn't exist. Life is pain. Of course, if you belong to the select few that live in a centrally-heated chocolate box, with immaculately turned out children, then, good luck. That's how Hollywood peddles dreams. But when the lights come up, everyone goes back to their own reality. You accuse me of being a slave-trader. How do you think large corporations get rich? Sweat-shops, cheap labour, avoiding regulations, bribery, finding loopholes in the law, avoiding tax and buying political support. America was built on it, Asia survives on it, and Africa has made it a way of life. You think America's a democracy? It's a hypocrisy. The land of the free was founded on robbing the Indians of their land, and enjoying the benefits of slavery. You don't know who you're dealing with. This is just a corner shop in the operation, and the people we work for will never die of a broken heart. What happened to Scrawn was unfortunate, but a minor inconvenience. Ours is not an organisation that encourages independence. It's not that I'm not sympathetic, it's just that I can't afford to be. Everyone will feel bad for a while. Then they'll forget about it, and everything will go back to how it was.'

The voice of Lily, Maria considered, had a cunning theatricality, and was intensely musical. It rose in quarter tones when she gave orders, and half-tones when she shouted. In attrition, she used semi-breves. 'No' did not just mean 'no'. It meant, 'how dare you'. Mostly, she dispensed charm in the manner of a rattlesnake. You heard the tonal implication, and waited to see if she would strike. Mostly, people heeded the rattle, if they knew what was good for them. She was tiny, with large hooded eyelids, that reminded Maria of Bette Davis, but with thin lips, surrounding a generous mouth and large uneven teeth, that dispensed poison in parcels of practical advice. But it was her eyes that persuaded. They were a luminous blue, and when they held you in their gaze, commanded complete obedience. But what Lily controlled by attrition, Luca enforced by might. Yet, at the heart of their criminal alliance was an irony that Scrawn, once referred to,

'When we're too old for the meat-rack, they really do use us as full-time cleaners!'

Lily sat back in the armchair of her lounge, refusing to give any indication of disquiet, yet at the same time demonstrated corruption was a parasite that also killed the soul of its host.

'You said your reason for this meeting was only partly about the girls' demands?'

'I want to do a deal,' said Maria. 'I will agree to work for you, but only if you release Yevgeny, and only until the amount you demand is paid back.'

'I'm glad that you've decided to be sensible,' said Lily. 'But first, we will need to see some proof of your loyalty. Until then, let us just say we are holding him as a security deposit.'

'He's a Ukrainian national, not a Thai import!' responded Maria.

Lily looked triumphant. Almost motherly. Maria could imagine how she could lure young girls with talk of a Western way of life, money, and the comfort of being part of a family.

That night she prayed that nothing would go wrong, and Stephen would fulfil his promise.

7.

THE NEXT DAY, accompanied by Lily and Luca, Maria set out with Hong, Kim, Mai and Apple to the other side of London. Maria hadn't been to the hotel before. It was close to Paddington station, which they passed minutes before, pulling up outside a four storey building set back from the road, that looked as if had been converted from two separate houses. One side served as the entrance that had a neon sign over the portico, displaying 'Bedfont Hotel', while the other had an illuminated box fixed to one of the colonnades that you could see if you approached from the side. The building itself looked run-down, and the inside was gloomy, foregoing charm in the interests of functionality. A once elegant set of stairs dominated the rear of the lobby, whilst set-back in a narrow recess to the left was a reception desk, manned by a chubby, middle-aged man of Asian appearance, wearing a white open necked shirt, but no tie or jacket. As they entered, he was reading a newspaper and smoking, and while Maria and the girls waited with Luca for the lift to arrive, Lily approached him.

'Well, what have you got?'

'It's slow today,' said the man. 'Thursday is always slow.' Maria and the girls were taken to a corner room at the end of a corridor on the top floor.

Like the rest of the hotel, the furnishing in the room was dated, and contained a double bed, a couple of tattered armchairs and a table, on which a jar of coffee, tea bags, a kettle and half filled boxes of biscuits were ready to be consumed. In the corner was a small cupboard containing soup, microwave meals for one, and packets of noodles, and underneath, a small fridge, on top of which stood a microwave oven. The small en-suite, with a shower and washbasin, included a solitary set of drawers, that in addition to accommodating the girls' make-up, included a large box of condoms. The whole room was reminiscent of an overcrowded restroom, complete with a solitary mirror, into which disappointed eyes peered into a future that offered little hope.

As soon as Lily and Luca departed, Kim and Apple slumped on the bed, whilst Mai, Apple and Hong applied lipstick, brushed their hair and made some tea. Hong looked despondent, and while the other girls were having an animated conversation in Vietnamese, Maria picked her brains about what to expect.

'The same as always,' said Hong. 'We sit here until Lily or Luca send for us. Then we get sent to a room, ask the customer to shower, and then strip to our bra and pants. Then after the customer has finished showering, we hand them a towel, and hopefully, by then, they have an erection.'

Hong then produced a condom, and demonstrated the most efficient method of inserting it on a man's penis.

'It works best if you slip it on before they realise what's happening!' she said.

She then advised Maria on how to accelerate their state of excitement, telling her it could be over in a matter of minutes, while other men took ages, and others just wanted to talk. Either way, the minimum charge was for half an hour, even if they stayed for five minutes. If they wanted extra time, or anything other than straight sex, they paid a 'special rate'.

But the girls never saw any money themselves, and Luca dealt with any complaints.

However, the most valuable insight Hong offered was how to deal with the mental torment of being used as the equivalent of a human vending machine.

'Switch everything off, and treat it as though you were giving pain relief.'

'Is that your state secret?' asked Maria.

'You'll soon see,' replied Hong.

As the organisation owned the hotel, the customers for the girls were booked in for a 'shower and massage'. Its salacious activity being mainly confined to the top floor, while the shoe-string backpackers and long-term asylum seekers occupied the lower floors, to give it legitimacy. But mainly, only the desperate headed in its direction. What amazed Maria was just how many of them there were.

From about midday onwards, they began arriving, and Luca would put his head around the door and call a name. Then the girl would disappear, and return about twenty to thirty minutes later, as if she had just popped out to perform a mundane chore, and then resume whatever activity or conversation she was engaged in before she left the room. Occasionally, they would exchange some raucous details in their native language and laugh. But mostly they appeared as bored as checkout operators between shifts, wishing they could be somewhere else.

Maria began to feel increasingly isolated. Before, she felt prostitution was just the enforced labour of the underclass. At best, a necessary evil. But now, the stark reality of being on the meat-rack itself horrified her, and she began to panic. Each time the door opened, she wondered if her name would be called, and became overwhelmed by a total sense of powerlessness. Between snacks and preening themselves, it was obvious the girls were curious to know when Maria's name would be called, and the waiting became unbearable.

Surprisingly, a sudden injection of humour, or a shared joke at the expense of Lily or Luca, could spontaneously erupt, but a state of enmity still existed between them. Especially Luca.

On arrival, he had distributed a small plastic bag of cocaine to each of the occupants, and had made a special point of giving one to Maria.

'It's your welcome gift,' he announced.

'Then it will make me feel even worse,' replied Maria. 'Especially coming from you.'

The girls fully expected Luca to retaliate, but in the light of recent events, it was evident he had been ordered to exercise restraint. Instead, his cheeks became flushed and his eyes narrowed, but he just smiled at Maria, and said nothing.

'Soon, you'll wish he had landed a right hook,' said Hong.

'Why don't you all walk out?' said Maria. 'All four of you. Out of the door, down the stairs and into freedom?'

'Why don't you?' said Apple.

'We'll be right behind you,' added Kim.

An awkward silence invaded the air. The girls looked at Maria as though she must have already known the answer to the question. There was no further discussion, and sometime later, Luca opened the door halfway, and beckoned to Maria.

'We've got a customer for you,' he said. 'Next floor down turn left. Room 310.'

'Who am I supposed to be meeting?' she asked.

'What do you think we are, an introduction agency? Room 310, and take a condom.'

Maria hesitated for several moments and then felt the outline of silver wrapping being pressed into the palm of her hand by Hong.

'Follow me,' said Luca.

On arrival outside the room, Luca stood a few feet away from the door. Maria approached, but had no time to prepare her mental state. She stood frozen at the doorway. Then Luca opened the door with one hand, and propelled her in with the other.

Sitting on the bed was a man of African descent, aged about twenty-five, who stood to attention as she entered the room. He was wearing a light blue pair of trousers that rode up above his long legs, and a dark blue T-shirt, several sizes too big. Together with scuffed trainers, he looked like an asylum seeker.

As Maria approached him, he started walking backwards, as if afraid of her.

'Speak English?' Maria asked.

'Yes a little,' he answered.

'Then you'll understand what *'get lost'* means, won't you!' she said defiantly.

Maria walked towards the door, and on leaving, turned right and headed towards the stairs, with Luca in pursuit. She could hear him on his mobile, as she propelled herself down three flights towards the entrance. When she reached the ground floor, Lily stood at the bottom, blocking her way.

'Where do you think you're going?' she demanded.

'I'm leaving,' said Maria.

'So soon?'

'Not soon enough.'

'You'll have to forgive that little incident, just now. It's just Luca's sense of fun!'

'He doesn't have one.'

By this time, Luca had caught up, and stood behind Maria menacingly. Lily signalled for him to keep his distance.

'Don't try and stop me!' insisted Maria.

Lily stepped aside.

'Then don't let me stop you. By all means enjoy the great outdoors. But if you do, I promise that, by tonight, your boyfriend will be found slumped in a doorway, somewhere in the West End, with a syringe in his hand.'

Lily held up her mobile phone and placed a finger over one of the buttons.

'Entirely, your choice of course.'

Maria looked towards the entrance and remained motionless. Lily walked casually up to her, and placing a consoling arm around her shoulder, spoke reassuringly.

'Luca will call the lift for you. No use in wasting yet more energy climbing all those stairs.'

When Maria returned to the room on the top floor, Hong approached her with a cup of tea.

'Here,' said Hong. 'Welcome to the club.'

'It was a hoax,' said Maria. 'Just Luca's warped idea of revenge.'

'Did he send you to room 310?' Hong asked.

Maria nodded.

'We call it the video room!' she exclaimed.

By now, it had turned four thirty. Suddenly, Hong was called outside by Luca, and returned with a blonde wig, and headed for the en-suite, emerging a short time later with her face covered in light pancake make-up, and the curls of the wig cascading down her back and shoulders. She then disappeared into the hallway, but returned less than five minutes later minus the wig, and sat on the bed looking bemused.

'Did he prefer a brunette?' asked Apple.

'He doesn't like Asians,' said Hong.

Not long after, Lily appeared at the door, and invited Maria into the hallway.

'You wanted a chance to pay for your boyfriend's freedom?' she said.

'Well, it's arrived.'

Lily asked Maria to accompany her downstairs, and when the lift doors opened, escorted her across the lobby to a small table, where Stephen Kline was seated.

'Will *she* do?' asked Lily.

Stephen's eyes met Maria's, but he showed no sign of recognition. Instead he looked her up and down casually, and then said,

'Perfect.'

Maria returned to the top floor, and was given instructions by Luca, accompanied by a warning.

'Mess up this time, and you can forget about seeing your boyfriend ever again.'

Maria was sent to Room 313, and awaited Stephen's arrival.

'I won't be very far away,' Luca reminded her.

When Stephen entered, she put her finger to her lips, and whispered,

'You're going to have to pretend.'

Stephen looked apprehensive, and was asked to remove his jacket and tie. Then Maria enquired,

'What do you want me to do?'

She spoke the words confidently, just loud enough to be heard outside the room.

'Everything,' said Stephen, with just enough authority to make him sound authentic.

'I don't do anything involving violence,' said Maria.

'Don't worry. I abhor violence,' he said, 'I prefer to teach.'

'First, you must take a shower,' said Maria, and handed him a condom.

'They'll need evidence,' she whispered.

It was an inconvenience Stephen didn't expect, but nonetheless he obeyed her instructions, entered the shower room and closed the door behind him. He ran the shower for over five minutes, and then returned carrying the condom between his thumb and forefinger, and handed it to Maria, as if she were a nurse collecting a sperm sample. She then wrapped it in a few tissues, and despatched it to the waste bin beside the bed, before declaring,

'Is this okay?'

'I'll tell you when to stop,' Stephen declared assertively.

Maria signalled her approval, as if they had rehearsed beforehand. She then motioned for them to lay on top of the bed, and announced,

'This is the part where I require a teacher!'

After a short interval Stephen asked,

'Am I making you feel wet?'

Maria turned her face away, and said,

'Yes,' but felt ill at ease.

'Good,' smiled Stephen, his voice more soothing. 'That's

very good.'

'Are you sure?' Maria asked.

'Just leave it to me,' said Stephen confidently.

In between their vocal subterfuge, both spoke in whispers. Planning the next stage of Maria's long odds gamble, Stephen produced a mobile phone, and handed it to Maria, along with a pen and paper, on which she wrote down the address where she was being held captive in East London, and drew a crude map, along with additional instructions in writing.

'I can't guarantee how long it's going to take,' whispered Maria.

'Let me worry about that,' replied Stephen softly.

Maria hid the mobile phone, and within moments he was back in character, adding some vocal authenticity to their coital engagement, and stepping up the climax of their charade, sounding suitably satisfied.

Then, without warning, he kissed Maria passionately on the lips, and she pulled away.

'You can't do that!' she said offended.

'Why not?' demanded Stephen.

'Because it's not part of the service!' declared Maria.

They looked at each other for several moments. Their fully-clothed encounter having the unintended consequence of revealing an undeclared moment of naked reality to slip from Stephen's sub-conscious.

He then prepared to leave, and told Maria,

'If its okay, I won't tip you. I've spent far too much already.'

Maria waited several minutes, and then washed her hands and face, making sure the towel looked as if it had been used. When she opened the door, Luca was leaning against the wall directly opposite, and gave her a look of approval.

'Very impressive,' he said. 'In fact, you're quite the performer.'

Lily was equally impressed.

'Luca tells me you have hidden talent.'

'I'm strictly an amateur.'

'It won't be for very long. Just until the debt has been repaid.'

'Exactly, how much are we talking about?'

'Just a few thousand. That's all.'

Corruption, Maria considered, involved a cunning alchemy, of which Lily was an established practitioner. The subtle and cynical calculation that had allowed her to manipulate others was now being extended to Maria.

'You know, you don't belong here,' said Lily. 'As from Saturday, you'll work exclusively for our upmarket clients.'

'Co-operation cuts both ways,' said Maria. 'I want something in return.'

When they arrived back in East London, Maria was granted permission to hand over her MP3 player for Ivan to deliver to Yevgeny.

'He must miss music so much,' Maria explained. 'Can you deliver it this evening?

'I want him to know I haven't forgotten him on his birthday!'

Lily examined the MP3 player to ensure it contained only music, and handed it to Ivan.

'It's good to see you using your intelligence at last,' she told Maria. 'That way any unpleasantness can be avoided.'

'Is that what happened to Scrawn?' Maria asked. 'She stopped using her intelligence?'

'She had intelligence,' said Lily, 'but only employed it on a part time-basis. There was also evidence she intended to elope.'

Maria felt sick. The punishment delivered on the body of Scrawn was really an attack on her spirit. Luca could have crushed her body with hardly any effort. Instead, it was meant to serve as a warning against the possibility of escape to some form of liberty.

Even a limited life, Scrawn must have known, was preferable to one that would persist in wringing out her existence, like a spent force, allowing her no joy. To exist for no other reason than to feed the inexhaustible greed of others.

Her real threat to the orderly housekeeping of the gang was not the minor infraction of hiding the mobile phone, but hope itself.

It was a contagion the gang had to eradicate.

'Do you want to know why she lost her life? She lost it, because she wanted to!' Lily claimed. 'After Luca had taught her a lesson, he was ready to let her go. But all she did was laugh in his face, and told him he was going to hell. He grew up in the suburbs of Grozny, so, he and hell are well acquainted. He therefore, gave her a warning, but she took no notice. All she did was look at him and laugh, like someone mentally deranged. Anyone else would have nursed their injuries and left. But Scrawn just had to have the last word. Pulling herself halfway up from the floor, and resting on one elbow, she told Luca that for a man with the brain of a dead sheep, he hit like a sissy.'

'Is that when you ran out and left her at his mercy?'

'Unfortunately, life doesn't happen on a theology course, or, in a climate-controlled environment. It happens in the rough, uneven current of everyday endurance.'

There was in her explanation no element of mercy or insight into the chaotic deprivation that had led Scrawn to her fate. Only the heartless reasoning of consequence and the irony of injustice. Even the loss of her meagre income to her family was of no concern.

Maria suggested that some kind of financial settlement be sent to Scrawn's family, in compensation, but the very idea was rejected by Lily as being tantamount to an admission of guilt.

'We will always have the poor with us. Even Christ said that,' she smiled.

'He was referring to the generosity of an admirer, not someone beaten to death over the ownership of a paltry mobile phone,' Maria replied.

Lily's eyes narrowed, and Maria felt in imminent danger of physical retaliation, except, just for a moment, she detected something behind her eyes that betrayed an inner torment. One Lily dare not admit. Then suddenly the spell was broken, and she returned to the conscious application of dominant coercion.

'If I were you, I'd get some sleep,' said Lily. 'You'll need all your devotion for Saturday.'

By now Ivan had disappeared with the MP3 player, and Maria hoped everything had gone to plan. The words of Lily, however, were prophetic. Saturday was only a day away, and Hong informed Maria it was more than likely she been selected as a Princess, someone whom she described as being white, European, and the proud owner of a high-priced cherry.

'The rest of us serve the needy. But the price for you will be high!' she said.

'Who knows! They might even try to market you as a virgin?'

Once again, there was clear water between Maria and how the rest of the girls were treated. She was to be preserved like some prize cow, owned and rented out to the highest bidder, like a stately home adds class to a property portfolio.

When she reported her discussion with Lily to the girls, they agreed to donate ten pounds each a week, and send it to Scrawn's family. It was a gesture of solidarity not shared by those who had taken her possibilities, and abruptly consigned them to history. Maria was also to learn that Scrawn was only eighteen when she died, and had been on the streets since she was twelve. The romantic idea they could escape was something on which they abruptly set the record straight.

'These people know our families and the villages where we live. If we don't co-operate, they will simply pay someone to visit our parents home one night with a can of petrol, and 'whoosh', or employ someone to kill them' Hong added.

Maria felt ashamed of naively believing they had some measure of choice, rather than being responsible for the life of a family member. She now felt the choice she faced was just as personal. The success or otherwise of her gamble was, however, still not a sure thing. Her hope of rescuing Yevgeny solely rested on the involvement of Stephen Kline.

Earlier, he had headed east to the address she had given him. From the roadside, it looked like any other convenience store. There was, as Maria described, a small alley at the side, accessed by an iron gate, but nothing to suggest the sinister connection Maria had confided. Eventually, an anonymous white van pulled up outside the shop, and Lily, who Stephen recognised from the hotel, got out, along with Maria, and three other girls, then disappeared into the side gate with two men.

Sometime later, he recognised Ivan, from Maria's description, emerging from the alleyway. But instead of getting into the van, as Maria had predicted, he jumped on the back of a Yamaha, and headed towards a roundabout in the opposite direction. Stephen did a U-turn, and followed the motorbike as it turned left, and continued along a main road for several miles at speed, weaving in and out of the traffic. Stephen continued to follow him, until suddenly the bike took off into the distance, approaching a long bend in the road that led to an intersection. At the intersection there was no sign of the bike, and Stephen knew the traffic ahead leading into town would be a lot heavier, allowing the bike to easily escape pursuit. He therefore decided to take a gamble, and turn right onto a long road, with a railway line on one side, and a series of run-down Victorian terraces on the other. The end of the road led to a small industrial estate. Stephen patrolled the area looking for the bike, passing a mixture of houses, boarded-up units and a scrapyard, until in the distance, he spotted a three-storey corner building, that appeared to be occupied. It was on the edge of the estate, and consisted of a ground floor shop with a yard to the rear, accessed by two large wooden gates. It was impossible to see into the yard, and the shop window was draped with heavy curtains. But chinks of light filtered through the fabric, from the skylight above the entrance. In the window was a crude sign painted on some chipboard 'C. P. Builders. Trade Only'. But most satisfying of all, parked up on the road outside, was the Yamaha.

Stephen made a note of the location, and then scouted

the area for any potential exit roads. providing the most direct route to make good their escape. In fact, he was so pleased with his detective work, he omitted to send Maria a message. She therefore spent the rest of the evening, intermittently glancing at the phone he had given her, wondering what had happened. She then heard the steel gate being opened at about midnight, and the familiar footsteps of Ivan climbing the stairs, and waited anxiously to find out if her gift had been delivered. Then, in the early hours, Stephen confirmed by text he had discovered where the delivery had been made.

The following day, the atmosphere was subdued. The news that Lily had refused to consider compensating Scrawn's family for her loss was taken as deeply disrespectful. Hong was nominated as their spokesperson, with instructions to demand that payment be maintained by their contributions. 'If that's what you choose to do. I have no objection,' said Lily. But it reflected the strength of feeling among the girls, to ensure that every payment would not only keep alive the memory of Scrawn, but also continually haunt the conscience of those responsible for her pointless slaughter. Again, the early warning signs of a possible rebellion loomed. But Maria had other things on her mind. When she encountered Ivan, and demanded to know the state of Yevgeny's health, he was surprisingly tight-lipped.

'He's not receiving any visitors at the moment,' he said, 'especially you!'

If there was one thing her captors knew it was how to keep people in a state of perpetual suspense. It was a potent weapon in maintaining subversive control, along with the threat of violence, and sowing seeds of dissent between different nationalities. In fact, it could be said that the major satisfaction of their captors' nefarious daily activity was devoted to the continual ingenuity of their subtle and calculated humiliation of others. Something to which they never appeared to grow tired. Is it at all possible, Maria wondered, that Ivan, Lily and Luca were a victim of circumstance, themselves. The fact that they never met anyone halfway in the normal navigation of human exchange gave rise to some internal speculation about what led to their desire to exploit someone else. Like an emotional blindness that elevated cruelty to an art form, it allowed them to dissociate any notion of care, and reduce individual worth to the level of everyday commerce. As if human greed was the main ingredient hard wired into every one of us. Fortunately, no one thought it was necessary to search her on returning from the Bedfont, and she was able to send a message asking Stephen to meet her within walking distance of the store at 1pm the following day.

Around midday on Saturday, when it was time for her and the rest of the girls to be paid, she waited for an opportune moment, and asked Lily what time she was required for work.

'We'll leave here at 6pm,' she said, 'but don't expect to be back early. In fact, you could be out all night.'

'In that case I'll need to do some shopping for clothes and get my hair done,' said

Maria.

'We'll take care of that!' Lily replied.

'No, you won't,' Maria insisted. 'If I'm working at a five star hotel, I want to choose what I wear.'

Lily looked at Maria, with a degree of admiration.

'Okay, I'll get Ivan to accompany you.'

'I hardly think Ivan would want to follow me around women's clothes shops and sit in a ladies hairdressers.'

'Very well then, *I'll* accompany you.'

'What's the matter. Don't you trust me? If I was going to walk out. I would have done it the other day, when you offered me the option.'

Lily weighed up the likelihood of defection, and after considering the matter for several moments, leaned forward and looked straight into Maria's eyes, adopting an almost motherly tone.

'I trust I can rely on increased evidence of your loyalty, in gratitude for my generosity, and the continuing welfare of your boyfriend. Be back no later than four. Have you enough money on you?'

The remark amused Maria. The same person who had refused to send a donation to the family of a murdered daughter, was now asking if she had enough funds to shop.

'I could always do with more,' said Maria.

Lily glanced at Maria and smiled knowingly, as if indulging a favourite daughter about to go on a shopping spree. Taking a hundred pounds from the cash box, she placed it on the counter before her.

'Buy something nice!' she ordered.

'You'd better inform downstairs I'll be going out,' said Maria.

Before leaving she placed the money under Hong's pillow, with a note telling her to give it to the family of Scrawn, and departed down the iron staircase. It was as if the doors of Colditz were suddenly being flung open, and she now had the enviable privilege of casually leaving the scene of her incarceration, without punishment. The other girls were quite envious, and must have considered Maria was being accorded special status, rather than being a victim of grooming. She walked through the steel gate, down the stairs, and for the first time, in weeks, sensed a freedom she almost forgot existed. It felt strange to be unaccompanied, and wondered if anyone was watching or following her. She therefore walked very slowly, and purposely stopped, and looked in several shop windows, casually glancing around, until she was sure no one was monitoring her movements.

She then spotted a vintage Jaguar parked on the opposite side of the road, and after walking for another thirty metres or so, crossed the road and walking back towards the car got in and sat in the front passenger seat beside Stephen.

'Do you know where you are going?' she asked.

'You just asked me to drive,' Stephen replied. 'What happens when we get there?'

They drove to the semi-deserted industrial area where he

had followed Ivan two days earlier, and Stephen pointed out the corner shop and builders yard towards the back of the estate. He then drove past the shop, and parked half way down the road, so as not to arouse suspicion.

'How long will you be?' Stephen asked.

'I'm not sure,' said Maria. 'But when I come out, make sure you have the engine running, and be ready to put your foot down!'

Maria alighted from the car, and walked back towards the corner. The gates of the builders yard were locked, and there was no sign of life. She then walked to the front of the shop, which had a half-glazed door, with a blind pulled down, and, at the side, a bell, with a white cover, secured to the door frame with a piece of tape. She pushed the button and waited, but received no response, so pushed the button several more times. Eventually, the door opened about twelve inches and the unshaven face of a man peered out from the semi-darkness inside.

'Can I help you?' he asked.

'Lily sent me. I am here to see Yevgeny,' Maria replied.

'Nobody has said anything to us,' the man responded.

'I can't help that,' said Maria. 'They need him back at the base.'

The man opened the door wider, and Maria stepped into a practically bare interior, apart from some boxes stacked up against a wall, several tins of paint and a few building materials, that lay scattered across a floor of aged linoleum. To the rear, there was a sink unit, and, nearby, a kitchen table, where two other men were sitting playing cards.

They both looked up as Maria entered. 'Where's Ivan?' said one of the men.

'He's outside on the phone, speaking to Lily. How do you think I got here?' Maria answered.

'Then, why did they send you?' the man asked suspiciously.

'Because I'm the only person he trusts. Now where is he? I haven't got all day.'

Maria followed the man through a door, and up two flights

of stairs, to a room at the top of a narrow staircase. He unlocked the door, and she followed him inside. The room itself consisted of a chest of drawers, a small table, on top of which was an uneaten plate of congealed pasta, and beside it, a camp bed with the shape of a body, hidden under a blanket. Maria went over, and pulled the blanket away, to reveal the emaciated body of Yevgeny, and then placed her hand gently on his shoulder, and tried to rouse him. He had his face to the wall, but then slowly turned around, and started blinking.

'He's useless,' said the man. 'Not good for anything. Why would they want him?'

Yevgeny recognised Maria, and smiled, even though he was clearly very weak.

'I've come to take you back with me,' said Maria. 'We need you strong again.'

The man stood at the foot of the bed, and gave a half smile.

'Yes. Your hands are becoming too weak to inject,' he chided.

Maria removed the blanket, and lifted Yevgeny's legs off the bed, and placed them on the floor. She then encouraged him to sit up, and instructed the man to assist her in getting Yevgeny downstairs.

'He has no strength,' said the man.

'Then we'll use yours,' Maria replied sharply.

Yevgeny, wearing only light trousers and a T shirt, began shivering. But Maria remained determined. She put some trainers on his feet, then placed her hands under his arms, and helped him to stand.

'I could pick him up with one hand, and deliver him without breaking into a sweat,' the man boasted. 'You don't believe me?'

The man picked Yevgeny up, and placing him across his shoulders in a fireman's lift position, carried him downstairs, with Maria following behind. On reaching the ground floor, Maria instructed him to lower Yevgeny to the floor.

'I'll take it from here,' she said. 'He'll be fine.'

Looking around, the man asked, 'Where is Ivan?'

'Outside waiting for me,' said Maria. 'Don't worry, it's only a couple of steps. Get back to your card game.'

The man looked at Maria intriguingly.

'So, what is it that you do for Lily?' he asked.

'What do you think?' she replied.

'And exactly what do they intend to do with him?' he added, contemptuously.

'Exactly the same as me,' said Maria.

The man thought for a second, and then began laughing out loud, nodding knowingly.

'Lily wastes nothing!' he exclaimed to the others, 'even a human pin cushion, with a crack running down the middle of his spine!'

The other men sniggered in the corner, as Maria put her arm around Yevgeny's waist, and guided him towards the door, as quickly as his strength allowed.

The man observed them thoughtfully for a few moments, then unlocked the door to let them out.

'Are you sure you'll be OK?' he enquired.

'He's as light as a feather,' said Maria. 'Enjoy your card game.'

She headed in the direction of Stephen's car. They hadn't got very far, however, when Yevgeny's head fell forward, and his knees began to buckle. Suddenly, he became a dead weight, and half-walking, half-carrying him, Maria began to struggle to ensure he remained upright. Unable to continue, he was about to collapse, when Stephen's car came into view, reversing down the road, coming to a halt alongside them. Stephen got out, and opening the rear passenger door, helped Yevgeny onto the back seat, whilst Maria got in the other side, and placing her arm around Yevgeny's shoulder, ordered Stephen to 'get going!'.

No sooner had she said this, than she turned around, and saw the man from the shop running towards them, with the speed of a sprinter, shouting for them to stop, with a hammer in his hand. Stephen took off, and all of a sudden, a large thump was heard at the back of the car. Then, out of the back window, Maria saw a car pull up beside the running man, and stop just long enough for him to board.

The vintage Jag was now hurtling down the road with the other car behind, in pursuit.

'Do you know where you're going?' asked Maria frantically.

Stephen turned left, and headed back towards the intersection. Instead of turning right at the junction, and heading to town, however, he turned left, and headed back in the direction they had come. 'You're going the wrong way,' screamed Maria as the car behind was rapidly gaining on them. Suddenly, Stephen performed a U-turn, narrowly missing several oncoming cars, and causing others to brake heavily, as they headed in the opposite direction. Likewise, the car in pursuit carried out the same dangerous manoeuvre, and caused mayhem, with car horns blasting away in anger on both sides of the road. Although Stephen's reckless tactic had managed to create more distance between them, it was clear their pursuers were not easily deterred, and as a result, Stephen significantly increased his speed, in the hope that his driving would attract the attention of a passing police patrol car. He also knew that the closer they got to the city, the traffic conditions would force him to significantly reduce his speed, and worst of all, they could hit stationary traffic. He didn't have long to wait. As both cars weaved in and out of the traffic, Stephen spotted a set of lights ahead changing to red, and three lanes reducing to two, forcing a temporary bottleneck at the junction ahead.

His and the other car both came to a halt, separated by at least a dozen other vehicles. Whilst he waited patiently for the lights to change, Stephen looked in his rear-view mirror, and saw the man who had thrown the hammer, alight from the car behind, and begin walking towards them. Faced with no other choice, he pulled out into the filter lane for traffic turning right, and drove into the path of oncoming traffic, sounding his horn to announce his incursion, and accelerated straight ahead. In the distance, he heard the riotous sound of car horns, and kept watch on the traffic behind him. He calculated that for the moment he had given the gang the slip, and after travelling a further mile or so, noticed the entry signs for a retail park up ahead. Pulling off the road, he headed towards the car park that, fortunately, was both spacious and congested, due to the number of Saturday afternoon shoppers. Looking around he drove to the far side, where he found an unobtrusive space, and reversed into it. For several minutes, there was nothing but silence. Stephen could hardly believe the way he had disregarded his, and everyone else's safety. Nothing else he had ever done had been so fraught with danger, or given him such an adrenaline rush. The sweat from his hands was still evident on the wheel, and his heart was pumping. He kept looking towards the entrance of the car park, half-expecting, any moment, the pursuing car would enter at speed, and pull up in front of them. If they had spotted him entering, it wouldn't be very long. A vintage Jag was easy to spot. Slowly, his heartbeat became more regular, and he slid down into the leather seat, as the tension began to leave him. Behind, Maria sat with her seat belt still fastened, nursing Yevgeny, who despite the turbulence of the chase, was fast asleep.

'Where do we go from here?' asked Maria.

'As far as the nearest strong cup of coffee,' said Stephen.

It took another hour before they reached the rehabilitation clinic, some twenty five miles away. When they arrived, a doctor, accompanied by a nurse, came out to the car, and placed Yevgeny in a wheelchair.

'How long has he been in this condition?' asked the doctor.

Maria wasn't certain. Since confinement, his condition had deteriorated considerably.

'What does he take?'

'Crack, heroin, amphetamines, skunk, plus anything he can find,' said Maria.

'OK. Let's get him inside.'

Yevgeny was wheeled into a small but bright room at the rear of the clinic, to be examined.

He was at last in safe hands, but his period of incarceration had no doubt been traumatic. He was shot, both physically and mentally, and while he was being assessed, Maria and Stephen were left in no doubt that his journey back to a drug-free existence was not guaranteed. 'Anything from three months to a lifetime,' said the doctor philosophically.

Maria broke down, and putting her arms around Stephen, began sobbing.

'I'm sorry. So sorry,' repeating it over and over, like a child whose guilty secret had been found out. Stephen tried to reassure her, but she wouldn't be placated.

'It was all my fault,' she confessed. 'All mine!'

It was the first time he could remember her self-protective shell open up to reveal the raw emotion inside. But it wasn't so much for the personal risk Stephen had taken, as the danger to which she had unwittingly exposed Yevgeny. He felt like an actor coming in halfway through the second act of a plot, of which he had only a vague idea of the complexity.

When she had recovered sufficiently, Maria asked,

'How much is all this costing?'

'At the moment, six thousand pounds,' he answered.

'What!' exclaimed Maria. 'We don't have that kind of money.'

'Treat it as a donation from a music lover,' Stephen replied.

Maria said farewell to Yevgeny, and Stephen drove her a short distance to a Holiday Inn.

His advance arrangements had exceeded all her expectations. All she had expected was some help for her and Yevgeny to get a room, and assist with funding a rehabilitation course. But instead, he had spent thousands on a private residential clinic, and was funding her stay at a nearby hotel. Maria suddenly realised that the dramatic circumstances of Yevgeny's rescue and the decline of his health had dominated her thoughts entirely. She asked for Stephen's forgiveness, and assured him that what he did was beyond anything that either of them deserved. Stephen offered no comment, nor even appeared to enjoy the measure of his own sacrificial contribution.

'I have to go now. Message me if you need anything,' he said.

There was neither joy nor jubilation in his response.

'But I don't know anything about you,' declared Maria, ashamed.

'And I found out a few things I didn't know about myself, until now,' he said.

'Is this the way all you English behave?'

'Only the lunatic fringe,' he responded.

Before he departed, Stephen handed Maria an envelope containing five hundred pounds, and told her he would visit them in a few weeks' time, the boot of his vintage car bearing the scar of a hammer blow, as he drove away. The dramatic high of the day's events now seemed more unreal, as she contemplated the tortuous journey of recovery that was just beginning for Yevgeny.

Tomorrow, she would need to acquire a change of clothes, and the practical accessories for survival. But tonight, there was something more pressing. Calling the emergency services, she asked to be connected to the department that dealt with human trafficking.

'Stay on the line,' she was told.

8.

ON PAPER, WITHDRAWAL is the physical eradication of opiates. In reality, the mind is in direct opposition to the body. If hell is what goes on in the heart, then Yevgeny's recovery was a series of major battles in the fog of war. The initial stages being beset with the symptoms of intense anger, paranoia, depression and fatigue, and the collateral damage of his incarceration.

Maria attended the clinic daily, and often did nothing more than sit at his bedside as he slept, vomited, shouted out in his sleep, or despatched food across the room. For a time, he was too weak to stand, so a nurse and Maria would walk him slowly around the room, and encourage him to eat. When she touched his shoulders or took his hand, it was clear how undernourished he had become. She was told that, like everything else in the treatment programme, his body weight would increase, as his health improved. But health to Yevgeny wasn't just a pharmaceutical remedy. It was something still missing in the heart. One evening, she brought in an audio player with some of his favourite piano music, placed the headphones on his ears and waited to see his reaction. He sat bolt upright, listened for several minutes, and then, after ripping the phones from his ears, violently threw the player at the wall.

'Stop it!' he shouted.

His initial response was to reject the very thing that gave him life. Even the encouragement she gave was received with disbelief and scepticism.

Maria enquired just how long Yevgeny would take to recover, and received an ambiguous answer. No one was prepared to put an exact date or result in her head. Except to tell her that Yevgeny's behaviour was normal. But this was not so worrying as some of the other symptoms he was exhibiting. Namely, a sorrow so profound that the spiritual despair he expressed was beginning to affect her own health. Maria was convinced something else had happened. She then began to reflect on just exactly what it was that drove him to destroy the very thing that kept him alive. It just didn't make sense.'

'Narcotics are amoral,' the consultant told Maria. 'They have an ambition all their own. Very often, the people that take them are longing to satisfy a deeper need, and use drugs as a fast route to mask pain or a situation they refuse to face. But the causes are nearly always as varied as the users.'

The noxious pleasure that led to destruction was the same flame that attracts a moth. Except, in Yevgeny's case, the moth was already a compulsive seeker after an inner metamorphosis. One that fell back on a temporary substitute, and got burned. Her visits were therefore painful reminders of issues that had refused to relinquish their hold on his life. His recovery required the constant reminder of their friendship, and the additional measure of psychoanalysis, to unearth the deeper conflict behind his habits. They were not to be given up lightly. His demons waged an interminable war of their own.

On one occasion, he had a very bad day, and Maria decided to stay with him overnight. He awoke on several occasions, and sounded as if he was reliving his past. It was the type of pain for which there is no anaesthetic. He already had the night sweats, but she sensed something different was happening in the dark shadows of withdrawal. In the end, his bony insubstantial frame sunk silently into the waiting arms of the bedsheets in defeat. After this, he slept for hours, only being disturbed long enough for an injection to be administered, or to be checked for incontinence. He showed no interest in food, and Maria's self-appointed task was to spoon-feed him like an infant, and assure him that his ordeal would soon end.

'And then what?' he asked.

'You'll recover,' she assured him.

She asked Yevgeny about some of the things he had shouted in his deepest torment, but his explanations were evasive.

'You think I don't know you?' she told him. 'I know that you're father mistreated you, and that your mother sought to protect you.'

'I was a disappointment,' said Yevgeny, 'and still am!'

In the torment of the night, the ghosts of his past came out to haunt him.

'I keep dreaming of a picture in two halves,' he told her. 'One side is of a neat and tidy house, with a path leading to the front door. The other side is derelict!'

'Obviously, you were torn between your mother and your father.'

'Quite often, after my father beat me, I would run across the field to my uncle's house, and he would sit me on his lap and console me.'

'Why not your mother?'

'My father told her she had made a sissy out of me. He blamed her for my melancholia, and said she had spoilt me. He was a simple man, unable to understand why he had spawned an alien.'

One day, Yevgeny got dressed, and ran, and ran, and ran. No one could understand it. Maria followed him as he ran along the road and down the hill. He ended up in a park, about a mile away, exhausted. It was pure frustration. The staff at the clinic were frantic, and thought he had run away. He had entered a stage of strange dysfunction, engaged in a private battle of his own. Was it part of his recovery, she wondered, or something else?

One thing she did know, and that was, without music, Yevgeny would not survive.

With some of the money Stephen had given her, she bought

an electric keyboard, and placed it at the side of his bed one morning, as a surprise. When he opened his eyes, he looked at it disdainfully, and said 'that's a toy,' and refused to lay a hand on it.

She then made a trip to Victoria station in London, and retrieved their belongings, and wrapped up the score of the Rachmaninoff 3rd Piano Concerto in the most beautiful azure blue paper, and presented it to him. When Yevgeny opened it, he placed his hand on the score, and, resting his head on the back of his armchair, closed his eyes, and began playing the opening bars of the concerto in his mind. His fingers moved as if on the keyboard, lost in the romance and intricacy of the score, and remembering the andante passages, orchestral interludes and melodic drive that reopened channels of communication that had, thus far, been all but purged from his memory. Maria looked at him, and was unable to control herself.

'Tell me you don't remember,' she said.

'Is that all you think I am,' said Yevgeny, 'a music box?'

He threw the score clean across the room, its cover partially destroyed by the impact. Maria gathered up the battered remnant, and left the room. The incident confirming that a wound to the mind heals far slower than an injury to the body. In Yevgeny's case, his trauma provided a refuge from the possibility of healing. That was something for which he wasn't yet ready. All Maria could do was patiently wait, and feed his mind with the distant and seductive charm of restoration, and for that there was no time limit.

She had regularly updated Stephen on his progress, but there was no point in him witnessing the jagged landscape of a recovery, that took no account of people's feelings. As Maria was sorely reminded, the beast that entered the bloodstream took prisoners, even as it departed. Recovery, in Yevgeny's case, left him stranded on a distant island, while she herself felt isolated with someone she no longer recognised.

'He still needs time before he's ready to see anyone,' she warned.

Stephen didn't raise any issues or display any concern over

money, but the initial period he must have envisaged Yevgeny would require for withdrawal had now entered its third month. The psychological withdrawal lasting longer than the physical, Yevgeny was required to remain in therapy as an inpatient, since neither he or Maria had anywhere to go except back to Ukraine. She continually apologised, and promised that one day they would pay back every penny they owed, but at present this looked a forlorn hope. Either by some irrational fortune of fate, or strategy of chance, Stephen had now become a distant benefactor, both caring and sworn to non-interference. But also a mystery? Something for which Yevgeny himself was both grateful and sceptical.

'Has he taken a down payment yet?' he asked.

'No,' said Maria, 'but you've been here long enough!'

'Then I suggest you propose a repayment plan?'

'Ask him yourself,' said Maria. 'He's arriving Saturday afternoon for tea.'

It was a warm day, and the clinic had prepared a table outside in the garden for them to have lunch. When Stephen arrived, Maria greeted him warmly. Yevgeny however, embraced Stephen like a long lost father. Holding him tightly, he broke down in tears, and thanked him in such an intimately personal way, that for a moment Stephen was both lost for words and unsure how to respond.

'Why you do this? Why you do this for me?' pleaded Yevgeny.

'It's a question with only one obvious answer,' said Stephen.

'It's just that we're both concerned about the money all this is costing, and neither of us has a future,' Maria explained.

'If you don't have a future, then all this is a waste of time. I don't want your money. I want you both to have a second chance. To be free of the obligation of money and realise your possibilities as performers.'

'We're an experiment then?' said Yevgeny.

'I assure you it's entirely selfish. It could be I'm completely mad.'

Stephen paused and looked at them both,

'And all because I visited the V & A to write some poetry.'

Yevgeny burst out laughing, and banged on the table. It was the first time Maria had seen him in such humour.

'Yes!' Yevgeny declared. 'The most expensive lunch you have ever had. And you are still paying for it!'

Soon, all three were laughing uncontrollably, then Yevgeny's face suddenly looked serious. 'Except, I can't play anything. I can't give you a mazurka, a nocturne or even a half competent waltz,' he said.

Yevgeny departed, like a wounded lion who had lost confidence in his ability. Afraid of facing the thing he most loved. The sickness may have begun to leave his body, but wouldn't leave his mind. That could only be solved by facing the ghosts of his pursuers. But, as Maria was told by the clinic,

'You can't save someone, unless they themselves want to be saved.'

In one of their intimate conversations during withdrawal, Yevgeny revealed he had been sexually abused by his uncle from the age of five, and beaten by his father, for the rebellion resulting from his own self-disgust. Being told he was responsible for the abuse of which he was a victim, he became both introspective and a loner. The symmetry was ironic. Worse, he was not just boyish, but pretty, with an androgyny, that later was to attract people like Szell and other predators. The strange course of events that had led him to the door of the Eshkol's had given him an unforeseen route to liberation. But now, the clouds of self doubt had once again reappeared.

Yevgeny told Maria that sometimes people climb a mountain, and when they reach the summit, instinctively know that nothing will ever feel the same again. But, if they make a second attempt, and fall on the lower slopes, then all subsequent attempts will fail also.

'You were never anywhere near the summit,' Maria told him abruptly. 'In fact you never even made it to base camp!'

His rejection of her belief, would, she told him, no longer

be tolerated.

When she returned, the next day, she noticed music from a Barcarolle laying on top of the small keyboard in his room. Yevgeny told her quite firmly that he wouldn't play in her presence. But, on consulting members of staff was told his playing was exquisite.

'Do you know that?' she reminded him.

Somehow, Yevgeny had passed himself fit for beginning the process of scaling his modest ambition to the lower slopes of a hill, rather than a mountain. During the next few weeks, he practised daily, for hours, and into the night. Compulsively and obsessively, with the headphones wrapped around his ears. In fact no one was able to hear him. He just sat and played on the restricted keyboard, familiar difficult passages, over and over. Rarely satisfied, he took on two roles, one as Popov, and one as himself. Remembering his very first lessons, and the discipline that Popov instilled in his daily routine. Without realising it, his recovery had begun.

Yevgeny was, once again, taking responsibility for himself. Maria joyfully relayed this to Stephen, along with the news that he was also due to be discharged in the next ten days.

A week later, Stephen contacted her with an invitation to meet him at Belsize Park station.

'I'm taking you to lunch,' he said.

9.

When Maria arrived at the station, Stephen drove her a short distance to a leafy road full of large stucco-fronted Victorian houses, and pulled up outside one of them. It had a rather grand entrance, with steps leading up to a large stained-glass door, whilst another set of steps led down to a smaller front door at the side.

'Is this where we are having lunch?' Maria enquired.

'You will be very soon,' said Stephen, and handed her a key.

Maria was not just overwhelmed, but embarrassed, as she followed Stephen down the steps towards the basement. Once through the door, a small hallway led to a kitchen, and a set of double doors at the other end, opened onto an opulent lounge, looking onto a small garden, screened by several large trees and a neat manicured lawn. The lounge was tastefully decorated, and exceptionally light. But that isn't what made Maria's heart soar. In pride of place, strategically positioned to the left of the large French doors, stood a Bösendorfer, eight foot, grand piano, inviting the occupants the unprecedented privilege of placing their fingers on its hallowed keys. In fact, the whole room was filled with light, and an overwhelming sense of calm. So different to anything she considered she would ever experience again. She looked at Stephen, who displayed neither excitement nor patronising condescension, and acted as if he were an estate agent, showing a potential tenant around a property. Maria sat in a nearby armchair, and sobbed.

'I can't believe it!' she said, over and over. 'I can't believe it! It is just the best.'

Stephen then led her up the stairs, leading off the lounge to the floor above, containing two bedrooms, a large bathroom and a study. With each step, Maria expressed her gratitude, by asking 'Why?' Stephen explained that he had used the services of an agent to find a place that would allow someone to practise eight hours a day. Fortunately, the owners of the house, who occupied the upper floors, were sympathetic.

'It makes no difference. We can't accept it,' said Maria, 'it's far too good for us.'

'Too late. I've already paid six months in advance.'

'But, we don't have the means to repay you.'

'Succeed in what you came here to do, a year ago.'

Maria placed her arms around Stephen and embraced him, admitting she was unsure how to respond and asked,

'Do you really love music so much?'

'No,' said Stephen.

'Yet you do all this for us?'

'I told you. It's for purely selfish reasons.'

Stephen claimed no moral superiority. It was, he said, a character flaw he couldn't control. An investment he could make in someone else, that they were unable to make for themselves. Suddenly, he paused, and remembered that in fact he hadn't heard either of them play a note, and burst out laughing. Maria realised he was right! He had placed himself in physical danger, spent thousands on rehabilitation for a pianist he hardly knew, and had now spent an equally large sum on a luxury apartment in order that they could practise skills he himself had never witnessed. The irony was too illogical and reckless. As a result, Maria began laughing too.

'Don't worry. We'll only disturb the musically illiterate,' she promised.

Although, deep down she felt uncomfortable, she was relieved and grateful that a Knight Errant had charged from the wings, and snatched herself and Yevgeny from the jaws of disaster, although was still unable to fathom the real reason for his remarkable generosity.

Before he retreated to the hinterland of suburban familiarity, they had lunch, and Maria questioned Stephen about the unknown space of another life he was reluctant to share.

She told Stephen she thought he viewed herself and Yevgeny as an interesting experiment, something he could influence from the distant shore of conformity and reserve. An insight into a world he had missed out on, and desired to enter in order to breathe new meaning into his own. His existence, he told Maria, was rigid and conventional, and that's why he needed to escape. For years, he had been trapped by circumstances, in which he had made no real impact, and had little influence. Teaching now bored him, and promotion had restricted his talents to the role of an administrator. He and his partner had not been blessed with any children, and it was this confession that offered Maria a revealing insight into a more complex motivation for his involvement.

Although it failed to explain everything, it was the first time he had revealed any personal details about himself, and the depth of her questioning made it impossible for him to offer the somewhat blurred explanation of moral responsibility.

But the real surprise was that he didn't indicate a desire to want an affair.

When Maria announced they would be moving to Belsize Park, and the idyllic surroundings Stephen had so generously provided, Yevgeny again broke down. He was both overjoyed, but suspicious.

'What does he want, in return?' he asked.

'He wants to adopt us.'

'Nothing is free. Not even freedom itself!'

'I know. You believe it impossible for anyone to have a pure motive for anything.'

'It usually arrives with a deceptive smile,' he replied.

Yevgeny found it hard to accept the generosity of a stranger, but when he set eyes on the piano, threw all objections aside, and could not be parted from the prized occupant of their new home.

It was as if the Almighty had reached down, and thrust him into a new and unmerited heaven, so unbelievable, yet so perfect. It had rekindled his passion, and lit within him a new urgency, as if he had been brought back to life with a blood transfusion. He began playing with renewed vigour, and the dedication of his old self began to return. In some ways, even better, relishing a new freedom and the adrenalin of survival. In fact, Maria had been so caught up with the excitement of Yevgeny's recovery and the unexpected joy and contentment of their new surroundings, she had to remind herself the reason why she had enlisted Stephen's help in the first place.

It was something she tried hard to banish to the shadows of misfortune, but it remained a part of her history, she could neither forgive nor forget.

For a long time, she had been searching for any news concerning the arrest of anyone from their former address in East London. It had been months since she had given the police a detailed statement and offered to give evidence, but had heard nothing. Now, when she had followed up the result of her allegation she was told… 'Matters of this type often take time gathering evidence, and are likely to involve other agencies…'

'*We* are the evidence!' responded Maria.

It poignantly underlined Scrawn's own pessimism, and Maria was enraged.

'What were you expecting?' asked Yevgeny.

'I can't just let it go,' said Maria. 'The wheels of justice don't just move slowly. They don't move at all!'

Maria decided to add some pressure of her own, and warned Yevgeny,

'I'm not giving up!'

The area in East London still held painful memories, and

Maria could feel herself shaking, as she observed the store from the other side of the road. She had purposely dressed down, and wore jeans, and a jacket with a hood covering part of her face. The store had been re-named, but in all other respects, looked just the same. She crossed the road, and walked past it several times, before deciding to enter. Inside, everything looked as it did before. Same products, same layout, even the same 'special offers'. Nothing had changed, except the face behind the counter. He barely looked up when she entered, and was holding a conversation on his smartphone, in between casually taking money, and asking 'Was there anything else?' Maria waited for an opportune moment, and walked up to the counter.

'I am here to see Lily about the cleaner vacancy,' she announced.

The man looked confused.

'You have come to the wrong place. We already have a cleaner,' he said.

'She lives in the flat upstairs.'

'That is my flat,' the man objected. 'You must have the wrong address.'

'Is Luca here?' Maria asked.

'There is no one here by that name either,' the man replied brusquely. 'Was there anything else?'

Maria studied him for several moments, and responded with a half-smile. 'Sorry to have bothered you,' she said, and casually headed towards the long aisles that led to the back of the store. She briefly wandered up and down pretending to shop, and could spot only one assistant stacking shelves from a large trolley. Then the man on the counter's phone rang, and while he answered, Maria quickly made her way to the large storeroom at the rear, and then exited through the side door leading to the rear staircase. Rapidly climbing to the first and second floor she arrived at the large steel gate leading to the roof area, and found it open. Then, as she slowly made her way up the iron staircase, was suddenly struck by fear. Memories of the past filled her with hesitation, as she began listening intently for signs of occupation. The roof was one flight ahead, and she slowly ascended the stairs. All appeared calm, except for the sound of passing traffic. Once her eyes were level with the flat open surface of the roof, she remained perfectly still, waiting to hear a familiar voice or some indication of activity. But there was none. Deciding she had come too far to go back, she entered the roof area and went straight to the cabin that had housed herself, Scrawn, Hong, and Noi.

To her surprise, the door was unlocked, and inside it was empty, stripped of everything. No bunk beds, bedside cabinet, chair, or curtains, even the nylon carpet was gone. It was devoid of any sign of life. She then went and inspected all the other cabins, including the isolation block. They were all the same. Nothing remained to indicate any sign of human occupation. Even the aged microwave in the kitchen and second-hand washing machine in the laundry room had been removed. Any sign of its former occupants had now been erased, except the shadow of Scrawn and Luca hung over it, like ghosts from its past, unable to escape the menace and culpability of what it represented.

'Too bad!'

She could hear the voice of Lily, laughing from the distance of her latest covert penitentiary, where a host of new Scrawns, Hongs and Baos had been kidnapped from the familiarity of home, and dishonoured. *'Too bad!'*

Maria returned to Belsize Park, feeling defeated.

Yevgeny told her she would only have put herself in danger, but Maria realised, it wasn't because he didn't care, all he wanted was to hide and bury himself in the escape route of music. In a way, she considered that this was in itself a gift. He was able to compulsively immerse himself in the beauty of music making, and complete his therapy with far less intervention. The world had intruded through his veins, and led to calamity. The only thing left to patch up his wounds lay in the overwhelming flame of his talent. Nothing else mattered to him now. Once again, it was the most singular and immediate remedy for remaining clean, and it began to clearly be displayed in his confidence. The quality of his playing gained momentum and polish, and his technique improved, like daylight filtering into darkness. But more than that, his interpretation had deepened, giving his playing a new maturity and insight. As bad as it was, they had escaped, and they owed it all to Stephen Kline. Suddenly, Maria was filled with guilt.

'Do you think you are ready to give a recital?' she asked Yevgeny.

Stephen was invited to dinner the following week. Maria planned to prepare some of her favourite Ukrainian dishes, and both she and Yevgeny were going to perform a recital in the lounge. It was, she said, the very least she could do, by the very least of the deserving!

Stephen quickly replied, accepting the invitation, and saying that both the company and the food sounded 'delicious'.

'We had better make sure it's good then,' Maria replied.

'Good is not good enough,' declared Yevgeny.

On the day, Stephen arrived carrying a large bouquet of flowers and a bottle of champagne. After embracing him warmly, Maria took him by the hand, and led him into the kitchen. The table was already laid with all kinds of Ukrainian specialities she had sourced from various places, including her 'speciality of the house', which was simmering on the stove, before leading him through the double doors that led from the kitchen into the lounge. Yevgeny was seated at the piano, dressed formally in a dinner jacket, dark trousers, a dress shirt, and black tie. When Stephen entered, Yevgeny leapt up and embraced him like an old friend. Stephen commented on the improvement in his appearance since their last encounter at the clinic, and congratulated him on his recovery.

'But before we sit down to eat,' said Maria, 'Yevgeny and I are going to give you a little concert. If it is okay?'

Maria led Stephen to an armchair by the fireplace, and fetched a small plate of dumplings, together with a glass of sparkling wine, and placed it on the table beside him.

'We call these Vareniki,' said Maria. 'They are to distract you from our wrong notes.'

She then stood by the piano, and announced that she was going to play Suite Number Two from Bach's English Suite. Her demeanour changed as she sat, in momentary contemplation, before performing as if the music had seized her whole being, and formed part of her inner conviction. It was both precise and yet weaved a pattern of absolute sublime musical simplicity amongst its complexity. The music, dancing and evoking a profound emotional response, as it connected so directly, opening the door to something uniquely communicated yet unsaid.

When she had finished, Stephen clapped enthusiastically, and shouted 'Bravo!' embracing her, with tears in his eyes. It was the first time he had heard her play, and the solemnity of the occasion had touched him deeply. He then sat down and placed his head in his hands, tears still streaming down his cheeks, and told her she had made him very happy.

Maria was bemused.

'If you are so happy, then why are you sad?' she asked.

When it came to Yevgeny's turn, he didn't announce what he was about to play, but simply stared down at the keys, looking hesitant for a moment, before launching into Chopin's Etude in C Sharp Minor. He then immediately followed this with Opus 10 and 12, before ending with a performance of Schubert's Impromptu in G flat minor. Throughout the performance, his concentration, and the intensity of his playing, forbid any interruption, as if to display any level of verbal or physical approval would have broken the spell. It completely disarmed any of Stephen's pre-conceived ideas concerning the person whom he rescued. Up until now, he had viewed Yevgeny as self-destructive and helpless, an anonymous footnote of fleeting musical acquaintance, who had aborted a promising career. But listening to him play, Stephen recognised immediately something beyond a flawless technique. A telling emotional core, that went beyond the notes to something more profound. A scintillating poetic delicacy of lyricism, that invited the listener to hear, not the pianist, but the composer, inviting the listener to share the intoxicating intimacy of his soul.

When he had finished playing, Yevgeny displayed no self-congratulatory impulse, but simply sat with his hands clasped together, and his head lowered. Stephen felt genuinely humbled, and lost for words, then stood up, and with yet more tears running down his cheeks, exclaimed, 'Bravo! Bravo!' and embraced Yevgeny like a long lost son.

'Now you understand exactly what you wasted your money on!' said Maria, before leading Stephen into the dining area of the kitchen, and setting before him an array of Ukrainian dishes, with an explanation of their names, recipe and their place in her ancestry.

It was, she exclaimed, 'peasant food for peasants', non-fussy, non-extravagant and ordinary.

Of course, it was the very opposite, and given with such generosity of spirit, accompanied by the one thing that had been missing for so long. The infectious laughter he had heard echo around the cafe at the V & A, the first time he saw her, complete with the lightness of her being, and the simple joy of her company.

His heart wanted to leap and break through his skin, just to sit and listen to her talk, and disarm him with her candid opinion, laced with enough modesty and a listening ear to allow an alternative opinion. Somehow, he felt less assertive in her presence, and fascinated by her intense curiosity and unpredictability. Something she herself appeared to be unconscious of. His spirits lifted, and inwardly he rejoiced. He was happy to feel stupid, and throw off all pretension. To rest and be content. To be able to fulfil even more of her demands. It was as if he was seeing her for the first time. But now understood something else: her considerable talent. The concert was all the reward he needed. Any doubts he had harboured had now been extinguished by the sublimity of their gift, and he felt supremely humbled and thankful he had responded to her plea to rescue Yevgeny, even if for selfish reasons.

After Stephen had departed, Yevgeny asked Maria,

'How much has he spent on us?'

'Over fifty thousand.'

'He didn't come just for the music though.'

'You should be thankful he didn't,'said Maria.

A week later, Maria asked Stephen if he was free to meet her for lunch.

'I still have fifty pounds left from my allowance,' she said. 'Enough for two plates of pasta and a glass of wine.'

When they met at the bistro she had suggested, Stephen presented her with a small bunch of daffodils,

'This isn't a date,' she reminded him.

Stephen took a deep breath and said,

'It's to reflect how I feel after you both played!'

Maria bowed her head, and remained silent. After such an uplifting evening, she now seemed quarrelsome and out of sorts. Stephen said nothing, and looked puzzled, as they both perused the menu. At length he asked,

'Well. Just why did you invite me to the smallest bistro in Haverstock Hill?'

'We are both very grateful for everything you've done for us. But at the same time, worried,' said Maria.

'Worried?' Stephen asked.

'About the amount of money you have invested in us?'

'Oh that?' said Stephen. 'It's not as important as you think.'

His nonchalance struck her as either bravado, or the reckless flippancy of someone who had too much money. Yet, as Maria was well aware, he was a teacher who was never likely to earn the large sums he had lavished on both her and Yevgeny.

'I know you are married and have no children,' said Maria,

'are you trying to adopt us?'

Stephen almost sprayed the water he was about to swallow across the table. But Maria looked serious.

'You think the money is a bribe?' he asked.

'You told me your mother died ten years ago. I presume she left you some money.'

'My mother was also a pianist. Her Bechstein still stands proudly in the lounge. But, it's not her money you have benefitted from. It's my fathers!'

Stephen explained he had been using the legacy left to him from his father's estate. A businessman, who had built up a large chain of chemists, and had deserted his mother, when Stephen was twelve years old, in order to marry a junior pharmacist, who he had made pregnant in his mid-forties. To add insult to injury, the girl, half his age, had twins, and both she and their children were the main recipients of his success.

'He died wealthy, whilst my mother died of cancer and a broken heart.'

As a result, Stephen vowed to spend the large sum his father left him on any cause he knew his father would despise.

'I can afford to be a benefactor,' said Stephen, 'because it allows me to reject his deathbed guilt in the most gratifying way possible. If my father knew his money was being used on the upkeep of an ex-heroin addict and a penniless student, he would rotate in his grave. So, you could say your good fortune is my revenge!'

'And what about your wife?' enquired Maria. 'How has your revenge benefitted her?'

'Now I understand the reason for lunch,' he said.

'Either your wife doesn't know about the money, or you haven't told her.'

'For practical reasons, we never made it official.'

'I'm not an expert on marriage, but have a fairly good instinct about women.'

'We're different from other couples. We give each other space to develop other interests, and to think independently. We don't need each others' permission to help someone else.'

'Then you could say your father had his revenge on *yourself.*'

'Why?

'Because he never asked your mothers permission to leave you both. He believed himself independent. Am I right?'

The breezy lunch Stephen had envisaged had now turned into a less sanguine examination of his motives, and for the first time Maria was beginning to pierce his natural reserve.

He could deal with the distant enjoyment of the subjective, or the thrust of opposing views, but the limelight of interrogation was something he had long avoided.

With Helen, he had succeeded in training her concerning the boundaries she was entitled to cross. But his openness with Maria, he told himself, had to be confined behind the steel door that led to the basement containing all the things he determined should remain hidden.

'Please don't let my lifetime of stupidity fool you,' he announced, 'I'm perfectly aware I have a weakness that occasionally sends a message that could light up a stadium.'

'I'm pleased to hear it,' said Maria. 'But we remain in your debt, and Yevgeny is unable to find any work. Are you willing to wait for us to repay what we owe?'

'Of course. But not with money.'

'What else?'

'It would be nice to see you both fulfil your ambition. I know our lives are often interrupted by circumstances and diversions beyond our control. You could call it one of the risks of life. Like love, you start out with an uncomplicated plan that you hope will run smoothly, until the journey gets interrupted by an accident, for which you had unwisely taken no precautions. I advise you therefore, to accept my fathers unintended charity, and reward me by becoming successful. If, however, your conscience won't allow you to do that, then I leave it up to you to dictate the terms of the compensation.'

They finished their meal in silence. Maria sensed a regret in Stephen. Not just a temporary regret at a thoughtless mistake or indiscretion. But something far more injurious and personal. An unhappiness to which some men and women are resigned. One they carry with them, that haunts their lives, even at their most productive. Stephens reaction to the music was testimony that something too personal to speak of in terms of language had occurred. A vulnerability that could make him defensive about his real feelings. What he had done, though, was demonstrate that life, too often, was on other peoples' terms.

When she returned home, Yevgeny was looking both sullen and intense. The hope that had shone a short time before in the Schubert and Chopin had all but evaporated.

'Well did you ask him?' enquired Yevgeny.

'He's intent on giving away the legacy his father left him.'

'He would have done better spending it on two performing seals.'

'What are you talking about?'

'After the concert the other night, I contacted Gorlinsky's office, and he wouldn't even speak to me. He even told his secretary never to let me into his office.'

'So what! There are dozens of agents in London. And if you don't get anywhere here, there are plenty across the channel, Berlin, Amsterdam, Paris or Prague. And there's always America.'

'The world of classical music is small, and he wields a lot of influence,' said Yevgeny. 'They look for a track record, and Gorlinsky has made sure I'll never find any work above the level of a cocktail pianist.'

'You give him too much credit.'

'No. You give *me* too much credit! It doesn't matter how good I am, or what critical acclaim I receive, the question on everyone's mind will always be how long before I suffer a relapse?'

Yevgeny reminded Maria that even Popov had disowned him. Gorlinsky, he maintained, kept everyone in line, by telling them that pianists were like diamonds. The only value they have depended on how long they sparkled. Once they lose that, he lost interest.

Maria sank into a deep depression. It had not occurred to her that Gorlinsky would extract such a high price for his revenge. To deprive such a prodigious talent the right to perform was, she considered, an act of egotistical spite by an autocratic self-serving power hungry parasite.

'He must have enemies!' declared Maria, 'a rival who would want to prove him wrong.'

'He has many enemies,' agreed Yevgeny, 'but none who are foolhardy enough to prove him right.'

For the first time in a long time, he became inconsolable. It was precisely in this state of agitation, Yevgeny had first sought solace in the use of narcotics.

'We have no possible way of paying the money back,' he insisted, 'none whatsoever. This has all been a waste of time!'

Maria understood Yevgeny's pessimism, but couldn't allow herself to share it.

'Stephen doesn't want the money. He wants us both to be a success. Besides, there must be other avenues we can explore. Gorlinsky doesn't own the world. He only owns the key to a side door.'

Yevgeny appeared to sink back into the isolation and despair, from which he had so recently emerged.

'What you've done once, you can do again,' Maria reminded him.

'Like negotiating the lower slopes of the mountain, you say I've never climbed?'

'Only this time, with a far better knowledge of the pitfalls.'

Yevgeny sat with his head bowed, and placed his hands over his ears, and refused to be placated.

'I can't' he said. I just can't!'

'In that case, we have no other choice than to go back to Ukraine,' declared Maria.

'What about our benefactor?' said Yevgeny, 'have you told him? After all, it's not me he wants. I have no reason to stay. But you do!'

Maria considered the impossibility of their situation, and informed Yevgeny she was unwilling to rely on the generosity of Stephen Kline any longer. She was disappointed they had squandered the opportunities they had worked so hard for, but they had to face reality.

'If you can't work, there's no point in us staying here,' she said.

10.

STEPHEN STOOD JUST inside the door of the Ritz, and when she entered, his face lit up, as the doorman raised his hand in a welcome salute. Stephen was unsure what to say.

'The smallest bistro in Haverstock Hill is closed tonight, will this do?' asked Maria.

'I don't know what to say. You look stunning!' Stephen responded.

'So you *do* know what to say.'

'It's too obvious.'

'Before we sit down to eat, let's have a cocktail,' she suggested.

Maria had never made such an entrance. The surroundings reflected the hotel's reputation for luxury. Her duty, she felt, was to pretend that it was all too familiar. Ironically, it was Stephen who appeared awkward and nervous. As if he were suddenly thrust before Royalty. To put him at ease, Maria ordered a cocktail, as if she were a regular visitor, while Stephen shifted awkwardly on his chair. Eventually, he relaxed, and allowed Maria to host both the proceedings and the conversation. First, she disabused him of the worry about expense, explaining it came from the pleasantly lucrative pastime of teaching the piano to the children of local families. Then, over dinner, she regaled Stephen with cameos of composers, people from her student days, Popov, compositions, technique, temperament and Yevgeny. It had been several weeks since their awkward lunch, and for once, he did not want to contradict, intrude nor spoil the insightful delivery of the moment, but simply be content to be enraptured by her company. She had, of course, planned the whole evening, from her entrance, the champagne ice-breaker and the subject of conversation over dinner. There were to be no loose ends. No awkward moments of conversational dryness, nor reference to her time in East London, or the clinic. It was, she determined, to be an evening of celebration. Maria felt his intrigue and anticipation, as he listened attentively, allowing her to dictate both the mood and direction of the evening. As a result, they left the hotel in high spirits.

Moments before, she had disclosed their next destination. At first, he appeared apprehensive and lost for words, then surprised, then delighted and at the same time confused.

'You said be prepared to spend the night away. You didn't say where?' he queried.

It was the reaction she expected. Surprise, followed by delighted disbelief, as she clasped him firmly by the hand, and guided him across Piccadilly towards New Bond Street.

On arrival in their hotel suite, Maria offered Stephen a glass of Horilka, and proposed a toast. Stephen looked nervous, and attempted a none too convincing apology concerning his inexperience, before allowing himself to sample the properties of Ukrainian alcohol.

The sudden jolt of the nearest thing to vodka initially numbed his senses, as it slid down his throat with burning efficiency. Maria followed suite, and shouted 'Budmo!' in order to loosen her own mounting inhibition. Stephen himself sensed her reluctance, and made a clumsy reference to being drunk. Their conversation and surroundings suggested only one thing, and Maria reassured him it was what she wanted, then sat on the bed and unzipped the back of her dress.

'If it's OK, I'm going to take a shower,' she said.

Maria took some items from her overnight bag, and departed into the bathroom, leaving Stephen alone. He had successfully contained his feelings, or so he thought, with a characteristic aloofness, that had allowed Maria to feel secure in his company. Her idea to spend the night with him came as a bolt out of the blue, and contradicted all his accumulated wisdom concerning how he understood their relationship. Funnily enough, his mother suddenly came to his mind, as a reminder of love-lost, never re-found. His own relationship had borne no children, and what passion there was had been replaced by the consequence of comfort, entirely mechanical, sex-less, and perfectly civilised. Like a synchronised watch that runs perfectly, but functions with no higher purpose than to tell the time. He wasn't sure what Maria was up to. But for once, he didn't care. Tonight, he told himself was about a journey he had long wanted to take. Delightful, warm and unexpected.

The effects of the Horilka had begun to make him feel relaxed, and almost dream-like. He had to remind himself this was really happening. Shortly after, Maria returned and told him the water was hot. Stephen dutifully entered the bathroom and turned on the shower.

Maria applied some Eau de Cologne to her neck, and climbed under the sheets naked. The moment had arrived. She had hoped that the wine and alcohol would make her feel relaxed, but her mind was filled with fear about her lack of experience. She decided, therefore, the only way to overcome fear was to appear confident. At least that was the plan following the champagne, the wine and a leisurely dinner. Instead she lay there, feeling vulnerable.

At length, Stephen emerged from the bathroom, wearing a dressing gown, his hair soaking wet, and looking like a child that had just ran from the sea. The towel was draped over his eyes, and he rubbed it from side to side vigorously, before testing it with his hand, to ensure it wouldn't leave any damp marks on the pillow. Maria smiled at him, and slid down towards the bottom of the bed, holding the sheets up to her neck. Then she took his hand, and held it to her cheek, as if nurturing him, in the slow progress towards her first encounter.

In so doing, she felt the depth of his passion through his fingertips, and then uttered a silent prayer. Seeing her lips moving, he asked, 'Is it about us?'

'Yes,' she replied.

Stephen got in beside her, and for a long time just lay on his side admiring her, as if she were an object of beauty he was too afraid to touch. Maria herself was too nervous to move. She had no understanding of intimacy, and not sure what to expect. She knew, of course, all about the rigours of sex: submission, penetration and the spent force of one-sided involvement. But this was submission of a different kind: willing, consensual, and expectant. Stephen, she assured herself, was both an experienced and considerate lover, who, she hoped, would also prove a sensitive teacher. He began by stroking her hair, before gently brushing her ears, and then her lips, with his fingertips. Barely touching the surface of her skin, he very slowly moved his left hand down her body, trying to sense any reaction to pleasure or rejection, until finally arriving at the forbidden part of her body, the one she most dreaded to be touched. Gently, she guided his hand back to her cheek, and then kissed it. He responded by kissing her on both cheeks, followed by her neck and shoulders. She remained perfectly still, and smiled back at him, as if making love was about consent, rather than returning affection. Stephen then kissed her on the lips, then again placed his finger just inside the forbidden area. It was a frontier that had to be crossed, and she now had no other choice than to allow him to explore the most sacrosanct and vulnerable part of her body. She closed her eyes, believing that entrusting something so personal and precious would demonstrate her heartfelt gratitude, and reward him with something he would recognise as sacrificial. That his eagerness would be tempered by maturity and tenderness, and to relax and accept a new experience, as he skilfully manoeuvred himself on top of her.

Suddenly a sharp pain intruded and she gasped. She wanted

to scream, but couldn't.

It was as if she had been pinned down, and had no choice but to remain calm, as she witnessed his breathing getting heavier, and his weight bearing down on her slim frame. It was then she remembered the one thing she had forgot, and immediately felt moisture between her legs, as Stephen let out a cry of fulfilment. He then rolled over on his back looking like a youth, who so energetic and playful moments before, was now becalmed and content.

She felt strangely unfulfilled, and waited for Stephen to say something, then placed her hand on his shoulder, and asked him if he was OK

'More than OK,' he replied, and asked her to give him a word in Ukrainian to describe how she felt.

'At this precise moment,' she whispered, 'it isn't possible in any language.'

For some time, they lay silently side by side, until eventually he took her hand, pressed it to his lips, and then fell asleep. Maria switched off the bedside lamp, and lay in the half light, still waiting, still thinking and feeling strangely restless, as the traffic hummed in the distance and the rain announced its arrival, by beating on the pane outside.

The next morning, when she awoke, Stephen was invigorated, as never before, and the energy of his attentiveness was inescapable. A new situation had been created, and a corner turned, that did not allow for reversal. The impact of Maria's sacrifice had already begun to make her reflect on the consequences. It was a voyage in which she had no former insight, or the experience to control. Stephen now felt liberated from the claustrophobic intensity of a life that up to now, he considered, only half-lived. His release from the obligation of conformity, rejuvenating him both mentally and spiritually. It had come late, but he considered, not too late for him to change the direction of his life. Over breakfast, he openly speculated about his new found optimism and hope for the future, but Maria remained strangely withdrawn. So different from her seductive diversion of the night before, following the champagne and Horilka.

'It was as if you had composed a wonderful overture, and gave the first performance without a rehearsal!' Stephen exclaimed.

'That's because I came unprepared.'

'We could have stopped celebrating at the Ritz.'

'I'm sorry if I let you down.'

'That's not why I'm asking.'

'You rescued two strangers, risked your life, and treated us like royalty. So, I also took a chance.'

'I kept hoping the purpose wasn't entirely unselfish.'

'Not so very long ago, I was close to being raped,' Maria confided.

The air began to leave Stephen's lungs, and the momentous exhilaration of moments before began to depart, leaving him feeling a strange mixture of disappointment and guilt. As if he had ultimately been the one responsible for her corruption. He sat on the bed and placed his head in his hands, suddenly filled with remorse.

'I apologise,' Maria said quietly. 'The only romantic quality I possess is intuition.'

'And what did your intuition tell you about me?' Stephen asked.

'That I would be safe in your hands.'

Her reply numbed the triumph he felt on waking. She was able to offer herself in the flesh, but unable to surrender the full measure of herself emotionally. In Stephens eyes, it reinforced the illusion of innocence, as if a barrier had suddenly appeared between them. The close confinement of the room now poisoning the atmosphere, as if to underline the misconception of their liaison. As a result, Stephen suggested they went for a walk.

They left the hotel, crossed Piccadilly, and headed towards St James' Park in silence. Stephen felt embarrassed, and suggested they visit the National Gallery. Maria asked if he knew anything about art. Stephen informed her he knew nothing about art, and had left university with a second class degree in literary history.

'Hopeless, if you nurse an ambition to teach anything technical. But useful, if you want to know why the Puritans boarded the Mayflower, or how many Popes died of syphilis.'

'How many?' Maria asked.

'Seasick Puritans or Popes that died of syphilis?' he asked.

'Popes that died of syphilis.'

'Officially, they think five. Unofficially, they lost count.'

'That makes sense.'

'So far, nothing else does,' he confessed.

'I've disappointed you,' said Maria.

'You gave me something more valuable than I've ever given you. I don't think you understand the effect it's had on me. But it was all my fault, for making you feel you were in my debt.'

'It's purely academic, since Yevgeny and I are going back to Ukraine. Last night was a parting gift.'

Stephen came to a sudden halt and looked at Maria in disbelief.

'Neither of us can afford to stay here any longer,' said Maria.

'Surely Yevgeny is ready to resume his career.'

'He's been blacklisted because of his past.'

'That's nonsense. I heard him play.'

'When someone locks the door on a soloist's career, it's very hard to break back in.'

'Then let me help you.'

'There aren't many opportunities left. And those that remain are highly speculative.'

'Let me decide.'

'Very well, but you may be taking a chance on someone who may still prove unreliable.'

'You need reliability more than he does.'

Maria hesitated, then turned and confronted Stephen.

'Would you hire the Wigmore Hall for Yevgeny to give a recital? Without the incentive to perform, he'll die. Not just musically, but in his soul. For him, nothing else matters. Right now, he'll return home a failure, and his career will be over.'

'What about your career? What's going to become of that?'

'You heard the evidence. Yevgeny's gift is unique.'

'If you want me to be his sponsor, then it will come at a price,' said Stephen.

'The lesson of last night is that I have an absent libido. You might demand a refund.' Maria replied.

Stephen told Maria he wanted to get to know her, away from Belsize Park and hotel bedrooms, and to embark on a friendship, with the aim of disarming her assumption of him as an older predator, and accept him as someone attempting to discover who she really was.

In the weeks that followed, the price of his support was the progressive probing of her intentions concerning a career, and more importantly, her feelings for him. This was accompanied by a succession of gifts she refused to accept, leaving him uncertain whether it was a rejection of him, or the question of his infidelity. When asked 'why?' Maria answered,

'Because you're giving them to the wrong person.'

At the heart of Stephen's justification in his pursuit of Maria was her own complicity.

Her parting sacrifice had badly misfired, and led Stephen to believe her frigidity was a protection against insecurity. He believed, in time, she would thaw, willingly, through friendship, and see him as something more than just a sponsor. In reality, his support had more to do with his own feeling of inadequacy. He had been undervalued and frustrated far too long, and still sought answers to a life that he once believed he owned the direction. Maria had come unexpectedly with energy and ambition, allowing him a precious glimpse of renewed hope.

What intrigued him the most was how willingly she would

commit a selfless act on behalf of others. He was also aware of the guilt Maria now felt over complicating his relationship with Helen.

'I think it's highly likely we will separate.'

'Please don't,' Maria pleaded. 'I've done enough damage already.'

'I'm on holiday for a few weeks,' Stephen announced, 'we'll continue this conversation on my return.'

Stephen's absence gave Maria some much needed space in which to think and consider her future. Not only hers, but Yevgeny's. From the initial euphoric return to form following his recovery, he had now fallen into a deep depression. As a result, she became fearful of the consequences of a relapse. Fortunately, Stephen had managed to secure the Wigmore Hall, due to a late cancellation. Maria therefore decided the time was right to carry out the most daring part of her rescue plan: Gorlinsky himself!

She contacted his office several times, and was rebuffed, and told outright that any matters to do with Yevgeny Dimitrov would not be discussed under any circumstances. Then, she telephoned the office, seeking an audition under an assumed name. She was politely informed,

'Mr Gorlinsky does not undertake auditions without an introduction from an international conservatoire or leading agent.'

Frustrated on every level at attempting to communicate through official channels, she was left with no alternative, than to ambush the elusive impresario outside his office.

She chose a day when the weather was warm. One of those days when people feel in a holiday mood, more light-hearted, and react to the effects of the sun's rays. Yevgeny, of course, would have laughed at the thought that anyone could change Gorlinsky's mind.

Maria wore her best cotton dress, that spoke of youth and spring. Something simple his daughter or grand-daughter might wear. She had decided to mount a charm offensive, aimed to disarm someone whose authoritative judgement and reputation for disposing of rivals was wisely feared. The little girl appealing to the charitable nature of a tyrant. With only the slimmest chance of success.

At his offices in Regent Street, a single entrance consisting of a rather grand looking door, with a large door handle in the middle, forbidding the casual entrant. Inside, an inner glass door required a security code for entry, and beside it, an entryphone, where callers were screened for admittance. Maria arrived shortly before midday, and waited for Gorlinsky to exit. After waiting for over an hour, she began to think he was either too busy to eat, or away. At ten past two, however, the door swung open, and Gorlinsky marched out, accompanied by an assistant, and headed north in the direction of Oxford Street. Maria followed closely behind. Like the man himself, he was a determined walker, and after several hundred metres, turned left down a narrow street tucked behind the grand Regency facade, and entered a small French restaurant. Maria hesitated momentarily at the door, as Gorlinsky and his assistant were greeted by a couple, and seated at an alcove table in the far corner. Without saying a word, she entered the restaurant, and squeezed onto the bench opposite to where Gorlinsky was seated, forcing the other dinner guests to accommodate her presence, and looking distinctly curious, as Maria proceeded to address Gorlinsky directly.

'My name is Maria Novotna, Mr Gorlinsky, and a personal friend of Yevgeny Dimitrov. I apologise for my intrusion, but could not reach you any other way. I am here to apologise on his behalf. I know that he let you down badly. But please, please, hear him. He has fully recovered from his illness, and is playing better than ever. I beg you, please spare him twenty minutes of your time, that is all I ask. He is a different person, and deserves another chance.'

Gorlinsky held up his hand, and signalled for Maria not to

continue.

'I know who you are, Ms Novotna, only too well! Have you any idea how many pianists seek my representation every week. How many requests I get from pianists, who could grace any concert hall in the world? I gave your friend Dimitrov a chance because of my friendship with Popov, and out of respect for his stature, as someone capable of nurturing great talent. But your friend threw it all away, and tarnished whatever small reputation he built, in one of the most hideous, irresponsible and destructive ways it has ever been my unfortunate duty to witness. When he first came to me, I told him there are some rules that a professional must never break, if they want to become a world-class performer. And he broke all of them, Miss Novotna. I could no more sell Yevgeny Dimitrov to the paying public, than make this table do a tap dance. He's finished. It gives me no pleasure to tell you this, but it's the truth. Please, tell him to go home.'

Maria bowed her head, and said nothing for several moments.

'Yes. You are right to remember his stupidity and his reckless stubbornness. But his talent is the truth, not his immaturity. He is just twenty years old, and he knows nothing but music. Nothing at all. All I know is that he deserves another chance. He has suffered too much. Should he be punished all his life? Is that what you are saying? You have a reputation of being a man of undeniable instinct, and knowledge of great talent. Sometimes that talent pays a price, due to the complexity and flaws in that person's character. But I defy you to deny his sublime gift. In fact, someone who believes in his talent is sponsoring his forthcoming recital at Wigmore Hall. He sent me here today to invite you personally. I know your inclination will be to turn down his offer, but I beg you, to please find it in your heart to forgive him.'

She placed the tickets for the recital in front of Gorlinsky, who stared down at them with disdain, and said nothing. Neither did anyone else at the table. Maria, feeling ashamed and embarrassed, arose from the table, and addressed Gorlinsky, with tears in her eyes, and her voice almost faltering.

'I apologise on behalf of myself and Yevgeny. He apologises for everything, and begs your forgiveness. Sometimes, talent is impertinent. But you deceive yourself. It wasn't Popov who persuaded you he has a supreme gift. It was the evidence of your own ears!'

Maria hurriedly left the restaurant, feeling frustrated, and more than a little foolish. Then, all of a sudden, she heard the voice of Gorlinsky calling in the distance. Turning around, she saw him walking towards her. He was neither smiling, nor for that matter, angry. But instead, calm and businesslike.

'My companions think your persistence is impressive.' he said.

'And what do you think?' asked Maria.

'Tell Dimitrov I'll attend his recital. But will arrive with very high expectations, and look forward to hearing him include some Liszt, Scriabin and Bach. But my attendance implies no guarantee of any work whatsoever.'

Maria threw her arms around Gorlinsky and wept. Embarrassed, Gorlinsky gently pushed her away, and then did something, that was for him very rare indeed,… he smiled.

'Miss Novotna,' he declared, 'it is not Dimitrov that has undeniable talent, it's you!'

On hearing the news, Yevgeny could have climbed the Empire State Building with his bare hands, and jumped over the Matterhorn on a pair of skis. He began working immediately on the repertoire that Gorlinsky had demanded, and together, they identified the pieces that should be perfected to accomplish Yevgeny's re-engagement.

'Its absolutely necessary you blow Gorlinsky's ears off!' Maria ordered.

When she informed Stephen that she and Yevgeny wanted him to be 'guest of honour' at the recital, he told her he had no intention of being in the limelight, and refused to attend, something Maria found difficult to understand.

'After all, it's your money,' Maria told him.

'But your idea,' he countered.

At the recital, Yevgeny, as well as including pieces by the composers favoured by Gorlinsky, gave a meltingly lyrical account of Impromptu number 3 by Schubert, included some contemporary works, and ended with a Transcendental Study by Liszt that exceeded all expectations. Beforehand, Maria had taken the precaution of contacting numerous music societies and academies in order that, whatever else happened, the place would be populated with discounted goodwill. She needn't have worried. Yevgeny came out like a lion, eschewing nerves, and completely conquered everyone by his sheer excitement. It was clear he loved playing before an audience ready to devour something he himself was obsessed with. He played with no affectation, and displayed humility, with simple introductions, and let the music speak for itself. Gorlinsky's attendance did not go unnoticed. But his welcome back into the fold was to be no walkover. Gorlinsky was clearly impressed by the manner of his courteous greeting. But told him, for now, his career would be short of prestigious engagements, and was ordered to undergo a series of provincial concerts and festivals, performing solo recitals and concertos with second-string orchestras. During this time, he was ordered to hone his performance skills, before he could gain entry to the inner sanctum. A space, Gorlinsky told him, few occupied.

To Maria and Yevgeny, the detail of the assignment didn't matter. From this moment on, their life was going to change, and nothing was going to impede it. On that question, Maria was resolved, and warned Yevgeny that if he had anything to do with drug use again, she would abandon him without a second thought.

Right now that possibility seemed remote. His enthusiasm and work rate had never been higher, nor more joyous. The repertoire in the solo recitals was going to be more adventurous and challenging. He would, of course, include the most important dishes on the classical menu, that's what Gorlinsky required, but he also had permission to be persuasive about the lesser known repertoire and especially modern composers.

'I wonder if Felipe Vargas is feeling inspired?' exclaimed Yevgeny.

Their ideas were brimming over to such a degree, that each day of their preparation brought some innovative new addition or suggestion. Bringing to mind the success of the tangos, Maria asked, 'What about the use of dancers?' But Gorlinsky was reluctant to spend any more money than was necessary, and declared, 'You're not at the Albert Hall yet!'

It was while this artistic restoration was in progress, that Maria was once again reminded of her guilty responsibility. In her newly inspired enthusiasm, she had almost lost sight of her last meeting with Stephen, until one day he unexpectedly called.

'I need to see you urgently,' he pleaded.

Maria did not expect to find Stephen in a conciliatory mood. Nor did she find one.

Instead, he looked tired and perplexed, and his tension was palpable. He explained that, if anything, the holiday had demonstrated more clearly than ever, how little he and Helen had in common, and was determined to end what he termed their '*love-less union*'. During the holiday, he had intended to break the news of his relationship with Maria to her, but when the moment came, lacked the courage.

'Are you sure about throwing away something that has proved so durable?' Maria asked.

The question required serious consideration, but in the end, her argument proved pointless. During the period of their meeting, Stephen navigated their conversation in one undeniable direction, their future together. She felt an unanswerable weight of guilt, and valiantly tried to encourage the possibility of his reconciliation with Helen.

'Everyone's relationship suffers from familiarity,' she told him. 'Everyone's! Often people think that life would be better with someone else, but it rarely is.'

Stephen remained unconvinced.

'You're not someone else!… ' he reminded her.

The conviction in support of his obsession was undeniable. But it was her naivety that had brought about his unfaithfulness. As a result, she pleaded with him to re-consider.

But Stephen's mind was made up.

'It won't make any difference,' he said.

'Then, please don't make me the cause,' begged Maria.

'Too late,' Stephen replied. 'You didn't separate two people who were in love. You provided the answer as to why we never were!'

When she confided her dilemma to Yevgeny, his mood darkened.

'What did you think would happen?' he demanded, and confessed it was all his fault, and entered into a deep melancholia she immediately recognised as his retreat into reflection, whenever he was challenged by a situation or event that disturbed him.

'I wanted to give him a gift. Something precious,' Maria explained. 'A reward to someone who had committed a wholly unselfish act.'

'Then you paid with something far more valuable than money,' Yevgeny replied.

It was an accusation made more in sadness than in anger, that reflected his own neglect and tainted history. But now events were about to take a course of their own.

Following their meeting, Stephen decided the matter could no longer be postponed. Up to then, Helen appeared to be content. She had crossed the rubicon of disappointment concerning lack of children with the distraction of work and outside interests. For the most part, Stephen had always been the reliable 'other half', who blended in with her busy schedule. Together, they had achieved the blissful state of non-interference in each others lives to such a degree that the malfunction of their emotional life was of secondary importance. In fact, it was a matter on which Helen no longer wished to dwell. She was content. So content, she hadn't noticed the change that had taken place in Stephen. His brooding and agitation she believed more likely the result of his lack of promotion and pressure of work. She therefore dismissed his admission of infidelity as a temporary mid-life crisis, and reassured him that having been together for so many years, it was the normal direction of travel. Except, of course, it was his direction of travel, and not hers.

In order to provoke a deeper understanding of the critical nature of their partnership, Stephen confronted Helen, by describing his relationship with her as bereft of a future, and his affair with Maria the potent, uplifting and giddy result of having at last discovered love. This painful and contemptible revelation leaving no room for truce nor manoeuvre. Only, the impossibly difficult and dismal consequence of rejection.

Since her pride wouldn't allow her to plead for justice, in a matter for which she had no case to answer, she reluctantly agreed to depart to the suburban hinterland of the singular unattached, hoping Stephen's affair with Maria would burn itself out.

But the damage had already been done. All that was left of her future was the outline of an existence for which she had made no provision.

'Infatuation is a pit-stop, not a destination!' she warned.

But it made no difference. Stephen allowed Helen time to transition to somewhere she could establish a new life, and was now eager to announce his new found status to Maria.

When they met, Stephen told her he had renewed the lease on the flat at Belsize Park, and to prepare herself for even more exciting news! Before he could announce the details of Helen's imminent departure, however, Maria told him she had some exciting news of her own, and regaled him with an account of her ambush of Gorlinsky, that had resulted in Yevgeny's re-engagement.

'I opened the window, and persuaded the owner to unlock

the side door,' said Maria.

'Then the same strategy worked twice!' exclaimed Stephen.

It soon became clear to Stephen that his role as a benefactor had dictated a new road map, as Maria revealed the extent of her self-appointed involvement in Yevgeny's return to full time concert performance. It was, she announced, going to keep both of them busy for the next six months.

'Both of you!' he gasped.

Stephen listened as Maria described the complexities and issues involved with a touring schedule in different parts of the country, and how impossible it would be for Yevgeny to undertake it on his own. She was to accompany him. He was a great pianist, she told Stephen, but completely impractical. She then added,

'It's all your fault! Aren't you pleased?'

Maria had skilfully distanced herself from his domestic situation, as she now enthusiastically outlined details of the repertoire they planned, and matters relating to Yevgeny's welfare, and effectively, signposted life in another direction.

'You see. We have vindicated your trust,' said Maria. 'But don't worry, I will make sure you are kept informed of every demi- and semi-quaver of the journey.'

Stephen had not expected Yevgeny's re-engagement to involve Maria, to the extent she was now happily confiding. In response, he gave a remarkable impression of someone delighted at both the inventiveness and shrewd conception that had allowed her to remain part of a career, that had both bought them together, and forced them apart. Maria announced she was now Yevgeny's tour manager, as well as his interpreter, and her enthusiasm spilled out of her like a young girl, reciting the details of some thrilling event she was incapable of keeping to herself. Stephen listened patiently and then during an opportune moment said,

'I have some news of my own, if you care to hear it.'

He announced calmly that he and Helen were parting on amicable terms. Maria had not expected the announcement to arrive so soon, and was uncertain how to respond. She couldn't pretend to be surprised, or even saddened. She had never met Helen, and in any other circumstance would no doubt spring to an emotional defence of her plight. Her only response was to ask if Stephen was sure he had made the right decision.

He assured Maria his relationship with Helen was beyond repair, and their parting inevitable.

'What if I hadn't made that call?' said Maria. 'What if your life had gone on, just as it was?'

'Then I would never have known true happiness.'

'Maybe your passion for me will fade in time as well?' speculated Maria.

'I doubt it. You are too talented and too interesting. You have roused me from rotting middle-aged bondage, promoted me as your getaway driver, and given me a taste for charitable causes.'

'As well as separating you from someone devoted.' Maria observed.

'Would you have preferred I waited ten years? Helen would have been almost the same age as my mother when she died, and likely missed the chance to start again.'

Maria considered Stephen had carefully disguised his own guilt, by asking a question that was inadmissible. Since he had effectively constructed a situation that, without her involvement, would never have arisen.

'Do you know what a musician's life is like? It's completely antisocial. Hours of practice, rehearsals, travelling and being away for long periods of time.'

'All the more reason for you to have an anchor then!' replied Stephen.

Maria bore personal responsibility for a situation she never intended, but six months was a period in which much could change. A period in which her own chances of success could be explored more fully. Fortunately, Yevgeny's schedule was busy, and most of the places on their tour were outside the capital.

The distance, she hoped, would provide much needed time for Stephen to reflect more fully on missing someone whom, from late spring to midsummer, he had depended on. She also agreed to keep him updated on everything that was happening. Stephen did not hide his disappointment. But her own direction of travel was now more assured.

Before they set off on tour, Maria told Yevgeny any lapses in his performance or behaviour this time wouldn't be forgiven.

'An old door, has closed, and a new one is opening,' she told Yevgeny.

'The trouble with old doors is that they can warp, and get wedged in the space they've become used to occupying,' he replied.

11.

Maria had now become Yevgeny's private secretary and organiser, overseeing everything in his life, from health, fitness, practice, travel and sleep, to energy, mood as well as mental preparation. In addition to being his travelling companion, she also took notes on every performance concerning repertoire and audience response, ensuring any flattering notices he received were preserved for inclusion in any press releases. The work was poorly paid, but it suited Gorlinsky that Yevgeny had a 'minder' who would ensure his protegee was supervised in many of the important areas of a performer's life, in which his own involvement was remote. Maria was confident that, in time, Yevgeny would not just mature as a performer, but eventually become a personality in his own right.

She wrote to Stephen,

There is perhaps nothing more precious than witnessing someone blossoming in front of your eyes. Yevgeny has not only grown in confidence, but in every respect is happier than I have ever seen him!'

Maria's communications were like the letter a person would write to an intimate friend, in which she described the daily routine of a musicians life, complete with descriptions of the venues themselves, mini-portraits of the staff, conductors, and fellow musicians.

In the solo appearances, the venue manager would introduce the programme with a brief outline of Yevgeny and the repertoire to be performed, written by Maria herself. This often began by praising the venue, and making reference to the region's musical culture, finishing with Yevgeny's fondness and love of whatever part of the country they were in, even if he didn't have any knowledge of where he was!

Playing with orchestras was to prove more challenging, with more time spent for rehearsals, and the conductor spending precious time getting the orchestral sound and balance right. Unlike the first rate professional orchestras in the major cities, some of the orchestras in the provincial towns were often not familiar with the same repertoire, nor under the capable hands of a sympathetic and experienced conductor. In some cases, Yevgeny was forced to follow the orchestra, and once in the Greig Piano concerto, the coherence between orchestra and piano became so adrift, Maria proclaimed it should be re-named Greig's Symphony No 1 with piano accompaniment.

'Ah yes. The Grieg,' echoed Yevgeny. 'The symphony is really outstanding, and the piano part is very nice too!'

Very often, Gorlinsky would arrive at a venue unannounced, and after the performance give Yevgeny notes. It was deliberately disconcerting, since Maria considered it would be more beneficial if he attended more rehearsals. But, she also detected there was a reason for it. She considered that Gorlinsky wanted to know what Yevgeny learned in performance, without being prompted at rehearsal.

'One day, it is you who will occupy the international stage, not me!' he declared.

'Make your mistakes here, and learn from them. You won't have that luxury later.'

She felt Gorlinsky was deliberately holding something back in his promotional and publicity expertise. So Maria decided to do some promoting of her own. Several weeks before he was due to make an appearance, Maria would call the venue, and ask what pre-publicity was being utilised. She was often asked to supply any additional information that would promote ticket sales. She decided that since classical music concerts attracted mostly traditional classical enthusiasts, she should add some spice to the usual low-volume fanfare.

'We need to entice more people into the theatre to hear you,' Maria insisted.

She did this by promoting the fact that Yevgeny was from Ukraine, and a finalist in the Odesa International Piano competition. Then she added that they should announce him as,

The Nureyev of the Keyboard!'

The young star of the Kirov had sensationally defected in Paris in 1961, to unprecedented publicity. With all the political uncertainty happening in Ukraine, she was tempted to suggest that Yevgeny seek asylum, purely for publicity purposes. But Gorlinsky shot the idea down in flames. So, instead, Maria persuaded him that her idea of using the ballet star's illustrious reputation for daring leaps would add glamour to Yevgeny's appearances, and give the local radio and television broadcasters something to talk about. The idea amused Gorlinsky.

Whatever he thought of her talent as a pianist, he admired her nose for publicity. The local newspapers and broadcasters lapped it up. Maria was now a one-woman publicity machine, and general manager of Yevgeny Incorporated.

Her happiness spilled out of every anecdotal insight and indiscreet revelation. Even during the impractical and logistical inconvenience of touring, and constant displacement, her excitement could not be expunged. She had become not only Yevgeny's minder, but Gorlinsky's eyes and ears.

Stephen had no other choice than to profess delight at both her innovation and Yevgeny's progress. He was though, merely a spectator. All he could do was to be patient and wait for her to become tired of being a chaperone.

One of the most pleasurable events in Yevgeny's busy schedule was in Bath. Host to the Festival itself, the city's location, restaurants, and the multiple delights of the city, were sure to attract Gorlinsky, and the intimate atmosphere of the Pump Room was, she considered, the ideal place for a debut.

'Why not surprise Gorlinsky with a 'special guest?',' asked Maria.

'Who do you suggest?' said Yevgeny.

'Me!' she exclaimed.

The idea immediately appealed to him.

'If I am the Nureyev of the keyboard, then you will have to be Dame Margot!' he said.

The pair entered into a routine that perfectly appealed to the subversive nature of Yevgeny's character. Like taking a cork out of a bottle. Once released, it spilled over into repartee, and for a time Adagio was now a Glissade, the Cadenza à Grande Jeté, and the Duet became a Pas de Deux.

Intuitively, Yevgeny felt a 'guest artiste' would be a refreshingly novel way of introducing Maria to a wider public. He also wanted to surprise Gorlinsky.

'You can knock their ears off with the Chopin, then join me for a duet,' he enthused.

'How about the Libertango?' suggested Maria. 'It celebrates the two things we both love.'

The recital was already sold out by the time they arrived. The programme announced included Bach, Beethoven, Chopin, Liszt, Rachmaninoff, Debussy and the Tangos composed for his Wigmore Hall debut.

Shortly before the concert began, Gorlinsky arrived and sat in an aisle seat towards the back of the auditorium. It was his custom not to make himself known to Yevgeny until the end of the performance. As Maria's appearance was not until the second half of the programme, she waited until the interval, and then changed into a split-front, full-length, off-the-shoulder, azure dress, that allowed freedom of movement, and her long auburn hair to make its own dramatic impact. Maria was to make her appearance following Yevgeny's rendition of a short piece by Barbosa, deliberately chosen in order to contrast with the dramatic energy of the C sharp Etude. She had first heard the Etude played on a recording by Horowitz from her parents record collection, and it proved to be one of the decisive pieces that made her want to become a pianist.

'If you mess up during the first five bars, forget it!' Yevgeny teased.

'Don't worry,' she assured him. 'I have no intention of fluffing my bar-lines.'

The music was indelibly printed on her memory, like one of the first classical milestones that mean anything to a young fertile mind. She now felt more than capable of putting her stamp on the composition in front of a paying public, and audacious enough to put her head in the lions' mouth, in order to surprise Gorlinsky.

'But isn't that what you are meant to do, to get noticed?' she asked.

When it came time for her debut, Yevgeny announced that there was to be a slight change to the programme, and told the audience that he had a very special 'guest artiste' he would like to introduce, and asked them to give a truly warm welcome to a fellow Ukrainian pianist…

When Maria walked on stage, applause spontaneously erupted from the audience, perhaps more for the way she looked, since she hadn't played a note. It immediately gave her confidence a boost as she sat down, and waited for absolute silence, before launching into the first electric bars, that ignited a collection of musical colours, like a firework exploding in all directions, before landing at the beating heart of the listener. The atmosphere, full of anticipation, at the introduction of an unexpected intruder, elicited a roar of collective approval, as the final bars died.

Then Yevgeny appeared from the side of the stage, clapping enthusiastically before seating himself at the piano to accompany Maria in the duet. As usual, although they had thoroughly rehearsed the piece, Yevgeny left a barely perceptible space into which they could both pour that remarkable and unspoken witness to an artiste's unique fingerprint, which, at the conclusion of their lyrical account, accorded a reception that demanded three curtain calls for Maria alone. If nothing else, Maria now felt justified in demanding Gorlinsky's attention.

When he came backstage, however, Gorlinsky entered Yevgeny's dressing room looking solemn, and announced that he would like to speak to Yevgeny alone. Maria waited outside while Gorlinsky no doubt pronounced judgement on Yevgeny's defiance, and several minutes later emerged unsmiling.

'Be at my office tomorrow morning 10 am sharp,' he announced acidly.

The next morning, Maria duly arrived at Gorlinsky's office, and was kept waiting in the reception area for over an hour. When she was ushered into his presence, he neither greeted her, nor invited her to sit down. Instead, he made her stand in front of him, like a schoolgirl being upbraided by a headmaster.

'Who invited you to appear in my concert?' he asked.

Maria said nothing. There was, she considered, little point.

'Where was your name printed in the programme?' he demanded.

Maria still refused to answer, and instead lowered her eyes. Her expression was not even one of repentance or shame, but of quiet defiance.

'If you had bothered to look above the programme heading, you would have noticed it states 'Viktor Gorlinsky presents'! Not Yevgeny Dimitrov, or Maria Novotna. Nor the general manager of the venue, or the ticket collector on the Magic Tour Bus, that takes visitors to sample the delights of Bath. But me, Viktor Gorlinsky! And I decide which artistes do, or do not, grace the stage under the banner of my name, no one else!'

Gorlinsky's voice rose considerably, like the crescendo passage from an aria, that acted as a prelude to banning her presence from any future venue in which Yevgeny was to make an appearance. But rather than give that final irrevocable order, he instead forbade her from performing for the duration of the tour. He was also too experienced and wily not to understand the cunning behind Maria's audacious strategy.

'You must think yourself very clever, Ms Novotna. You chose the timing of your unofficial debut, knowing full well that critics from the national and musical press would be present to report your performance. That is rather unfortunate, because I will have no alternative than to tell them you were simply an amateur friend of the artiste. An interloper who has nothing whatsoever to do with this agency. I know full well that Yevgeny has been very successfully manipulated by you since the beginning of this tour, and I deliberately let you have your head. But when this tour ends, all that is about to change. Your efforts have been wasted. Knowing Yevgeny, and looking desirable in a gown, do not qualify you as a performer in my eyes. Only as someone who has the singularly unique and unashamed talent to hustle. Good day!'

Maria said nothing for a few moments, and then cleared her throat, and walked towards the door of his office. On opening it, she declared in a loud voice,

'Thank you so much for your advice, Mr Putin. The next time I ruin a concert by taking three curtain calls, I hope it will be under a more enlightened management.'

That was it. As cold and abrupt negation of her talent that he knew perfectly how to orchestrate. As a result, Gorlinsky did not visit Yevgeny directly, after attending any of his future performances, but instead insisted Yevgeny meet him at his office, on the days when he was free. Nonetheless, Maria did get mentioned in the arts section of a financial broadsheet, and reviewed in a classical magazine of some repute. The broadsheet briefly mentioned her appearance in the duet, but the classical magazine described her as '*a fellow Ukrainian of some considerable promise, in her performance of the Chopin*'. This did not constitute the critical acclaim she hoped for, but she had learned to live on a little. The fact that Gorlinsky proved fractious was a disappointment, but in time she would have her revenge.

For now, she could claim she had appeared as a 'guest artiste', and able to quote a respected journal as saying she had shown '*considerable promise.*'

Yevgeny himself had received some excellent reviews. He had expanded his repertoire, and gained in confidence, and as a result, was now more assertive. In addition, he was more precocious in his professional dealings with others, and although his English was far from perfect, made use of his incomprehension to avoid argument, and insist on his knowledge and conception of the work be given the utmost consideration by conductors. He had also learned some valuable lessons on how to handle what he termed 'the beasts of the baton' from Popov, and would often demonstrate the value of some small adjustment in tempo and nuance of the orchestral accompaniment, and how it affected the piano part, in order to realise the composer's intentions more clearly. He was, in fact, growing up both as a musician, and artistically forging ahead.

Just at the point when her ambitions were frustrated, and her morale was at its lowest, Stephen called Maria, and asked if she could meet him for dinner, when she was next in London.

She had hoped to be able to give Stephen a triumphant account of her own bid for stardom, but Gorlinsky had ensured for the moment this would be delayed. Instead, she gave him an enthusiastic account of Yevgeny's progress, and the highlights of the tour, including the useful publicity generated by the association with Nureyev, carefully avoiding her own delinquent attempt in the limelight. Stephen appeared amused, but Maria suspected he was agitated and unsettled. The more positive she became, the more his self-esteem suffered from the challenge of being subordinated to the role of a passive sponsor.

Maria suddenly remembered she was discussing the wrong subject…

'I'm so stupid. Please tell me everything I have been missing about the brilliant talent of Stephen Kline!' she demanded.

'I'm finally free,' said Stephen. 'Helen finally moved out of the house last month.'

'I am sorry to hear that,' said Maria.

'Sorry?' queried Stephen.

'You spent so many years together.'

'But were never happy.'

He was like a man full of purpose, but at odds with how to be at ease with himself.

Having consciously discarded someone for whom he considered he had no future, he was now eager to discuss his future with Maria.

'Even the best laid plans can be derailed!' Maria warned.

There was a silence, then Maria told Stephen about her falling-out with Gorlinsky.

'Sometimes, to prove you're not invisible, you have to disappear,' said Stephen, and suggested they escape, and take a short break to somewhere mysterious.

'It just might provoke Gorlinsky into a realisation of your value,' he told her.

'Yevgeny, too!'

Maria considered they had relied on her too much, and appreciated her too little. Gorlinsky needed to be taught a lesson. Losing her services at such a crucial time in the tour, just might allow Yevgeny to insist on the value of her being his 'special guest.'

Either way, she considered she had nothing to lose.

When she announced her impending trip, Yevgeny declared it was one of their busiest weeks.

'Tell Gorlinsky to advertise for a new assistant then,' said Maria. 'I'm off on a tour of my own.'

'Where to?' demanded Yevgeny.

'Somewhere I'm wanted.'

12.

As STEPHEN'S CLASSIC Mark 2 Jaguar pulled up outside the flat in Belsize Park, it instantly reminded Maria of Yevgeny's rescue, and reminiscent of a bygone age. Stephen had prepared for their time away with the utmost care, planning every detail like a military operation. Their trip included vintage champagne and a picnic basket containing caviar, smoked salmon, artichokes, sauerkraut, Ukrainian cheese, biscuits and the ingredients to make a half-decent borscht.

As they left the London suburbs, and headed eastward, Maria was intrigued.

'Are you kidnapping me?' she asked.

'Of course!' Stephen replied.

After several hours, the fringe of the metropolis had disappeared, leaving only a sparsely populated landscape, served by long winding roads, that unfolded towards a horizon of low-lying clouds, that fused with the failing light. Beyond this, an even more startling discovery awaited them. Like a giant Dalek, signalling for them to stop, the car progressed down a long narrow lane, and reached the very threshold of an imposing structure, before coming to a halt. Maria looked both bemused and stunned.

'What on earth is it?' she asked.

'Rest,' said Stephen.

Stephen located a small wooden box by the entrance, and

extracting a large key, opened the front door, and invited Maria to step across the threshold. Under the large cone-shaped interior, the ground floor contained a lounge area, complete with a sofa, dining table, bookcases and walls filled with watercolours, plus a kitchen with a double oven, and cabinets full of groceries. A large rug covered the stone floor, and nearby a wood burner, surrounded by several piles of neatly cut tinder, waiting to be lit. Stephen had chosen somewhere there would be no distractions. A private domain, in which two people had no other choice than to explore the possibility of co-existence. Even in late summer, the air was chilly, and the location exposed. Stephen, therefore, lost no time in both warming the air, and allowing Maria to fill it with the familiar aroma of borscht. He also became, for a brief moment, like a small boy, running up and down the spiral staircase, and opening cabinets and drawers, hunting for extra blankets. There was, anyway, a different scent in the air, and Maria felt she could almost taste the chaff that blew from fields, moistened by frequent showers. A secret kingdom, a million miles from being responsible for a career that wasn't her own. For the first time, in a very long time, she felt relaxed. But something more,… homesick. Those days of youthful summers, when she would sit curled up in Mariinsky Park, or at home with a favourite book, discovering the world with a serene feeling of security. Her parents were comparatively well travelled, and loved Italy. Often they would cook pasta, and for their own amusement, use Italian words and musical expressions to describe the preparation and enjoyment of the meal. Spaghetti *Sforzando*! Cannelloni *Pizzicato*! Lasagne *Giocoso*! To cries of *Bravo, Encore* and *Bellissimo*!, her parents Italian expressions allowed the meal to be enjoyed with some Mediterranean brio, that evoked memories of Venice, Rome, and Positano, but at the same time, had stimulated her appetite to visit Paris, London, and New York, and get her feet wet on distant shores.

There was no doubt that the passport to all this was music. She had won numerous competitions, appeared in local Ukrainian concerts dedicated to young performers, and had framed her diplomas. But at twenty-three, she should have established some small but important foothold on a career in music. Her experience on tour with Yevgeny had given her a much greater insight into the business of performing, and moreover a taste for being within a finger-width of a breakthrough. She felt the time was now right to make her own reputation. England was that tiny idiosyncratic outpost of Europe, where the inhabitants had a reputation for being eccentric, like Stephen. A people who hid emotion behind words that required you to interpret their inner world. Up to now, it was to be the longest time she would spend in Stephen's company.

In the wide open spaces of the countryside, it was conversely both claustrophobic and intense. There was no television, piano, hi-fi, nor any other distractions. Stephen's purpose was clear. He told Maria he wanted to get to know who she really was, not just the 'minder' of a prodigy, but the free spirit that had first aroused his interest. As a result, she revealed to him her inner thoughts, and the ideas that had dominated her direction.

'Up to now, there has been no other direction than music,' she told Stephen.

'Based on someone else's career,' he observed…

More and more, her thoughts returned to Ukraine, and the sacrifices her parents had made.

She owed it to them to prove a career in music wasn't just a vain hope. If nothing else, she was determined not to return empty-handed.

'That,' she said, 'would be a defeat, after everything Yevgeny and I have been through…'

'What about Putin then?' asked Stephen, referring to Crimea.

'He's unpredictable,' said Maria. 'He'll smile at you one minute, and stab you in the back, the next, then he'll lie, and say he ever knew you!'

Like Putin, the weather was unpredictable, and it rained for several days. As soon as the sun came out, Stephen suggested they went for a picnic. When they reached Aldeburgh, he spread a blanket on a shady area of the vast beach, and began to unpack the provisions he had dutifully been carrying in a hamper. It was reminiscent of a mini-Fortnum and Mason, with smoked salmon, Brie, soft cheeses, wholegrain bread, olives, duck pate, pickles, truffles, and a half bottle of champagne. He then proposed a toast to Maria's future.

'I want to be a soloist,' she asserted. 'Do you think that's too ambitious?'

'On the contrary, I think if you don't do it, then you will resent the world and everything in it. But you'll need the kind of help Yevgeny could never provide.'

'Why not?' asked Maria.

'Because he already has a career of his own.'

'He taught me a great deal.'

'About rejection. You need someone to provide the conditions to be creative, the finances to survive, and the security of someone devoted.'

Maria looked deep in thought, as Stephen outlined the future as he saw it. Her future, filled with his constant and unswerving purpose and intent. The type of support that allowed her the opportunity to finish her studies, promote her talent, and pursue an entirely new and independent path to becoming an established pianist in her own right.

He noted she was already experienced at handling publicity and creating opportunities. The one thing she lacked, he told her, was… security!

'You've already proved the effect you have on an audience,' Stephen declared. 'It's the same effect you've had on me, ever since I set eyes on you.'

Stephen studied Maria's face. Or rather, scrutinised it, like someone who was convinced it contained an uncommitted truth she had failed to utter. Then he moved even closer, inclined his head slightly, and kissed her with the most exquisite tenderness and feeling. Her response was tentative, but he sensed she was longing to invite an intimate connection that had for so long been missing in her life. To satisfy a desire she herself could never quite fathom, and the strange abandonment of the moment she was unable to control. She was a late developer, who was both frightened and excited by an instinct she had rejected, and had never fully discovered her own body. Yet, when so many other things found her capable, highly intelligent, and fearless. She remained emotionally incomplete. For Stephen, she was a mystery waiting to be solved. He longed to refine and reassure her, by the measure of his tenderness and affection. To ignite in her a passion that, in every other way, he knew she possessed.

The isolation had allowed her to examine her motives more fully, and the intensity of Stephen's reasoning persuaded her that the key to unlock her frigidity was in the certainty of a future he was able to provide. The emotional and financial security, that would allow her to concentrate, and avoid the pitfalls that too often choked a performer's survival. She was also aware that behind every truth is a motive, and wanted to help ease Stephen's pain. What he had revealed about his past left her in no doubt he felt both a failure, and regretted he was childless. If nothing else, she decided their time together had to do with helping each other heal, and find new meaning. Yet, whenever they had made love, Maria was unable to fully participate, and give herself to the moment. This communicated itself to Stephen, who felt he was in receipt of something he didn't deserve. A guilt accompanied the act, as if he had been caught stealing in plain sight of the owner. He was longing for her to surrender the very thing she had always withheld. That most private, personal and secret inner sanctum that stood guard over her privacy.

'You hold it back,' said Stephen. 'Is it because of something that happened to you in the past?'

'What is it I hold back?' she asked.

'You!' he announced.

If anything, her time with Stephen had underlined her distaste of physical intimacy. As the last days of their time in Suffolk approached, Maria regretted she had foregone caution, and was aware that Stephen demanded something she was unable to return. It was, she explained, only in music she was able to express an emotional depth denied her in almost every other aspect of a personal relationship.

'Is it a rejection of me?' Stephen pleaded.

'No,' said Maria, 'just something, I forgot to pack for the journey.'

When she returned to Belsize Park, Yevgeny was rather aloof, like a child who had suffered the desertion of a parent. She had always known a precocious temperament was part of the necessary inventory of his character, but now began to sense something new. He was curious about her trip to Suffolk and, more importantly, why? Previously, the time she had spent with Stephen had been fleeting, and to Yevgeny's mind, social. But now, in view of their time away, it amounted to something like courtship.

'I needed to get away and escape,' she told him.

For so long, Yevgeny had relied on her efficient and meticulous conduct of his affairs. She reminded him however, it was a role she had undertaken with neither encouragement, nor just reward, from Gorlinsky. Yevgeny agreed. According to Gorlinsky, recitals were a business, and had to meet the test of market share.

While she was away, Gorlinsky had called Yevgeny into his office, and disclosed his plans to launch him on the international stage.

'Up to now, you are simply a Ukrainian prodigy. But I want you to become something more. You know that people are interested in others' rise to fame. In your case, you have a remarkable story. A promising career almost ruined by addiction, and a life that could have ended at nineteen…'

He spoke as if he was pitching a script to a producer, keen

to soak-up the synopsis of a Hollywood biopic. It was not only a good story. Yevgeny's recovery from addiction could serve as a powerful testimony of victory over adversity, and as a warning about the devastation drugs wreak on society, especially the youth of a country. This coming from a youthful prodigy would, Gorlinsky predicted, provide not only useful publicity for his future public appearances, but in addition, have a far more universal appeal. Wide-eyed and in youthful bloom, he was the complete prodigious package: tall, blond, androgynous, awkward, complex, charismatic, and sensationally gifted.

All Gorlinsky had to do was give some thought on how to present him to the public.

Yevgeny knew he could not remain supported by the generosity of Stephen Kline for much longer, and informed Gorlinsky he now wanted a place of his own. Gorlinsky agreed.

Maria had served her purpose, and now it was time for her role to be guillotined. Any continued involvement with the tour would not be welcome. Maria was therefore informed by Gorlinsky that in future his needs would be met by a 'professional' tour manager, appointed by him. It was clear Gorlinsky intended to take Yevgeny's career in a new direction.

When Maria next met Stephen, she informed him of Gorlinsky's plans to launch Yevgeny as an ex-addict protege. A hybrid between a serious classical artist and a pin-up, to save the youth of the country.

'Gorlinsky is phenomenally ambitious,' Maria affirmed, 'and will suck him as dry as the Atacama in a bid to make more money.'

'Then why do you persist in wanting the same thing?' Stephen enquired.

'To see how far the journey takes me!'

'It's full of corpses and disappointment.'

Stephen announced that he wouldn't be renewing the tenancy on the apartment in Belsize Park, when it expired.

'You must surely know the reason?' he asked.

Suddenly, Maria felt trapped. She realised their time away had been a rehearsal.

'I'd make a poor replacement for Helen,' said Maria.

'I don't want a second-hand Helen. I want a newly invigorated Maria.'

'Gorlinsky has dispensed with my services, and Yevgeny no doubt will be moving soon. Domesticity is not the right career move for me right now.'

'Nonsense, you'd be free to do whatever you want, and I have the means to make it happen!'

'I'm not sure I can give you what you want. More to the point, I'm not even certain I can achieve what I want for myself. Your offer is generous. It's just that I'm not ready to be buried in a suburban cemetery right now!'

Stephen did not attempt to disguise his disappointment. The intimacy that had, over time, developed between them, and to which he had devoted so much attention, had for the moment, been liquidated by the sudden chill of her response. After they parted, he therefore decided to take the unprecedented step of writing Maria an old-fashioned personal letter. Something she did not expect. His letter was both passionate and businesslike. He painted a picture of her being nurtured under his care and protection, like a rare bloom, that in order to blossom, requires the ideal conditions to be created. His words confirming not only an unswerving and wholehearted belief in her talent, but assuring her that he '*knew her*' in a way that only someone destined to love only one person in their life possibly could.

It was, amongst its wild and romantic portrait of support and declaration of love, a letter of intent. Something for which she hadn't been prepared, requiring a delicacy of response, in which she hadn't been tutored. A trap of her own making. Like being offered the security of a father, combined with the ardent attention of a lover. Most alarming of all, Stephen had assumed her continued financial security and happiness would be solely dependent on him.

Her reply acknowledged the help and support he had given, and the sincerity of his intentions. When it came to addressing Stephen's invitation to share her life with him, however, she referenced Putin's illegal occupation of Crimea.

'*Some decisions that look attractive in the short-term inevitably fail, when you consider the long-term consequences….,*' she told him.

In its brief and subtle communication, Maria delivered a decisive blow for independence. For once, Stephen chose not to challenge her reasoning, but signalled his bitter disappointment in a short formal reply, advising her of the day and time he would require the flat to be handed back. She knew, of course, the penalty for creating distance between them would be costly. This was to be no exception.

Yevgeny's twenty-first birthday was only days away, and Maria persuaded him to celebrate by doing something reminiscent of home. She wanted to cook a simple meal for him, watch a favourite film and enjoy some Ukrainian music. He had already received a letter from Madame Eshkol, and a card from his mother, which had made him homesick. He was far from home, the familiarity of his adopted family, the love of his mother, and the estrangement of his father. It was a burden that weighed heavily, reminding him of an injured past he was unable to escape. During these times, he became unconsolable. His birthday, rather than being a joyous occasion of youthful excess, was in danger of being clouded by issues that had drilled deep into his psyche.

For once, Gorlinsky came to the rescue, informing them both he would be taking them to his 'club' to celebrate the occasion.

'Does it serve Ukrainian food?' asked Yevgeny.

'No. But it is both humble and accommodating, just like myself,' replied Gorlinsky.

Gorlinsky's 'club' in Pall Mall was not in the least humble, and its accommodation rather grand. The preserve of the rich and entitled, it announced itself in the elegance of a sumptuous interior that Gorlinsky referred to as a 'home from home'. In its own way, it made the same kind of statement as stepping out of a Rolls. Its very Englishness, and rather snobbish self regard, amused Maria, and intimidated Yevgeny, who felt distinctly like a fish out of water. They passed through an elegant 'resident's lounge', and were given a tour of the library, boasting the collected wisdom of Archimedes, Shakespeare and Samuel Pepys, among over two thousand years of sophisticated philosophical and political insight, and were then led into the large 'dining room', with high ceilings and gold leaf pillars, complete with plush red carpet, Edwardian lounge chairs, and portraits of past illustrious members, that gazed down on elegant dining tables.

Gorlinsky felt very much at home, as no less than two waiters and a maître d' pulled their respective chairs out, and once seated, stood behind them. The maître d' greeted Gorlinsky like one of their most esteemed members, and presented him with the wine list, whilst the two waiters stood at attention behind Yevgeny and Maria like guardsmen.

'What would you like to drink,' enquired Gorlinsky, handing Yevgeny and Maria the wine list, containing a bewildering array of fine French, Italian, German and English varieties.

'We don't drink,' replied Maria.

'Nonsense,' said Gorlinsky. 'Never mind. We'll order the food, and then decide.'

The a la carte menu housed in a cover the size of a tabloid newspaper was then presented to all three. Maria and Yevgeny opened its leather facade to discover it offered a limited range of four 'starters' and six main dishes, together with a 'cold plate' and 'dessert trolley' of patisseries, jellies, trifles, and puddings. Yevgeny and Maria studied the menu for several minutes. Its starters consisted of foie gras and parsnip terrine, mussels, braised pork cheek and liver pâté, and for the main course, a choice of Scottish beef, grilled calves liver, breast of wood pigeon, roast venison and Dover sole.

'Well,' said Gorlinsky. 'Have you made your mind up?'

'Can I have goulash or spaghetti?' asked Yevgeny.

Gorlinsky looked quizzically at the maître d'.

'We may have some spaghetti somewhere,' winced the maître d' '.

Gorlinsky looked at Maria, and raised his eyebrows in contemplation.

'Do you have a vegetarian option?' she enquired.

This time, Gorlinsky did not refer to the maître d', but addressed Maria directly.

'The beef comes with roast and creamed potatoes, cabbage, spinach and green... beans. I suggest you have the roast beef, minus the roast beef.'

'That will do nicely,' said Maria.

The maître d' bowed politely, and Gorlinsky ordered a bottle of vintage Claret, three bottles of carbonated water, a large jug of orange juice, plus soup and pate for starters, without any further reference to Maria or Yevgeny. Both sat before him like two unruly children, that signalled their rebellion at the formality of their surroundings. In Yevgeny's case, Gorlinsky had no doubt, he felt like eating spaghetti, but Maria's request bore all the hallmarks of insolence.

'Now, let's get down to business!' ordered Gorlinsky.

'Business? This is celebration,' said Yevgeny.

'A double celebration,' replied Gorlinsky.

'Why double?' Yevgeny enquired.

'Because there are at least two more presents to be unwrapped. One is an appearance at the Festival Hall in July of next year, and the other your debut at the Proms a month later!'

Yevgeny's face lit up like a thousand candles, and his eyes glistened like lasers, fighting to come out of their sockets. If he were not in such decorous surroundings, he would, no doubt, have danced on the dining table. As it was, he jumped up and pulled Gorlinsky out of his chair by the shoulders, and kissed him, as if a childhood of missed Christmases had been redeemed in one spellbinding and unforgettable moment. Gorlinsky, for once, was lost for words, and momentarily froze. Then Yevgeny took the bottle of Claret by the neck, filled his glass and shouted 'Budmo!' at the top of his voice. The whole dining room suddenly came to a shocked silence, as Gorlinsky, with as much dignity as he knew how, sat down and patted his mouth with his serviette. Meanwhile, Maria not only enjoyed the spectacle, but felt the first real pang of envy. She had always been the sharer of his joy. But not yet the recipient of its fruit.

When Yevgeny had regained his composure, Gorlinsky outlined the immediate steps he had in mind to prepare him for his most auspicious debut.

'How exactly are you intending to promote him,' asked Maria.

'That is something I soon intend to take care of,' said Gorlinsky. 'But right now, I order you both to enjoy yourselves. Outside is a car, waiting to take you to a nightclub in Knightsbridge. It plays the kind of music that people of your age appreciate. The driver has orders to take you back home at whatever time you choose to leave. Meanwhile, just to ensure you enjoy the full facilities of the club, here is a small gift of my own. Please forgive the rather inelegant wrapping.'

Gorlinsky took from his pocket an envelope, and handed it to Yevgeny. Inside the envelope was a thousand pounds, and a birthday card on which Gorlinsky had written,

'The best years of your life are ahead of you'

Yevgeny suddenly became silent, and holding both the card and the money in his hand, began to weep unashamedly. Maria went over, put her arms around his shoulders, and began to comfort him.

'I don't deserve it,' said Yevgeny. 'I don't. I don't.'

'Believe me, in time you'll not only get used to it, you'll demand a lot more besides!' exclaimed Gorlinsky.

Aided and abetted by the news from Gorlinsky, and flush with funds to celebrate the occasion, Yevgeny ordered champagne, and for once entered into self abandoned party mood, that no power on earth could shake. He was simply re-energised, ecstatic, uninhibited and quite beautiful. A new man.

His concerts, of course, had been well received, and every appearance had produced some subtle ingredient into his performance. But a soloist appearing at the Festival Hall on London's South Bank, and the Proms, with one of the country's finest orchestras being broadcast live, was something that a half-beaten, confused, and what his father considered to be an insipid peasant, could never have imagined. It is one thing to be swept up in desire, but to be gifted with the very nature of your destiny, after lying outside the gates of destruction, was like the flight of a once-injured Phoenix, now ascending with the undimmed sanctification of a higher power.

Maria herself, had a double reason to celebrate. She felt that Yevgeny was her own protege. After all, she had believed in him in a way Gorlinsky had not, and as such, he was a tribute to her own success, in rescuing him from the jaws of inevitable self-destruction. His hallowed path, owing as much to do with her belief and character, as Gorlinsky's enviable ability to scheme.

As such, she entered into the celebration at the nightclub with the same infectious optimism.

In the early hours, they arrived home, elated and insatiably hungry. Maria cooked Yevgeny Pampushka, one of his favourite Ukrainian dishes, while he delighted her with a spirited rendition of a rousing folk song, before falling at her feet, and looking up at her through eyes half open and full of nostalgia. Whether it was due to the excess of alcohol, or the high octane assurance of being released from his normal inhibition, Yevgeny probed Maria about her feelings for Stephen Kline. Rather than respond to his question directly, she told him that Stephen wouldn't be renewing the lease on their apartment.

'That's okay,' said Yevgeny. 'Gorlinsky has found me a home with the family of a fellow musician.'

'Gorlinsky has thought of everything then, hasn't he!' said Maria.

All of a sudden, Yevgeny stood up and, drained of the optimism of a few minutes before, began to shake Maria violently.

'You can't love him. You can't!' he repeated.

'He wants me to share his life,' said Maria.

'Then you'll be trading yours for the dull lecherous insanity of domestic abuse.'

Yevgeny had reverted to his native tongue to convey the depth of his argument, and in doing so. conveyed a personal hurt and conviction, so far unexplored in both their personal and professional relationship. Previously, any opposition to Stephen Kline's provident patronage had remained unvoiced. Now, fuelled by alcohol, he gave life to a resentment he had evidently been harbouring for many months. In fact, it was the first time Yevgeny had so openly challenged the absolute sanctity of her private affairs.

'I do believe you are jealous,' said Maria.

'This is serious,' he said.

'I didn't say I would,' said Maria. 'Quite the opposite.'

Yevgeny, once again responding in Ukrainian, and taking flight, ascended the stairs to his bedroom. She followed close behind, and found him collapsed on his bed, part-exhausted, part-elated, part-emotionally overwrought.

'I don't understand,' said Maria.

Yevgeny, sat up and faced her directly.

'Don't you?' he asked. 'Don't you really!'

Maria lowered her eyes. Whatever it was she knew, she didn't want to know it. She hadn't expected this most potent issue to arise on such a night of celebration.

'It's just the drink talking,' she said.

Yevgeny looked at Maria intensely, and stripped off the carefully assembled armour that had so carefully disguised his thoughts.

'When I first met Gorlinsky, he interrogated me thoroughly,

especially about my private life. He wanted to know everything. Who, what, why, dates! I do mean everything. Then, he asked me if I had ever slept with a woman. I have a strange sex drive, I said. It's something I learned to use in exchange for a favour. I don't expect you to understand. 'Then why not let a women enjoy it too?' he asked. 'I don't know, I've never tried, I said."

'He asked because he was curious about us? Why our relationship was platonic?'

'I told him, I thought it was a line that two working professionals shouldn't cross. He agreed, but it has always troubled me!' said Yevgeny.

'Why?'

'Because it's one of the few experiences I've never tried.'

His mood was now serious, far removed from the bonhomie of their excursion to the club and the light-hearted, intoxicated post midnight nostalgic feast they shared.

Shorn of pretence, the fragile youth appeared once more, unconfident, unsure, unseasoned, a volunteer bathed in innocence.

Maria just smiled at him, and laughed unconvincingly, attempting to play the role of the big sister. But when he held out his arms to embrace her, she sat down on the bed, and began stroking his hair, until he became very relaxed. She then teasingly began stroking his lips and face very gently, until he closed his eyes. He looked like a young boy, slumbering on a summer lawn, yearning to taste his first youthful embrace, ready to be tutored in the sensory delight of a new intoxication. He briefly opened his eyes, and then closed them again, in order to signal a common agreement that neither of them need say anything further. Maria took his hand, and held it to her cheek. A few minutes later, his eyes opened wide, and they looked at each other with an intense acknowledgement of something that can only be communicated by instinct.

She then slid silently into the bed and lay beside him.

13.

STEPHEN ARRIVED PUNCTUALLY, and stepped inside the flat. It had now been de-populated of many of the items that had made the surroundings familiar from his previous visits. The kitchen was practically barren, and the student-like decoration of music and books had all but vanished, leaving only the inventory inherited at handover. The carefree and idyllic time in Suffolk now seemed like a distant memory, replaced by estrangement, following her subtle but decisive rejection. Maria greeted Stephen politely, like a departing tenant meeting a landlord on the day of departure. She gave him a guided tour, and told him that she and Yevgeny had left everything just as they had found it.

'Everything, that is, except you!' declared Stephen.

Maria informed Stephen that her plans were about to radically change, but didn't say why. He sensed that all was not well. She behaved cautiously, and handed him a letter from Yevgeny, who had already departed, thanking him for everything he had done, and promising to pay back every penny of support he had received.

Stephen displayed annoyance, and reminded her that it was she who was the catalyst that liberated Yevgeny, not him. Reacting like a man who had been deprived of a relationship, and now stung by her seeming indifference, he demanded an explanation, and reminded her of a future only he could provide.

Maria told him she had found alternative accommodation,

and had something to tell him that would very soon change his mind. She then asked him to sit down, and sat opposite with her eyes downcast.

'Well!' Stephen demanded. 'What is it?'

Maria paused, indecisive, and hardly able to speak, and then nervously whispered…

'I'm pregnant!'

At first, her voice was so quiet, the news didn't register. Stephen wasn't sure what he had heard, and asked her to repeat it. Then his spirits soared, as the implication of fatherhood bubbled-up inside him, like sulphur about to ignite. His mind doing somersaults, and his excitement mounting, as the longed-for family had at last arrived, despite the unexpected, surprising and strained circumstances of the announcement.

Stephen jumped up, hoisted Maria up from her seat and hugged her, overwhelmed and stuttering. He then slowly turned her face towards him, puzzled by her impassive and strange detachment. She turned her face away again, and soberly stared into the distance, as his mind made plans for the immediate period of her pregnancy, and how perfectly its timing suited the renewal of their future.

'It's the most perfect unplanned plan…!' Stephen enthusiastically announced… 'Except, this time, I have no intention of taking a back seat…'

Stephen's mind was racing, ready to take charge of the many organisational issues that would require his attention…

'Why aren't you excited?' he asked

'Call it self protection,' she said.

'It wasn't planned. But, so what!'

'So long as it's a baby. Is that it?' Maria questioned.

'So long as it's *ours*!' Stephen declared.

'Don't you mean yours?' Maria replied coldly.

'I understand. But it won't spoil any of your plans. In fact it will make them even better!'

'Ownership is very important to you, isn't it ?'

'Yes, when the cargo is so precious. You don't need me to tell you the value of something only a womb can produce. In fact, it's the most perfect way of repaying me you could possibly conceive!'

Stephen laughed out loud joyfully at his own joke, and kissed her on the cheek.

He then looked at her seriously, in order to comprehend her disquiet.

Maria avoided his eyes.

'You're worried. I can see that. But you shouldn't be.'

'Why. Would you accept the baby on any terms?'

'You mean there's something wrong with the baby?' he queried.

Maria remained silent.

'Or there's something you're not telling me? Whatever it is, I don't care!'

'Are you sure about that?'

'I have a perfect right to know.'

After a long pause, she answered,

'... It's Yevgeny's!'

The colour drained from Stephen's face, as he studied her expression for some explanation of the idiocy of the statement. As if she was playing some elaborate joke, before confirmation of his paternity. But she neither smiled nor changed her expression. Her eyes were not bright, but cloudy, and she looked away in a manner he had come to recognise as guilt.

'I don't believe you!' he said abruptly. 'Yevgeny is incapable of impregnating anyone, ...least of all you!'

His anger rising, he started shouting through a fog of incoherence, unable to absorb the consequence of what he was hearing, or comprehend the meaning of her words, His voice dry, emotionally distraught, and breaking, he searched her face for an admittance of deception, and declared her real aim was to deprive him of paternity, and demanding the proof of a DNA test.

'I've had a paternity test,' said Maria, 'and it confirms that

Yevgeny is the father!'

'That deception is worst than the last one, and you know it!'

Stephen again began shouting and declaring her a liar, as she explained, at length, how Gorlinsky had treated her and Yevgeny to dinner on his twenty first birthday, and used the occasion to announce Yevgeny's debut at the Proms. As a result they had both ended up at a club, and got very drunk.

'Yevgeny being drunk, I believe. Being drunk and capable. I don't.'

Stephen reacted in mocking disbelief, as Maria's words described their arrival home, the late night nostalgic supper, and the unlikely outcome that even she couldn't have foreseen.

'Do you mean to tell me that you have become pregnant from one drunken encounter?'

Stephen desperately hoped to hear the explanation of a victim, now confessing guilt. But instead, Maria lowered her eyes, and said defiantly,

'No. Not from just one!'

Within moments, Maria found herself pinned to the wall, with Stephen's hand gripping her tightly by the throat, leaving her fighting for breath. The coldness of his eyes, and the strength of his grip, taking her by surprise. In one brief moment, he could find no other expression than in the unbridled act of violence, as if nothing more mattered to him. In her struggle for survival, and unable to loosen his vice-like grip, she was on the point of collapse, until finally she had the presence of mind to place her hand under his chin, and pushing as hard as her remaining strength allowed, forced his head upwards, causing him to slowly release his grip and stumble back, as if he had been in a trance.

A sudden realisation came over his face. He looked dazed, and began examining his hands as if they were an unwilling accomplice, ashamed for losing control.

Now sorrowful, he retreated to the sofa, and sat with his head buried in his hands, weeping, repeating over and over,

'It's not true! Tell me it's not true!'

Maria's first instinct was to flee the house and recover. She had been violated, and totally unprepared for his uncharacteristic use of violence. But, she considered, he was just as equally unprepared for her announcement. The shock having driven him to the extremity of an emotional eruption he was ill-equipped to deal with, and one in which she herself was complicit.

Humiliated, he became in turn, remorseful, apologetic, and repentant. Attempting to come to terms with a situation that confounded him.

Maria explained she had never intended for it to happen, but Stephen was disconsolate. Like a child, he now kept repeating,

'Don't talk to me… please… don't talk to me.'

Her feelings, strangely enough, were now directed more towards his worrying state of mind, than the demonstration of his blazing anger. It was as if Stephen had reached a cliff-edge, and had no direction to go but down. It was the parting she most dreaded.

She stood quite still for some time, like a servant waiting for the right moment to interrupt the private agony of a soul who, for the present, no longer knew how to function. Then she sat next to him, and taking his hand, informed him,

'There is an answer. Yevgeny has agreed that you can claim paternity. No one but us will ever know!'

Stephen didn't respond for several minutes. Then, without lifting his head or looking up, declared,

'I will…'

Through tears, he dismissed the suggestion, as if breaking down every chapter and verse of a theory, in order to prove its impossibility. He wouldn't be adopting just her child, not even any child, but most wounding of all, Yevgeny's. Someone who could inherit the character and traits of not just unruly talent, but everything he considered vain, weak and self-destructive. Someone who could once again return to claim ownership of something precious that belonged to him.

'But, that is what you most enjoy, isn't it? The performances you give in private. Ones in which you have no emotional involvement. Just like a *whore*!'

Maria slapped Stephen hard across the face, but instead of retaliating in kind, he took her by the hand, and holding it to his cheek, declared he still loved her.

'I can't help it!' he declared. 'My jealousy won't allow me to compromise. I'm just not strong enough.'

There followed several moments of hesitancy, in which Maria felt she couldn't abandon his sad broken presence. Stephen was now crying, unashamedly. Not in the normal way of sadness, but a far deeper grief. Something that can only come from the core of deep regret and loss. Something beyond repair. Maria, instead of departing, therefore, sat close to him and waited. Waited for him to stop. But instead, he cried and cried. She had never heard a man cry like it before, and felt completely helpless. He refused to look at her, and after some time, she heard him taking short breaths, and then all of a sudden he raised his head, and addressed her in a sentence barely above a whisper…,

'You know…' he said quietly, 'it's just a foetus. Right now, that's all it is.'

Maria wasn't sure if she had heard him correctly. It was as if the momentous course of events that had just occurred meant nothing. What type of miserable human being could assert such a thing?, she asked herself. But Stephen delivered his argument with such calm, logical authority that, as horrendous as the idea sounded, offered a solution, that before she would not have remotely considered. He spoke almost as if he was addressing the issue with himself. His words delivered like small explosive parcels of self-doubt, concerning responsibility, sacrifice, lack of freedom, and opportunity…all the things that pregnancy represented in place of personal growth.

Worst of all, he claimed, it was a journey she would largely undertake alone.

'Can you see a child looking after a child?', he insisted, 'because that is what would happen. You would end up as a single mother of two.'

Maria didn't reply, but listened as Stephen spoke of the promise of a career and a future unburdened by circumstance. Single motherhood was avoidable.

Stephen proclaimed a solution existed, unenviable, but nonetheless one that offered time for her to experience the possibility of something she had been waiting all her life. She suddenly felt faint, and started to shake. Like delayed shock, all her energy suddenly began to dissipate. Then Stephen said,

'I forgive you. Do you hear me? I forgive you! That's something you understand isn't it? he insisted, 'Forgiveness.'

14.

STEPHEN PULLED INTO the car park of the private clinic, purposely selected for its discrete location, and reputation for professional care. For a few moments, they sat silently and said nothing. Their understanding was that Maria could change her mind. But instead, she sat staring ahead, and displayed no emotion. Stephen then placed his hand gently on her knee.

'What's the time?' asked Maria?'

'Ten past ten,' he said.

Alighting from the car, he then got out and walking to the passenger side, opened the door like a dutiful chauffeur. Maria remained motionless and said nothing.

'I can easily cancel the appointment,' he reassured her.

After several moments, Maria followed him into the entrance to the clinic. It was in appearance something in the order of a very upmarket surgery, with a reception area containing two leather Chesterfield sofas, a large coffee table, on which were scattered Country Life, Home and Garden and similar magazines, a water fountain, and a vending machine, with a selection of tea or coffee. After taking her name, the receptionist invited Maria and Stephen to take a seat and enquired, 'What would you like?' Stephen asked for coffee, but Maria shook her head. 'Shouldn't be very long,' the receptionist smiled, as if they had just popped in to order a takeaway. Presently, a doctor appeared. He was tall with a congenial air, and greeted Maria like an old friend. Shaking her warmly by the hand, he asked,

'How was the journey?'

Maria and Stephen followed him into his consulting room, where he formally introduced himself, and offered a brief explanation concerning the procedure…

'You'll likely get some stomach cramps and some bleeding, but the procedure is surprisingly simple. We use a suction method, which is normally over in five to ten minutes, and if you choose a general anaesthetic, I doubt if you'll remember anything. 'Does that sound okay?… ' he asked.

'Is it that simple?' asked Maria.

'Yes, it's that simple!' replied the doctor.

He asked if either she or Stephen had any further questions, and offered Maria the services of a counsellor, if she needed one. They were then ushered into a side room, to ensure they were completely certain of their willingness to proceed.

'It's your decision,' said Stephen. 'Of course, you could take a pill, if you wanted to, but this takes less than ten minutes, and then it's all over!'

Maria assured him that this was the one thing for which he wouldn't be blamed.

'Even though it was your choice,' she confirmed.

'After you're through here, I'm taking you home,' said Stephen. 'Then we'll put this behind us.'

'Pick me up at about ten tomorrow morning,' said Maria. 'I'll need some time on my own.'

Stephen embraced Maria tightly, and pressed his cheek into hers. But she displayed neither affection nor emotion. His own emotions were anyway coloured by his conviction that the course of action she was about to take was the only sensible option. It was after all, only a foetus, nothing more than the yolk of an egg, he had maintained. As yet, without form or personality, nor fully flesh.

'You're doing the right thing,' Stephen reassured her. 'Deep down, I think you know that.'

Maria said nothing, as Stephen withdrew, and headed in the

direction of the car park. A few minutes later, a nurse entered the room, and enquired whether she still wished to go ahead with the termination. It was one of those moments in which with a nod of the head Maria made a life-or-death decision.

'You know if you have any doubts, any doubts at all, you are perfectly free to reconsider!' she was told.

'It won't damage the possibility of having another child, will it?' Maria asked.

'At your age, highly unlikely.'

The procedure was as efficient and relatively painless as promised, and the consultant extremely gentle, and well practised in the clinical art of termination. The whole strategy, it seemed to Maria, being to divorce the physical practicality of extraction from the delayed shock of the termination. It had nothing so much to do with any complication arising from the procedure, as with the trauma of finality. She was assured she was perfectly healthy, and time was on her side. But the seed of life that was developing at the root of her womb, had now begun to have its own conversation with her conscience. The nascent promise of a life she would never know, or be fulfilled, whose character would never form, know sadness, joy, or the pain of loss. The child she will never hold in her arms, chase, or boast to be the better part of her nature.

She rested for several hours and was given a light lunch. She had her own private room, and midway through the afternoon, wandered into the lounge, where she was invited to have tea and some Victoria sponge.

Half a dozen other women were resting or otherwise walking around, some socialising, others silent. Several men were present, either husbands, or boyfriends, who came to reassure or comfort, perhaps relieved they didn't have another mouth to feed. She heard one women say 'three's enough!', confirming termination was the economic solution to a budget crisis, or relief from the emotional and domestic strain of hosting another life. She herself was now relieved of that responsibility. She could start again, without the burden of relying on either Stephen or Yevgeny. Various plans had not come to fruition. But the complication that would have dictated the course of her future had now been removed.

It was, in the simplicity of its execution, barbaric but necessary, if her future ambitions were to amount to anything.

At 4pm, she sent a message to Stephen, saying she was recovering perfectly well, packed her overnight bag and discharged herself.

Before the lease in Belsize Park had come to an end, and armed with the money she had saved from giving private piano lessons, she had rented in advance a room at a flat in Camden Town. Somewhere she could be both independent and anonymous. Most of all, …anonymous.

The flat was owned by a thirty-something civil servant, who had advertised for a 'similar professional'. Maria presented herself as a final year student at the Royal College, and offered to pay three months in advance. Meanwhile, Yevgeny had begun to settle into the home of a professional cellist and his wife. For, even though he could now afford a place of his own, Gorlinsky calculated what he needed was stability, and somewhere offering paternal guidance.

Maria's response to her dilemma had been to escape, knowing she would be trapped by the one, or force the other into an obligation for which he wasn't prepared. As a result, she wrote to Stephen a letter thanking him for all he had done, stating she needed time alone, away from any persuasive interruption, to contemplate the next phase of her life. Her communication contained many compliments concerning his generosity and care, but failed to offer the assurances he desperately felt he was owed. Including a return address.

Her life so far, she felt had been wasted. Everything she had sacrificed had amounted to nothing more than an empty gesture. She had even begun to doubt her own talent.

But, just when it seemed the green shoots of her future had all but evaporated, and the world was suffering a paralysis, courtesy of Covid and lockdown, Yevgeny informed her that Gorlinsky had commissioned a professional writer to undertake his biography, believing it was the ideal time!

'Since you cannot fulfil any concert engagements at present, due to the pandemic, we might as well use the time working on publicity!' Gorlinsky advised.

He was told the biographer had a shrewd eye for the youth market, and at the same time a highly tuned nose for the populist angle.

'The audience of the future is playing video games!' he said. 'I want them to identify with someone they can relate to.'

'Relate! How?'

'For people to try something new, first you have to design the package.'

Yevgeny reported to Maria that the writer lived in Hampstead, and worked from home. But he felt ill-equipped to deal with any searching questions and missing details of his time in captivity.

'You were vital to my rescue,' Yevgeny pleaded, 'and an important part of my recovery.'

'I'm trying to escape the past,' Maria explained.

'Then liberate mine too!' he ordered.

Judy Cavendish had made her name writing biographies of boy bands. She shrewdly calculated the bands popularity, fan base, and sales figures, then sought the co-operation of their agent to put together a publishing deal. What emerged amounted to a scrap book, full of memorabilia, behind the scene photos and 'exclusive' anecdotal padding, marketed as a 'must have' no self-respecting fan could resist. She was extremely good at networking, and pre-sold her concept so successfully, she was often invited onto radio and television programmes to comment on some indiscretion or controversy of the moment. She also had the knack of making her subjects far more interesting than they really were, and often spun some basic sporting skill or innocuous pastime into the realm of brilliant achievement or passion for danger, avoiding, of course, the less wholesome subjects of casual sex, drugs and any other character traits that violated the sanctity of fandom.

Gorlinsky invited her to write a biography of Yevgeny, to coincide with his plans to launch him internationally. He was to be promoted as coming from the wrong side of the tracks, and overcoming the odds by virtue of his talent. Appealing not only to classical enthusiasts, but the vast untapped market of youth. Like many teenagers, he had experimented with drugs, and his life had lost its purpose, but, with the right guidance, had triumphed against adversity.

Gorlinsky didn't want Yevgeny's drug use overstated, but used artfully to prove he had his pulse on the prevalent counter-culture. A classical musician who was also '*cool*'.

Drugs, he considered, may not be uncommon in the jazz fraternity, but as far as the general public was concerned, almost unknown in the world of classical music. Yevgeny's story contained a significant message, and it was this that Gorlinsky ordered Judy Cavendish to exploit, using her contacts in the media, and suggesting coverage in the popular press, ahead of his Proms debut.

In this regard, both Gorlinsky and Cavendish sang from the same song sheet. Since both knew how to get a premium bang from a promotional buck.

Following their discussions, Judy Cavendish arranged for a series of interviews with Yevgeny at her home in Hampstead. Gorlinsky wanted a candid portrait, but not too intrusive.

The message was important, but it mustn't obscure the real objective.

'Make him interesting,' said Gorlinsky. 'Not Cobain. More like Bowie.'

The first thing she noted was how photogenic he was. His current publicity portraits were aimed to decorate the hallowed bastions of classical culture. What she wanted was to set light to the dress code, and allow him to appear fashionable, in order to appeal to the prevailing youth culture, while playing up the more accessible features of the classical repertoire.

His addiction and renaissance was a good combination she knew full well how to present. Essentially, a piano-playing version of a rock guitarist. The trouble was, Yevgeny had no following, and, as she was soon to discover, was far more complex and introverted than any boy band. In addition, his English was poor, and Judy Cavendish knew next to nothing about Ukrainian culture!

'Not that it matters,' she told Yevgeny. 'The public have no interest in farming or the politics of an ex-Soviet state.'

Of course, both were pertinent in the DNA of a prodigy. But there were other things she didn't understand. Mainly, the personality of Yevgeny himself. And it was here she was at a loss to transfer the subject to the page. For although Yevgeny was self-evidently gifted, he didn't understand many of the questions she asked, and very quickly began to withdraw into himself.

By the time of the second interview, she had undertaken more basic research into the history of Ukraine, and its illustrious roll-call of prominent musicians, but found it impossible to penetrate the private and precocious inner world of her subject.

Yevgeny himself was bewildered, and insisted Maria accompany him to all the remaining sessions. When they met, Judy Cavendish told Maria she was not an expert on classical music, and would instead concentrate on Yevgeny's poster appeal, with the romanticism of his repertoire thrown in for good measure.

'Aren't you growing tired of producing all those non-alcoholic cocktails?' Maria replied. 'For once, why not take the chance on something far more intoxicating!'

Judy Cavendish wasn't used to opposition. Especially from a student. She was known for being a media hustler, chosen by Gorlinsky because she was the old school in a new wrapping.

A postgraduate, with a background in public relations, and possessing the scruples of a fly-tipper.

However, she sat intrigued, as Maria related the details of Yevgeny's childhood, his relationship with his father, and his natural and miraculous gift for music. She then gave a detailed account of their arrival in London, his attempt to cover up addiction, and the events leading to their descent into the underworld of people-trafficking, and the painful journey to recovery.

In all, Maria revealed Yevgeny to be far more intense and enigmatic than the prodigy Judy Cavendish was initially asked to publicise. Therefore, when she reported back to Gorlinsky, she told him the story of his protege went far beyond the scope of her original assignment.

'What the story suggests is not so much a publicity drive, as a suitable subject for film noire,' she told him.

Gorlinsky disapproved of Maria's involvement, but Judy Cavendish found Maria's account far more challenging and controversial than anything she had so far attempted. She was also shrewd enough to know that the story Maria urged her to tell could take her career in a completely new and rewarding direction.

A few days later, Judy Cavendish contacted Maria, and told her she felt as though she had been ambushed…

'I've told Gorlinsky that if you insist on taking this story in a darker direction, it comes with more scrutiny, extra work and additional risk. Just like the ingredients of a meal, the more you add, the more there is to chew on. Could you both face that kind of exposure? Because publicity is like cannibalism. When it's hungry, it eats its own!'

A few days later, Judy Cavendish told Gorlinsky she had decided to enlarge the scope of the book, and that it now would become her own project. The story Judy Cavendish now prepared to tell, related to a different kind of landscape, other than the superficial chic of brief fame. One complicated by the dynamic of others. Not just the enslavement of narcotics, but the greed and depravity of people trafficking, and the corruption that financed crime, and collaborated in the systematic destruction of innocent lives. Like a mutating virus at the heart of society, in which there were no easy answers, the complexity of the narrative was made authentic by an eye-witness account

In this respect, Maria had proved invaluable by not only giving her an insight into the social and political history of Ukraine, but by being able to recall the events she witnessed in detail. Most of all, for getting inside the head of Yevgeny himself.

'I don't know if you realise it, but you'll likely end up the heroine!' Judy exclaimed.

Yevgeny himself, was far less happy about the exposure the book could arouse.

'Why should I explain my life to anyone else!' he complained. 'Why would anyone want to know?'

Yevgeny's debut was, in any case, some way off, and newspaper serialisation was thought to be a far more sensible pre-publication route. As far as Maria was concerned, her part could, over time, be profitably developed. Right now, they could only wait, as the pandemic forced Yevgeny to spent time with his new found 'family', while Maria returned to the flat she shared with the isolated civil servant.

It was over three months before they heard again from Judy Cavendish, who reported that she had completed the first draft of the book. Maria couldn't wait to read what had eventually ended up on the page, and wasn't disappointed. If anything, Judy Cavendish had made the story even more exciting. She had given more than a colourful description of Maria's account, but somehow managed to add some unexpected ingredients of her own. Inventing characteristics, and painting in much more of the background to both concert performance and the repulsive trade in people trafficking. In this she gave a potted history, criminal cases, and facts and figures from organisations involved in its abolishment, and had also done her homework on the history of Ukraine and the Soviet Union. She also included a vivid account of Kyiv and Odesa, referring to their rich legacy of world famous musicians, especially pianists, and even included an account of the importance of farming in the community where Yevgeny was born. In short, she had framed the dramatic events of Yevgeny's life in a style that read both part-history and part-fiction. And it worked. What is more, from Maria's point of view, she emerged not only as Yevgeny's contemporary and saviour, but as a pianist in her own right!

'What are you going to call it?' Maria asked.

'I'm thinking of calling it 'Obsession',' replied Judy Cavendish.

A week later, Maria rang Gorlinsky and asked him if he had read the first draft of the book. He suggested they meet at his office, and sat behind the large polished monument of his desk, as if subpoenaed to listen to unwelcome testimony.

'I know the book wasn't the one you had originally commissioned,' said Maria, 'but at least, I hope you think it's worthy.'

'I noticed you managed to highjack a very generous word count.' he commented drily.

'Then you must realise that people will be curious about me. They will know me as a pianist that has accompanied Yevgeny to various venues and shared a platform with him. When the book is published, it could create a demand to hear me play.'

'It's also the kind of book I wouldn't authorise. The real problem is the narrative drive of your harrowing melodrama asks more questions than it answers, and Yevgeny will be seen as weak and easily manipulated, none of which will appeal to the youth market. However, what the book so admirably demonstrates is the infallible depth of your nerve. Something, so abundantly reflected in your playing.'

Maria had come armed for criticism. And Gorlinsky didn't disappoint.

'True. The book isn't the cosy pin-up endorsement you wanted,' she replied, 'but I can play, you know I can. If you don't use me, then somebody else will!'

Gorlinsky sat quietly, looking deep in thought. The one thing Maria knew about him was the devastating attraction of the box office, and what lengths he would go to, in order to capitalise on an idea that attracted the public's imagination. Finally, he said,

'Okay, but don't think I am going to pay you a fortune. Because for now, I consider you just another mouth to feed. And I'm not giving you anything more than a six month contract, nor guaranteeing any other billing than as a 'guest artist'. And only then, if the book proves a success!'

Gorlinsky escorted her to the door, and before she departed warned,

'You know, publicity is a double edged sword. It cuts both ways!'

Maria did not inform Yevgeny of her triumph immediately, but waited until conditions allowed them to meet for coffee, on a day they were both free. She hadn't seen him since their last meeting with Judy Cavendish, and the pandemic had severely curtailed social interaction. When they met, she was immediately struck by his sense of aloofness and detachment.

For once, she felt intimidated in his company. He was infallibly polite, and businesslike, but instead of old friends, it felt as if they were familiar strangers with a shared history. She began by referring to the contents of the book in the broadest terms, noting the background work Judy Cavendish had done on the social and political reforms since Perestroika, and the dangers posed, following Russia's annexation of Crimea.

At first, Yevgeny avoided any reference to the book itself, preferring instead to listen, as Maria referred to her meeting with Gorlinsky, and his offer of a provisional contract. Yevgeny then informed her that Gorlinsky had already told him about the meeting, and praised her ingenuity,

'From your point of view, it has worked out very well!' he said.

'What about the book?' Maria asked

'Gorlinsky wanted a cautionary tale about how I overcame

drug dependency, by finding meaning in music. With your involvement, the meaning of music was replaced by my dependency on you to save me.'

Maria reminded him they had a duty to 'Scrawn', and thousands of others, to expose the subversive undercurrent of drugs and human-trafficking.

'It also makes a direct connection between crack addiction and prostitution.'

'Is that a problem?' said Maria.

'For a long time, casual pick-ups allowed me to pay for my supply. After I was kidnapped, they enjoyed watching me being raped for a tiny rock they named my 'silver reward'. It wouldn't take very long for an experienced journalist to discover a catalogue of even more lurid stories.'

Maria was totally unprepared for Yevgeny's confession, and the way he viewed the book as an invasion of his privacy, rather than a celebration of his survival.

'What do you suggest? We clean you up, in order that people can listen to Rachmaninoff played by someone never willingly penetrated?' she asked. 'The point of the book is about how one filthy trade corrupts many.'

'You're quite right. The book is full of accuracy! The kind that will grieve my mother, and convince my father he was right!'

The memory of his humiliation made Yevgeny pause, and there was a silence between them. He then addressed Maria, almost as if by Gorlinsky himself.

'Believe me, no one will ever disagree what a heroine you are. The book makes that perfectly clear. In fact, I owe you everything, and that's my problem. I can never now escape. It will always be there in black and white, to follow me around. Everywhere I go, people will ask about you, and I will have no choice than to acknowledge your talent, guts and loyalty. You will always be sitting next to me on the piano stool, or accompanying me at a public appearance. Since I already have enough ghosts from my past pursuing me, I have decided from now on, our friendship is to be strictly professional. We will rehearse together, share a platform with each other, and I will endeavour to co-operate in any public appearance that demands our attendance. But there, it ends. Our relationship will no longer contain any personal involvement, and be according to the terms of your contract with Gorlinsky. As you're aware, he's a keen advocate of keeping our private life separate. I hope you agree. It's the most sensible way for us to maintain a working relationship.'

'You talk as if it was the end of our friendship,' said Maria.

Yevgeny, stood up, took some money from his wallet, and placed it on the table.

'By the way, it was me who suggested that on publication of the book, you should be given a contract. But as a soloist, not merely as a 'guest artiste'. It appears your brinkmanship with Gorlinsky was a waste of time. As usual, he short-changed you!'

Yevgeny told Maria he would always be in her debt, but left her in no doubt he felt betrayed.

His departure, however, revealed something more profound. That the two parts of her couldn't be reconciled by a cunning strategy. What he had underlined was something far more revealing than the temporary hurdle of miscommunication. Something for her, far more devastating: abandonment.

After a couple of days, Maria made an appointment with Judy Cavendish, and told her she wanted all references of her involvement in Yevgeny's life deleted. This revelation came as a shock, since it was Maria who had made such a convincing case for authenticity.

'This sometimes happens,' said Judy Cavendish, 'They call it 'first draft' nerves.'

'It's a joint decision,' said Maria. 'I suggest you go back to the original idea, and promote Yevgeny for his performance skills, rather than his talent with a needle.'

It wasn't unusual for people to get cold feet, but for something that meant so much a short time ago, Judy Cavendish wasn't convinced by Maria's change of mind. She also enquired about the people she had described as victims, and her compelling argument for truth. In reply, Maria told her that Yevgeny realised his life in print would keep reminding him and others of all the things he was desperately trying to escape, and that it was something he wanted to bury, not keep alive.

'What you're really telling me is that Yevgeny wants me to abandon the book?'

'If you insist on going ahead, then he won't co-operate. Nor will I.' confirmed Maria

'In that case, I'll change the names, and turn your cautionary tale into a novel. Then, if Yevgeny does happen to make a name for himself, people can make up their own minds.'

'You mean you won't scrap the project?'

'You mean disown my own work? I don't think so.'

Judy Cavendish had no intention of abandoning the project, and knew perfectly well how to re-package the salutary tale as fiction. Sacrificing her monumental challenge to the level of a pin-up who recovered from a drug habit was no longer an option. She had no qualms whether a story was true or untrue. It simply presented an opportunity for her to take her career in a different direction. If nothing else, she could now lay claim to being a serious novelist, and if Yevgeny did gain some recognition, it wouldn't do the book any harm either.

Once again, the narrow door of opportunity for Maria had been slammed shut.

She now spent her time listening as well as playing. Searching for the subtle but defining effort that led to the enlightened reading of the gifted, rather than the worthy workmanship of the merely talented. Both familiar and modern works that could elevate her above the graduates, who year upon year poured out of the colleges, with diplomas, degrees and awards, all purposed to thrust them towards the hall of fame, to which very few were admitted.

'Why? Why? Why? And why not?' she once screamed at Popov, in frustration.

'I don't know!' he exclaimed. 'If you are completely obsessed and nuts, the world is your oyster. But forget an ordinary life. That's why it's for so few, especially a woman.'

His sentiments echoed what Gorlinsky had once confided to Yevgeny, who told him that whatever direction a woman's career takes, it's almost always interrupted by the urge to have children.

'After that, the instrument of her affection are the people who call her 'mummy!'

Maria had been pregnant, and rejected the pleasure. Her objectivity began to desert her, and she recalled the words of Judy Cavendish when she first discussed the success, or otherwise, of the book.

'Basically, there are two headlines', she was told, ' *'The tragedy and triumph of sensational child prodigy'* or *'The promenaders enjoyed good weather'.*'

'Right now, we have the transport. All we're waiting for is the driver to pass his test.'

Maria's own headline now took up space in her own feeling of self worth…*'Unknown Ukrainian pianist… remains unknown! Life on earth continues!'*

Although it hardly mattered. The ultimate prize had been taken away. Yevgeny had believed in her more than she believed in herself. Popov's words resonated in her head more than ever.

'What is it that makes life worth living? Let me listen to you play, and you'll tell me!'

Up to now, she thought she knew. But warning bells had started to ring. She observed her thirty-something-year-old flatmate turn forty, and began looking at the years beyond. So far, she had only seen her career, nothing else had mattered. But the one thing she had never contemplated was the loss of Yevgeny's friendship. The effect of his rejection had left her feeling isolated and disillusioned. The doubts in her mind advanced, and had begun to undermine belief in her own talent. More and more, she began to miss the protection of the cavalry that came to her rescue.

One night, with only the company of distant laughter, she called Stephen.

'I know you have a thousand questions,' she said nervously.

There was a long silence at the other end, before Maria realised Stephen was crying. When he did speak, he didn't ask any awkward questions, and insisted he would not seek an explanation concerning her absence.

'None of it matters,' he said.

When they did meet, he looked apprehensive. But almost immediately told her that he thought the termination of the baby had been a mistake.

'I was wrong,' he confessed.

Rather than recrimination, he was instead filled with remorse for encouraging her to go through with it. Especially the emotional consequences.

The more Stephen confessed guilt in the part he played, the more it penetrated the thin and delicate veil of her own complicity. Unable to construct an explanation that could restore simplicity to so painful a subject, nor a true understanding of its psychological imposition. He insisted there was no point in reviewing a past that could not be re-invented,

'I've changed. From now on, you'll see a new Stephen Kline. I promise!'

Maria longed for peace and restoration. A place to withdraw and reassess. To be delivered from the emotional pull of circumstances she could no longer navigate. Once the moon was hers for the taking, but now looked an immoveable object from which no one smiled.

Stephen assured her he was a changed man, and together they could put the past behind them.

'A new beginning *is* possible,' said Stephen. 'All it takes is faith in the future.'

15

When Maria entered Stephen's home, it felt like going back in time. The mark of his mother shone from the rugs on the floor to the lampshades on the ceiling. The Bechstein stood grandly in the corner of his through-lounge, on which the silver-framed reflection of his journey from baby to bachelor was on display. A handstand on the beach, official school photos, catching a pike from a lake, having a picnic, at the wheel of a mini-Clubman, and his graduation. Most included the presence of his mother. Only one displaying any evidence of his father. His mother's marriage photo. It was in black and white, and she looked slim and touchingly fragile. Stephen had inherited her bone structure, and mirrored some of her physical characteristics, especially around the eyes. In the photo, his father didn't smile, and appeared haughty, tall, but nonetheless quite handsome. The photos of his mother in later life, holding a puppy, somehow reflected the enduring bravery of a solitary life. Yet somehow, the very Englishness of its familiarity was re-assuring.

Each and every incidental decoration, and the space either side of it, a reminder that Stephen needed its unchanging permanence as an anchor that harnessed his identity to a time and place he felt secure. There were no photos of Helen, now relegated to a footnote of history. Although interestingly, Stephen testified it was Helen who had updated the kitchen. A reminder of the demarcation her predecessor enjoyed. Now Stephen invited

Maria to do the same thing.

'Although, don't go overboard!' he said playfully, as though his mother was still the owner. It was something she didn't yet feel either entitled nor qualified to do.

'Let the house grow on me first,' she told Stephen.

The house itself was a handsome Edwardian detached property, set back from the road behind high railings, with an impressive drive, marked by both an 'In' and 'Out' entrance.

It occupied a prime position opposite Chorleywood Common. Stephen's father had bought the house after the acquisition of his most successful enterprise, a pharmacy in Edgware. Stephen remarked his fathers success had bought them no pleasure at all. But his mother had always loved the house.

In Maria's eyes, it wasn't so much Stephen's home, as a shrine to her memory.

It both captivated and captured. Its five-bedroomed extravagance never realising its original intention of family growth. It would now, Stephen promised, be filled with new life, melody, and the most important ingredient of all... love!

Her first objective was to please him, and allow herself a period of tranquillity. A period in which to absorb the fundamental shift in her life and ambition.

At present, she had no idea where her future belonged, and sought some much-needed rest. In this regard, she insisted on occupying a room at the back of the house to give her some privacy. Stephen acknowledged the dramatic sequence of events that had so dominated the core of her emotions, and begged her to find peace in the unoriginal, staid and undervalued purpose of routine.

A life with no surprises Maria found surprisingly satisfying. It avoided complication, and produced an inner security that the world around her might change, but she could remain permanently rooted. In addition, she found she enjoyed becoming a homebody, keeping the house looking clean and well presented, experimenting with new dishes, learning the art of gardening, and enjoying long walks with Stephen. In fact, for a while she almost felt English. The one small detail that lay buried at the heart of this domestic utopia was Maria's insistence that she wasn't yet ready to resume a physical relationship. It would, she insisted, be an additional burden for which she was not yet prepared.

Stephen had learned patience. It had a discipline Stephen hoped Maria would eventually recognise as commitment. But whenever he drew closer or unthinkingly traduced the line between affection and what she considered physical trespass, it produced a response he immediately came to recognise. She explained it as 'being dry', intimating that the condition was a physical manifestation of her earlier trauma. As far as Stephen was concerned, it was psychological. But in this, as in all other things that had characterised their relationship, he felt he could provide the answer.

Maria had began teaching again, and had built up a small but loyal following. Mostly local schoolchildren whose parents were keen for their children to be taught the 'Russian' method. Maria, of course, made no such distinction, yet didn't discourage the attraction of being thought someone capable of imparting 'specialised' knowledge. She told herself to be thankful. After all, Stephen's words made sense. Hadn't she always been chasing a dream? And wasn't she always going to end up as a teacher?

Slowly, her old life and ambition began to recede, and the conformity she once derided had offered itself up like a warm blanket, to protect her from the cold. Stephen preached that freedom was to be found, by taking control of the situations that governed a person's life. The safe, sensible and sober reasoning of protection against life's surprises. Although she felt Stephen had been at his best when forced from under the blanket of his own rigid submission, and had risen above his own subversive desires. She also felt relieved of the burden to believe she had been gifted enough to perform in the most prestigious arenas of music excellence. Her legacy would be she once came close to it.

Yevgeny was never very far from her mind, though, and following her meeting with Judy Cavendish, she had written him a tearful goodbye, telling him she was starting a new life. Yevgeny's response was to fail to respond. Ironically, she was grateful there had been no contact. He would be the first person to penetrate the true state of her happiness. But, she knew, no bond forged from a history so perverse could be broken completely.

By now, the restrictions that had blighted so many lives had been lifted, and emerging from the pandemic, she realised that the ambition and energy of her past had now been replaced by a genteel indolence that demanded little. As a result, she began to search for new interests, and accept her life must take a new direction. As well as starting to teach again, and to please, Stephen, she had avoided reminiscing about the hope she once cherished. She even told herself that ambition was about vanity, and that her real life was the one she was living now. In fact, she considered she had successfully retreated from her past.

One day, she received a message from Yevgeny, asking her to have lunch with him.

Their last meeting had left a bitter memory, and her first response was to turn the invitation down flat.

'I'm busy teaching, all next week,' she replied.

'Then unteach!' he demanded.

Invitations of this sort usually had the effect of making her do the opposite. But Yevgeny's was different. She was too intrigued to refuse. Like a current she was too inexperienced to avoid.

'I'm meeting an old friend from the college. Do you mind?' she asked Stephen.

'Is there any reason I should?' he replied…

Maria hadn't seen Yevgeny since their brief acrimonious meeting the year before, and was almost bursting at the seams to discover his latest news. When they met, they both agreed that Judy Cavendish's decision to use her biographic skill for the purpose of a work of fiction, was, in the end, the most sensible compromise.

'Just as well,' said Yevgeny. 'Living down to peoples expectations is just as hard as living up to them!'

Maria excitedly gave an account of her new life, the reward of teaching, and of her contentment. Yevgeny listened attentively, then took her hand, and carefully studied Maria's face.

'Are you trying to tell me that you're happy? Or is the question too delicate?' he probed.

'It depends on how deep you want to explore. I killed my own child, and began a new life with Stephen. How delicate do you prefer your news?'

'It was all my fault. If it wasn't for me, none of it would have happened.'

'Don't worry. It was all very civilised, just like all the other decisions I've had to make.'

'Except you didn't learn from it!'

'You asked if I was happy. On the satisfaction scale, happiness is froth, and contentment the real prize. On that basis, I'm content.'

'According to Popov, happiness is a mysterious ingredient between two slices of pain.' Yevgeny replied.

'Was Popov ever happy?' Maria asked.

'He is now,' announced Yevgeny. 'I have in my pocket a ticket for my Prom debut. And you are to be my guest of honour!' he declared.

Yevgeny bowed to Maria, and producing an envelope from his pocket, presented it to her, as if she was royalty.

'What are you playing?' she asked.

'The Rach two.'

'Oh Yev, I am so happy. Do you remember how proud Popov was of you? He cried like you were a son, when you left the academy. Like he would never see you again.'

'Promise me you'll come?' pleaded Yevgeny.

Maria touched his hand, and examined his fingers one by one.

'Funny, everyone has fingers, but only yours can make me

cry. We are such strange creatures. Imagine you were trying to describe yourself to a Martian. What would you say? 'Well, Mr Martian. I spend my life plunging my fingers down on pieces of plastic and ivory attached to a strange and elaborate mechanism that strikes strings inside a big wooden box.' 'What's clever about that, Earthling?' asks the Martian.'

'Ah,' says Professor Yevgeny. 'I manage to strike the strings in such an exquisite combination. It creates a magic no one can explain... Least of all me!'

When she arrived home, she waited a few days, and then told Stephen she had received an invitation to join Gorlinsky's party on the night of Yevgeny's Proms debut.

Stephen's demeanour suddenly changed, and he withdrew into himself, and went for a walk on the common. It was something he did whenever he felt challenged, or wanted to think. The meeting with Yevgeny had produced in her a new found restlessness. The truth was she could clearly identify everyone's future except her own. She knew that if Yevgeny kept his nerve, he was on course to achieve a breakthrough. She also knew it was only a matter of time before she would have to accept, or reject, Stephen's offer of marriage.

She considered the culmination of all the passive sins that had led to her own loss of direction, and sought Stephen's assurance. Her instability, he insisted, was entirely the result of her disappointment in believing she had been denied a career as a soloist. But she wasn't. She had taken part in many local concerts, and proved to be an excellent teacher, he reassured. Above all, she had at last achieved both peace and security.

'Security isn't a direction. It's merely somewhere to park,' she replied.

This question repeatedly occurred to her as the day of Yevgeny's debut approached. She shared these thoughts with Stephen, and he told her that after all the emotional upheaval she had suffered, it was a good place to admire the scenery.

'You've gone from a terminal condition to recovery. Part of the healing process is to accept change. You may not think our life together is the answer. But in time, you'll see I was right. We don't get the past back. That's the pact we're obliged to make with the present. Trust me. I'm an educator. The only thing that we get to influence is the future!'

When the day came to attend the Prom performance, Maria made a particular point of not looking excited.

'What time will you be home?' asked Stephen.

'I'm not sure what Gorlinsky has planned,' she answered. 'He mentioned something about a reception!'

Stephen drove her to the station, but made no reference to the performance. Instead, he observed how appealing she looked.

'Are you sure you're not the one participating?' he asked.

Maria wondered if he could sense the intensity of her expectation. To be present at such an auspicious occasion, was as much a triumph for her, as it would be for Yevgeny.

As she walked into the station, she felt Stephen's eyes following the eagerness of her steps. Smiling, she turned and waved him goodbye.

'Don't be late home!' Stephen shouted, as she disappeared into the entrance.

His words were delivered like a pernicious fingerprint around her throat. Attempting to pull her back from the very thing that made her pulse and senses race.

When she reached the Albert Hall, she was directed to a box in the Grand Circle. It gave each spectator an enviable view of the stage, and Gorlinsky sat centre-front, like an ambassador.

'Is this your first time?' he asked, when she joined his party.

'Yes,' said Maria. 'How's Yevgeny?'

'He is what I would call nervously excited.'

'Not beating his brains out?'

'All artistes of any measure beat their brains out. Hopefully, he will leave his guts on the stage. And they will love him.'

'Is that what you like?'

'Of course. The Albert Hall is a boxing ring with musical accompaniment!'

Maria was introduced to the others sharing the box, as a friend of Yevgeny's, who studied with him in Odesa, rather than a pianist in her own right. As usual, Gorlinsky was subtly adept at telling her something publicly, without the need to address the matter privately. But apart from this slight, Maria was thrilled by the atmosphere in the Hall. The high domed ceiling, and the arena filled with promenaders, was something she had never experienced before. It was not just full of the usual middle-aged, middle-class aesthetes, but included young people of Yevgeny's age, all crowded together laughing, jostling, chatting, sharing stories, and on the evidence right in front of her, in high spirits. She wanted to push her way to the front and stand pressed up against the stage, looking up, and willing Yevgeny on. To be near enough for him to hear her shout and clap, and go mad, and cheer.

The evening started with the overture from Tannhäuser, and continued with some Berlioz, before the interval. In the second half there were only two items. The Serenade for Strings and Rachmaninoff. By the time of Yevgeny's arrival on stage, the air was electric with excitement. There had been some pre-publicity, but no one really knew who Yevgeny was. It was. no doubt. prudent of Gorlinsky to let him get some recognition, before the planned assault on the public. If nothing else, both Gorlinsky and Yevgeny knew this was the 'big one'. If he fluffed his lines on the stage of the Royal Albert Hall, and the millions of radio and televisions viewers, then the critics would no doubt carp about any pre-publicity stunt. But if he triumphed here, then the stage would be set for the slight, blond, publicity-shy youth to land on a star, and wink at the moon. She knew what he had to do. She had seen it many times. He would go deep into himself. No one could talk to him. He would fight all his inner demons, and make them suffer. He would tame them, and make them dance and sing, and bow and beg, and scream and laugh, and shiver. There would be no surrender. He would show them. All of them. Often he would shout 'Budmo!' before he went on stage, to give himself the courage to face the audience. It was for Yevgeny a love-hate relationship, as much about defiance and overcoming his private introverted torment, as it was about performing. That is why he liked the challenge of the more complex and intricate compositions. He wasn't figuring out the composer, he was figuring out himself. That is what Popov had discovered hiding in the shadows, and knew if he could present Yevgeny with the ultimate challenge, then he would come back to face it again and again, like a chess player who is obsessed by the challenge of the complexity. Yevgeny saw himself as a gladiator arriving at the arena, to overcome the possibility of defeat. Tonight, especially.

When Yevgeny stepped onto the stage, he could hardly look at the audience. In fact he didn't look up at all. It wasn't what he was used to. The flamboyant promenaders shouted and screamed, and the conductor on the podium attempted to calm them. There were whistles, and a few hurrahs, and then someone shouted 'Bravo', and some laughed.

Then suddenly, there was a hush. The opening chords played from pianissimo to fortissimo, immediately sending the entire hall into a conspiracy to listen, before the strings emerged and engaged with the piano. He opened with a brilliant cadenza, introducing us to the irresistible theme that leads to a lilting melodic conversation. Like a coiled snake, his playing came and bit right into the marrow of the audience, demanding a response to their feelings, unblocking them, and making them rejoice, as he led them through peaks and valleys, and dancing icicles, that sped up and down our spine, and took them to lavish hot springs, and luxurious meadows of rich texture, that sparkled and danced, and punched and kicked, as they bit deeper and deeper into our psyche, before delivering a great fiery exaltation of melody, that stretched out into the deepest recesses of the audience, conquering all in its wake, charging without fear or hesitation, to the concerto's victorious finale that loudly and clearly declared… 'Victory!' … Once again, Yevgeny had slain his demons.

The audience reacted like an explosive force, fracturing the air with clapping and screaming, and throwing streamers onto the stage, and even some flowers. Yevgeny, finally looked out into the audience, surprised, nervously, unassumingly, and almost apologetically. He disappeared down into the tunnel at the rear, and then was coaxed back by the conductor, who, along with the orchestra, stood and gave their approval. The conductor encouraged Yevgeny to stand right at the front, but he quickly withdrew, as if the audience would mount the stage at any moment. Maria, along with Gorlinsky and his party, stood and applauded as Yevgeny disappeared, and was brought back five more times, to receive yet more applause.

Eventually, the noise died down, and all that was left was the excited talk of the departing audience, musically satisfied, refreshed and uplifted. Maria clearly detected a buzz in the Hall. From where she sat, Yevgeny looked like a little boy when he walked on stage. Almost as if he were lost, and afraid to acknowledge anyone in the vast confines of the hall. But when he played, it was as though he was playing for each individual personally, willing them into his musical ideas and purpose. For although the concerto was well known, Yevgeny had delivered a performance of such bold and sensitive insight, Maria was convinced, many had now only heard it for the first time.

Maria asked Gorlinsky if he was pleased.

'He delivered,' replied Gorlinsky. 'That's all that matters!'

He spoke as though Yevgeny had produced a knockout punch in the tenth round of a prize fight. Gorlinsky's assistant had bought a hamper, and he and the other guests had devoured a dozen sandwiches and two bottles of champagne, during the interval, as if they were taking part in a musical picnic.

'Are we going back stage?' Maria asked.

'No, to the Dorchester,' said Gorlinsky. 'Yevgeny will join

us there.'

Gorlinsky had hired a private room. When his party arrived, there were already about a dozen or more people in the room. A buffet had been prepared on a long table, consisting of fresh salmon, turkey breast, oysters, and exotic fruit, together with wafer-thin sandwiches, pastries and cakes and nibbles of every possible description. All the while, the fluted glasses of guests were constantly being replenished from bottles of champagne that lay around chilling in ice buckets throughout the room. On a separate table, at one end of the room, was a large chocolate cake in the shape of a grand piano, with the inscription '*Maestro*' in bold white lettering across the top.

An hour later, Yevgeny arrived, looking lost, and ignoring Gorlinsky, immediately approached Maria.

'Was alright?' he asked, as if he were a child contestant in a piano competition on the outskirts of Lviv.

'Did you not hear the audience?' exclaimed Maria.

'No. Only my mistakes,' said Yevgeny.

Maria felt Yevgeny's isolation, and his battle with a disappointment few would understand. Gorlinsky took Yevgeny to one side, and they had a discussion. Gorlinsky did most of the talking, whilst Yevgeny studiously listened with the same serious intent an athlete would listen to a coach, following a major competition. Neither Gorlinsky nor Yevgeny smiled during this exchange, and before Maria knew what was happening, the head waiter tapped on an empty champagne glass, and announced those assembled to prepare for a toast.

Gorlinsky gave a speech of breathtaking superlatives in favour of the performance Yevgeny had executed, and of his undoubted prospects as one of the foremost pianists of his generation.

He proposed a toast, and invited Yevgeny to cut the cake made in his honour. Several journalists, and other industry professionals, then took it in turns to talk to him. Yevgeny looked bewildered, and Maria felt an instinctive urge to rescue him. Although his English had greatly improved, she felt he was unlikely to cope with any complex questions, especially about his background. In the end, he signalled for Maria to join him, and she became his de-facto spokesperson, helping him carefully guide the questions into uncontroversial areas of performance.

Afterwards, Gorlinsky thanked her for her assistance. She said she thought it was the right decision to make Yevgeny less controversial, and his talent more appealing.

'It isn't the controversy that's important, Ms Novotna,' said Gorlinsky, 'it's how you control the information.'

He then smiled faintly, and did something even more unusual for him. He winked at her.

At midnight, people began to drift away, and Maria told Yevgeny she had to leave.

'Stay here,' said Yevgeny.

'I have to get home.'

'Gorlinsky has reserved a suite for me.'

'Here?' said Maria. 'At the Dorchester?'

'Yes.'

Maria wanted so much to stay and talk with Yevgeny. Just to be alone with him, while he shared his thoughts with her. Maria called Stephen, who immediately answered, sounding concerned.

'Where are you?' he demanded.

'At the Dorchester. The reception has gone on far longer than planned. Gorlinsky has invited me and some other guests to a party, and arranged the transport home. I can't very well refuse.'

Stephen grudgingly gave his approval, without any reference to Yevgeny, or the performance, and instead mentioned tiredness, and the difficulties of travelling past midnight.

'How often do you think I'll be invited to the Dorchester?' she said.

The call abruptly ended, and shortly after, Maria found herself alone with Yevgeny in his private suite, generously furnished with a grand piano, champagne, flowers and cards from well-wishers, including one from Gorlinsky, attesting to his faith and confidence on his debut.

'I'm going mad,' Yevgeny confessed. 'All day, I practise, and all day, I'm alone. Everything is about my career! Gorlinsky treats me like an old-fashioned record. Put on. Play. Take off. Rest. Put on. Play. Round and round. Everything is about my future. Nothing is about now! Even tonight's now is over!'

'But Yev. This is what you dreamed about. What you always wanted. Shortly you'll have the world 'at your feet'.'

'The other day, during the rehearsal, I walked out, and went into Hyde Park. Gorlinsky screamed at me down the phone. 'Where are you? I want you back here in two minutes!'

'I want to hear a bird sing,' I told him. 'I want to feel fresh air.'

Maria laughed. It was so like him. To elope from the pressure, and search for the lost boy, who ran away from the farm. But at a deeper level, she realised something more. Far from being elated by his triumph, he behaved as if he were a detached participant.

'After every performance, I feel abandoned,' he said.

'People only know you through layers of lyrical expression,' said Maria. 'And what Gorlinsky wants to tell them. He sees you as a commodity. Rescuing you from obscurity, and turning you into a celebrity. He diluted your past in order to make you acceptable. Aren't you thankful?'

'Only as long as I can play on my own terms.'

'They won't be yours for very much longer!'

Yevgeny fell silent. It was a silence full of unanswered questions, and the absence of the camaraderie they once knew. Eventually, Maria said,

'Stephen will be worried.'

'You don't love him. You can't,' said Yevgeny.

Maria looked out onto the crowded road below. Full of slow-moving traffic, soon to be heading in different directions. She knew, and Yevgeny knew, they had plotted different routes to escape the uneven path that had shaped both their lives.

'Leave then,' said Yevgeny. 'Leave, for that dull, suburban desert, in which nothing will grow, and nothing will change.'

'It's indestructible,' said Maria, 'which is why no one wants to change it.'

Yevgeny looked intense and profusely sad.

'Then I feel sorry for you,' he said.

'That's your immaturity talking,' Maria replied. 'That's all it is. You're light-headed, and feeling homesick. I did what I promised Popov. From now on, your life is going to be very different. In a short time from now, you are going to be stepping on and off planes, and monitored like a railway timetable. You've been groomed for a life you can't imitate, and a solitude only you can inhabit. And all because your one true love is so demanding that no one, least of all me, could compete!'

Yevgeny suddenly took Maria by the shoulders, and shook her like a boy remonstrating over an unkept promise.

'It's you who needs releasing from captivity,' he declared, 'not me!'

'The time we spent travelling, I realised something,' replied Maria. 'The moments of triumph are short, and the years of sacrifice long. I'm sure Gorlinsky has already found the perfect replacement for me!'

As the early hours approached, they both confessed to being homesick, missing people they'd left behind, and the familiarity of the places they knew. They were also mindful of recent history. They rarely discussed it, but it had followed them like a black cloud.

The communications back home had reflected a distinct pessimism. Yevgeny, who rarely displayed any interest in politics, suddenly reverted to a state of melancholy.

Maria recognized his malady, and repeated all the reasons for him to celebrate, and how Popov and everyone back home would be so proud of him.

'Tonight, you waved the flag for Ukraine! And I absolutely forbid you to be sad,' she ordered.

'Of course, I am not alone,' Yevgeny declared. 'There is another rising star. One of the most exciting talents to emerge from Kyiv, although her name escapes me. Never mind. Let's raise our glasses in anticipation of her debut!'

Maria sat at the piano and posed, as if she had just given a recital, then stood up and took a bow. Yevgeny clapped wildly, and presented her with a bouquet of flowers. She gracefully accepted, and curtsied to Yevgeny, both realising time was precious.

'Popov thought very highly of you,' declared Yevgeny.

'The most I could hope for now would be to play for a local music society. A few Bach or Chopin favourites, or an accompanist for the occasional Fischer-Dieskau impersonator who wants to sing about a galloping horse!'

'Not everything that appears permanent grows. Sometimes it rots,' observed Yevgeny.

Maria reminded him it was time for her to return home, and kissed him goodbye.

Gently, at first, on the cheek, and then again to console him. He looked helplessly at Maria, and pleaded for her not to abandon him, then tearfully embraced her, and began kissing her passionately on the lips.

'This isn't a very good idea,' she warned.

'At heart, you're a coward!' mocked Yevgeny.

'You think so?'

'You're afraid of yourself and your talent. You're afraid of true love, and you're afraid of your real feelings. That's what's been missing from your playing. It's precise, highly-accomplished, and cold. You see everything from the remote distance of your protective shell. Even your virginity is selective. You can hide almost everything except the insecure person hiding beneath a frigid interior. You want love, but can't return it, and you wanted fame to please others. You're driven by duty, not by instinct!'

'That's a complete lie, and you know it!' Maria said, defiantly.

'Is it?'

Yevgeny took Maria's hands and held them firmly, looking directly into her eyes. She turned her head away, and refused to look at him. Yevgeny released his grip, but she didn't move. She waited for something she was too afraid to acknowledge. Then, when it happened, Maria did not resist, but allowed him to reveal in the tender unexpectedness of a single moment, a purpose beyond the luxurious predictability of their surroundings, and the irresistible intoxication of the champagne. The very thing she had distrusted most: to be lost in the tender and brittle chemistry of being physically and overwhelmingly desired. This time, not as a big sister, or as a reluctant participant. But for once, fully, intentionally and emotionally alive.

The next morning, when Maria switched on her phone, there were already a dozen messages from Stephen. And almost, immediately he called… She answered, half-dazed…

'I'm at a hotel…In London…It got too late, and I drank too much…Gorlinsky paid for it…No. It's okay…I need to do a few things…I'll call you after breakfast…'

Yevgeny was slumbering. He looked peaceful, and somehow complete. Maria also felt different. It wasn't the kind of awakening she had ever experienced before. Then suddenly, Yevgeny's eyes opened. He just looked at her, as she made faces at him, and observed his eyes, they were wide open, but displayed a look of disapproval.

'What's wrong?' she asked.

'I heard you talking,' said Yevgeny. 'You didn't tell him you had been liberated.'

'It's too early for surprises,' she answered.

He opened his arms wide to embrace her, like a child seeking assurance. She sat on the bed beside him, and after gently stroking his hair, kissed him on the forehead.

'I'll order breakfast,' she said.

Maria called room service, and then took a shower. She needed to think. When she returned, Yevgeny was negotiating a calorific English Breakfast.

'I would prefer your souffle instead,' he joked.

He then got up from the table, leaned forward, and kissed her passionately on the lips.

'Are you happy?' he whispered.

'I feel strange,' Maria replied.

'Guilty?'

'Yes.'

'I don't care. From now on our lives shall be powered by that selfish and most delicious inspiration known to mankind, and anything that either walks, talks, or swims. That dances to a waltz, or reacts to a melancholy nocturne, or simply wants to stand in the rain, and thank God for their existence!'

Yevgeny was animated like never before…hungry, eager and talkative. As if the applause of the previous evening was still ringing in his ears. He then sat down and poured himself another coffee.

'Aren't you excited?' he asked.

'About your debut?'

'About us, except, from now on, we'll make it official. You will be in charge of all my affairs, share my triumph's, organise my diary, and be there to encourage me at those times when I need convincing, I'm still good enough to face the public.'

'You mean keeping you in the groove, like a needle that goes round and around. Put on, take off. Ensuring the speed of your career keeps perfect time with Gorlinsky's plans.'

'If you like.'

Maria placed her half-eaten souffle to one side, and stared down at the table.

'I don't think I'd be suitable.'

'Why not?'

'Last night, during the interval, Gorlinsky discussed his plans for your future. They're phenomenal in both scope and ambition. Later, when someone asked him about the pitfalls of a twenty one year old prodigy, he gave a straightforward answer. 'Marriage!', he said.'

'That's just the kind of thing he would say,'

'Gorlinsky may be many things. But so far, his predictions have proved correct. Just like your opinion of my cold, precise playing.'

'I said that, to make you confront your true feelings. And I was right!'

'So too is Gorlinsky's brutal forecast.'

'I don't understand?'

'After Gorlinsky mentioned the word marriage, I asked him why? He replied, 'Anyone at the start of a significant career has no time for marriage or children! After all, you can only do one thing well.'

'What else did he say?'

'He didn't need to add anything. He's far too skilled at suggestion for that.'

'Gorlinsky isn't against motherhood. Except you can't have parenthood and a career. It's a choice you have to make early on. You decided motherhood wasn't for you.' said Yevgeny.

'So instead you want me to watch you become Gorlinsky's monkey. Put on. Play. Take off. Round and round. Soon, you'll even need permission to hear a bird sing!'

'That's the price we pay for the ticket. '

'You're even beginning to sound like him. Not that I'm surprised. You've finally found the father you've always wanted. Either way I'd end up a cuckhold having to share you with someone else, which, even for someone used to scaling locked gates, is too high a price.

'Then it's for nothing,' he replied. 'For you, it's just sound without reason, a mechanical act. Like running towards something that doesn't exist. Pointless and empty, as if Chopin had written a polonaise for no other reason than to function as a composer, but had nothing to commit to the heart, except an empty collection of notes. Is that what you hear? When we embrace and makelove. Is that what it is? A noise you are unable to respond to, or make sense of. Once again you're running away. This time from something inescapable: yourself!'

Before Maria knew it, the plate that had once played host to

Yevgeny's breakfast shattered against the wall of his elegant suite. Then his phone rang, and he immediately switched it off. There followed a knock at the door, and a member of the hotel staff entered, carrying a bewildering array of Sunday Newspapers, and neatly arranged them on a nearby table. The phone in the suite rang. It was Gorlinsky. Yevgeny listened politely, as he was instructed on what would likely happen following the reviews, and precisely how to answer certain questions. When the conversation had concluded, the disappointment on his face was palpable. Maria kissed him gently on the cheek, and bid him farewell. It signalled the seismic shift between two worlds. One she had decided not to enter:

'Just for once I've decided what little happiness I've found I'm going to try and make work for me' she told Yevgeny.

'And what kind of future, do you think you'll have, with Stephen Kline.' Yevgeny screamed. 'Tell me that!'

'Predictable!' said Maria. 'Suburban, unexciting, underrated, and predictable.'

On arriving home, Stephen was expecting an explanation for her overnight absence. But instead, she concentrated on the atmosphere of the Albert Hall, and the reception, telling him that the performance had justified Gorlinsky's faith. Stephen listened patiently for a short time before he interrupted her colourful description…

'I phoned the hotel. Gorlinsky's reception ended at midnight. The party you attended must have been very short of guests… Some parties are like that… they start off crowded…, and then only two people are left…'

'Am I not allowed out after midnight?' Maria asked.

'For all I care, you can dance with a Prince until morning. It isn't just the lie to save embarrassment, it's the deceit behind the lie that angers me. A party to which I have never been invited!'

Stephen's words dismantled Maria's excuse with the cold efficiency of a professor interrogating a novice. To her surprise, however, his real anger centred on the part he himself had played in Yevgeny's rehabilitation, and how it had shifted the entire focus of her life. It had resulted, he told her, in her insecurity and confusion. Sacrificing her career for his, in her blind, impulsive, and incomprehensible loyalty, towards someone who had proved himself irresponsible and destructive. At every turn, she had placed his needs above hers, and threatened her own chances of happiness. He didn't spare Maria's feelings, and waited for her to respond to a distress call, from someone crippled by the wasted energy of regret.

In reply, she told him that fame requires 'a particular kind of valour!' and if she married Yevgeny, she would become a mother of two: him and his career.

'I couldn't cope with both,' she admitted…

Stephen told her he 'lost his father's love', because his father was obsessed with someone else. In his fathers case, he succumbed to the blackmail of pregnancy. In Maria's case, he believed she could only accept him as a consolation prize, something he told her he would refuse to accept. Not until he was certain she was emotionally free to love, to love him, and not the embodiment of someone else's career.

'So far, all I have ever been to you is a harbour for you to take shelter. More fool, me. Trapped, just like my mother. And just as unloved.'

In this mood, Stephen felt abandoned, and as a consequence, departed to an emotional island, incapable of listening, and instead addressing the injustice of old wounds.

'It seems you are still unable to resist the very person who has no need of you.'

'How ironic? So, I will just wait. I will wait until you recognise my weakness and stupidity as not just selfish, but something I am unable to let go of. Something, that even though I have only received a grudging amount of its warmth, I refuse to be parted from. I will wait for that moment. That moment, when you finally come home.'

Stephen departed in disappointment, and a remorse she recognised only too well.

In the following weeks, Maria attempted to take the most compassionate route back into his favour, and had softened to a degree that Stephen didn't think possible. Almost all his habits and annoying character traits remained unchallenged, and she refused to be drawn into the more controversial areas, where he chose to dictate his opinion. The one exception being music, where Maria was able to govern her small fledgling principality unhindered.

She now had a growing number of pupils she was able to teach at home, during the hours he was absent, and took the step of applying for a resident visa. This change of heart gave Stephen the confidence to explore the future, especially as Yevgeny appeared to be no longer part of it. As a result, he began to relax. He had also reluctantly agreed to Maria's demand that, for the present, physical intimacy was to remain a prohibited part of the life they shared. Although it served as a barrier he found hard to accept.

One evening, Maria plucked up courage and asked Stephen,

'Would you do the same for me as you did for Yevgeny, and hire the Wigmore Hall for me to give a recital?'

Stephen agreed, on condition that she would accept it as a wedding present.

Maria insisted on some conditions of her own.

One, was that her parents were to attend the wedding. The other, was that she had no intention of becoming pregnant.

'If we are going to be married, then it will be done properly,' she said, 'and since my parents knew nothing of my pregnancy, I intend to have a white wedding!'

Maria also insisted that she became Stephen's tenant, and not his lover, as it would appear to be more acceptable to her parents. And there were other practical considerations.

'Namely, a date when my parents would be free to travel!'

Nowadays, she called them more frequently, mainly due to the political situation. Putin's annexation of Crimea, and his underhand tactics of subversion, had cast a long shadow over the future of Ukraine. Lately, his troops had begun to appear in increasing numbers on the border, causing mounting speculation at home, and in the capitals of Europe. Putin claimed he had no plans to invade, but her parents were sceptical…

'When a man jails his critics, assassinates the opposition, and whose favourite export is Novichok, you can take his promises with a pinch of salt!,' her father said.

Nonetheless, they all agreed it seemed inconceivable, and more in line with his rhetoric of intimidation. They therefore set a date for the wedding, to coincide with the Easter holiday the following year.

'It will arrive in no time…' declared Maria.

Stephen at last appeared content. Christmas was coming, and there was a distinct flavour of goodwill in the air.

'Are you happy?' he asked.

'I've stopped asking myself whether I am happy, but to simply make the most productive use of the time God has given me.'

'I'm surprised you still believe in God,' said Stephen.

'Why?'

'Because, of all the cruelty you've witnessed!'

'Maybe, I believe in a hope beyond suffering.'

'Well, in that case, ask God to grant you a mild winter, and for Easter to arrive with the kind of weather that will allow our guests to have lunch on the lawn!'

'The trouble with God is he doesn't always give you what you want, when you want it!'

'Then, for once, we are in complete agreement,' said Stephen.

Maria rarely spoke of her once flowering ambition. Her pre-occupation with her domestic situation was now so complete that her intense love of the piano was pursued in the practice time she spent in the hours Stephen was absent. However, she longed for one last chance to give a recital. Not only for her parents sake, but before she settled down, and became someone only capable of nurturing the possibility in others. Just as she would do in time, with her own children.

One day she reminded Stephen about his promise,

'You mean your Wigmore Hall debut?' he asked.

'Yes. Who knows, I may even prove, that failing to have a career, was no fluke !'

16.

FEBRUARY TURNED OUT to be the cruellest month. Christmas had passed, and spring had yet to deliver its promise. The turf on the Common opposite the house choreographed its own seasonal compass, and the frost this particular day was apt. For just when it appeared the gloom of the recent past was receding, the second month of the year delivered its own bombshell. Something far too audacious, improbable and harrowing to be thought credible. As Europe slumbered on its bed of false security, Maria awoke to the news that Russia had launched a full-scale invasion of Ukraine, and that Kyiv was under attack.

In one brief moment, it was as if her whole life had been thrown in the air, and landed in pieces. In desperation, she called her parents, who reported they had immediately volunteered for front-line duty, whilst members of her family had either enlisted, or were taking refuge in one of the many hastily convened shelters. She attempted to contact her student friends from Odesa, including Moiseiwitsch, who told her he had no choice but to enlist. At first, it made her smile, since he was the least suitable of anyone to be considered for active duty.

'What are you going to do?' she asked. 'Line the Russians up, and play Paganini?'

'Worse!' he said. 'Play them a recording of my four year old nephew. He can kill anything you put in front of him.'

Maria then asked him about Popov. Moiseiwitsch paused for

a few seconds.

'Haven't you heard…? Popov died!'

He explained that, shortly after he arrived back from London, Popov had failed to turn up for his classes one day, and the academy raised the alarm. He was found slumped in his lounge, with an old vinyl recording of Horowitz on his turntable. When Maria enquired about the cause, Moiseiwitsch answered, '… heart failure. He died listening to a Chopin waltz!', and added, he thought it was the most appropriate music at the most appropriate time.

Maria felt a mixture of relief and sadness. With all the madness going on now, she believed Popov was in a better place. Unfortunately, he hadn't lived to hear of Yevgeny's triumph. Although Moiseiwitsch told her he would be OK, she knew by his voice, that he was deeply concerned for the future. Right now, confusion reigned, as missiles were reported to be landing in Kyiv, Mariupol, Kharkiv and many other places, along with rumours that Russia was sending an amphibious landing force towards Odesa.

'It may be a while before we speak again!' said Moiseiwitsch. 'Shalom!'

'Only for now,' pleaded Maria.

'Of course!' answered Moiseiwitsch. 'Until I next make a clumsy effort to pursue you!'

When Maria told Yevgeny about Popov's death, he cried in a way she had never heard before, and then terminated the call. So far, they had discussed events as they unfolded, and attempted to glean any extra knowledge via family or friends. Meanwhile, President Volodymyr Zelensky, now acting as Ukraine's spokesmen, pleaded daily for practical help, and badly needed weapons, to combat the missiles and mind games of Putin, who described the invasion as a '*special military operation*', denying Ukraine was an independent democratic nation, and treating it as a breakaway province of Russia. Fancifully dressing up his warmongering, by asserting that in order for Ukraine to be liberated from bullying and oppression, the most neighbourly thing he could do was bomb apartment blocks, hospitals, and schools, along with innocent women and children. Alongside this, his pretext concerning the threat of NATO expansion had precisely the opposite effect, and within days, Ukraine sought NATO membership. The scare tactics didn't appear to be working.

Just as Hitler had attempted to liberate Europe, before heading in the direction of Stalin's backyard, the Kremlin's attempt to capture Kyiv and install a puppet regime had also failed.

'You don't know Ukrainians,' Maria told Stephen. 'They are going to surprise everyone!'

Stephen was not so sure, and stated that Ukraine was hardly in a position to defend itself against the might of Russia.

'You have swapped realism for hopeless optimism,' he told Maria, citing Russia's superior armoury and nuclear capability. 'Do you think Ukraine can defend itself against that?'

'Yes, I do,' replied Maria. 'And what's more, they must. For your sake, as well as mine.'

Although Stephen declared his support for Ukraine, Maria suspected he felt obliged to prepare her for a compromise, or worse, inevitable defeat, with the reluctant acquiescence of America and its allies, in order to avoid the war's enlargement. His educational perspective overruled his emotional grasp and first-hand knowledge of what she knew to be overlooked in the corridors of power and among those whose fingers had never touched the soil of Kyiv, Odesa, Lviv, Uman, Chernivtsi, or Zaporizhzhia.

'Do you know the difference between someone fighting for the survival of their country, and the territorial ambitions of a psychopathic narcissist?' asked Maria.

'Of course,' answered Stephen. 'One uses the weapon of fear, and the other may run out of bullets.'

It appeared they both experienced the action through a different historical lens, but Maria still believed the carnage Putin had unleashed would come back to haunt him.

When she discussed it with Yevgeny, he was unable to express it in anything other than sarcasm.

'Russia is, after all, a tiny country desperate to protect its borders,' he mocked.

He had spoken to his mother, and she told him his father had immediately volunteered to fight.

'As you know, he is strong and determined,' she told Yevgeny. She herself had decided to remain where she was.

'If the Russians come here, I'll welcome them with a tray of Molotov cocktails. Putin and his followers talk about de-Nazification, and behave like the Third Reich!'

His mothers response, and his fathers patriotism, left him feeling impotent. Maria reminded him that from now on, he wouldn't be playing for himself any more, but for Ukraine.

'All I'm doing is performing a concerto, when others are sacrificing their lives,' he said.

As the first weeks of the war began to recede, it was clear that the drama unfolding wouldn't be short-lived. Stephen felt like an outsider, dispensing moral support, whilst ensuring Maria's participation didn't extend beyond the safety of her domestic role. More than likely, there would be a refugee crisis, he advised, and she could always help with that?

'I agree!' said Maria. 'After all, we have the space!'

'You mean turn my mother's house into a refugee centre?'

'Our house,' corrected Maria. 'Does that not appeal? Other people's messy lives intruding on the manicured lawns and tidy suburban hedges of Chorleywood Common?'

'Very well,' Stephen replied. 'Since your parents are no longer able to attend the wedding, let's have a registry office ceremony now, and a church service, when the hostilities have ceased!'

'That's unlikely to happen anytime soon,' said Maria.

'What are you talking about?' argued Stephen. 'Didn't I tell you that, one day, Ukraine will run out of bullets. You don't surely believe that America and Europe are foolhardy enough to save you!'

'Then where would you and Mr Putin like us to go?' asked Maria. 'The Antarctic?'

'I care about you and our future,' argued Stephen.

'That's just the point, isn't it?' said Maria. 'What we both care about!'

Stephen told her that he had found the perfect place for them to be married. A peaceful village in Suffolk with a luxury hotel, not too far from where they had stayed previously.

'I've told everyone, I'm going on a special military operation to rescue someone from Ukraine,' he joked.

He had arranged the ceremony and booked the hotel in advance, telling Maria she needed respite from the almost hourly updates, frantic calls home, and little rest from the constant barrage of media reports and commentary about the war.

'For five days, I forbid you the use of any outside communication.'

'Are you being serious?'

'Perfectly,' said Stephen.

He then excitedly explained that although their honeymoon would be short, he didn't intend that it should lack any of the trimmings. They would stay in a historical luxury hotel, dine extravagantly, relax in the countryside, and close the door on all the negativity and disaster of the hour. For a brief moment in time, they were to be alone together, among peaceful surroundings, and prepare for their future without any outside interruption.

'We are returning momentarily to the past, in order to clarify the future,' he said. 'I want us to start married life as if none of this ever happened.'

'I'm afraid that's not possible?' Maria responded.

When the day finally arrived, Stephen polished his beloved Mark 11 Jaguar, and carried out some mechanical checks, whilst Maria prepared for the journey. Every so often, he popped into her room, to check on her progress, and suggested various items from her wardrobe that would be suitable for the honeymoon. He also presented her with a diamond necklace, but she told him she preferred to wear the small-heart shaped locket Popov had given to her on graduating from the academy in Odesa.

'It contains a few mustard seeds, to remind me of hope,' she told him.

Stephen was in high spirits as he packed their cases into the back of the car, along with as many convenient luxuries as space allowed. Maria insisted the light cream, organza wedding gown was to remain in its protective cover until the ceremony. When they set off, he opened the passenger-side door for her as if she was a VIP, and carried on a conversation concerning the hotel, and hinted at the surprises he'd been preparing, in order to make their wedding as memorable as possible.

'If you and Yevgeny hadn't moved to London, you could be in danger right now! As it is, you're in the right place at the right time,' he declared.

'You mean avoiding conflict?' said Maria.

'Exactly,' said Stephen. 'After all, with conflict? Nobody wins. Nobody wins at all!'

'Although, inevitably, somebody always loses?' Maria observed.

'Or has to compromise,' replied Stephen.

As they proceeded along the common, and turned into familiar streets towards the motorway, Maria requested they make an alteration to the route.

'I've just remembered, I've forgotten something. Can we head for the High Street?'

'The traffic's heavy this time of day, and the High Street's in the other direction, can't it wait?' asked Stephen.

'No,' said Maria. 'I don't think it can.'

As they approached the centre of town, the traffic slowed considerably, and came to a halt at a set of traffic lights. Maria glanced at Stephen, then unfastened her seat belt, and walked away from the car. Stephen looked puzzled, lowered his driver's side window, and began calling after her. Then the lights suddenly changed, and the cars behind began sounding their horns. He shouted for her to come back, but she turned into a one-way street, where he couldn't follow. Unable to park, he then abandoned the car, and tried to pursue her on foot, but the noise of the traffic behind him was insistent. He repeatedly called her name out loud, as she disappeared into the distance, and headed for the station.

An hour later, Maria called Stephen and begged him to continue the journey to Suffolk.

Confused and in distress, he pleaded for her to meet him, and discuss the issues that had so far remained unresolved. But Maria insisted that the things that disturbed her couldn't be fixed by any further meetings. She acknowledged her own emotional fragility, for which she bore full responsibility. But there was something she still had to resolve, she told Stephen.

'It's not your fault. It's mine.'

'Where are you?' he demanded.

'I've come to hear a bird sing,' she replied.

'What are you talking about?' said Stephen.

'That's one of the things I have to resolve.'

'What is?' he insisted angrily.

'The voice in my head,' she answered.

Stephen grew even more alarmed, and tried to reassure her.

'I understand,' he said. 'It's normal. Lots of women have doubts. And you're missing the support of your parents. It's only natural. I understand. I honestly do. I promise.'

He tried to reason with her on a question and answer basis, in which she could do nothing but agree. But it was hopeless. She therefore begged him to continue his journey to the hotel, and told him she would join him later. Maria then terminated the call, and waited by the Albert Memorial for Yevgeny. Eventually, he appeared, looking solemn.

'Where's the confetti in your hair, and the stars in your eyes?' he asked.

'They're waiting for new supplies,' she insisted.

'That's not the real reason.'

'I've decided I want something more important.'

Yevgeny told Maria the doubts she had now were no different from the ones she had in the past.

'You returned because you believe you owe him fatherhood, but you followed your ambition, not your heart. Now, even your willpower has doubts.'

'That's why I need your advice.'

Yevgeny questioned her uncertainty, and told her it was character that was predictable.

'You like the idea of feeling comfortable and safe,' he said. 'Well, you can't have it! Freedom isn't just a nice idea. It's a dangerous concept! We can't just sit in a nice armchair, and accept we're powerless.'

'Then use your talent as a weapon!'

'You mean, wave the flag from a distant shore, while others bleed. I'd rather perform on a bomb site in Odesa.'

'Except you're not a hero! The only thing you could kill is a waltz.'

'That's why I'm joining the army of the insignificant. To make myself useful, and volunteer for the less glamorous acts of valour. Who knows, I may be good for something. Even if it's only helping to keep up morale. It isn't only bombs that win wars. There's also that strange mystery of endurance called the human spirit.'

'Then endure by performing.'

'Do you think I could sit in the air-conditioned comfort of a concert hall, play a Beethoven sonata, and pretend I was doing something worthwhile? The penalty for not going would be worse than going.'

'Then take me with you,' pleaded Maria.

'And leave your cosy prison with all its creature comforts? An hour ago, you were on your way to become a bride.'

'Suddenly, I feel home-sick.'

Yevgeny told Maria he would be leaving straight after the concert that evening, and joining other Ukrainian volunteers on the Polish border.

'If you're serious, meet me at the airport terminal before midnight,' he said.

Maria was startled.

'So soon?' she gasped.

'It's up to you. If it's a hard decision…, don't go. If it's an easy one, join me! Just bring your passport, and a change of clothing, nothing else!'

Maria placed her hands on Yevgeny's cheeks, and kissed him passionately.

'You damn fool!' she told him.

'Don't worry, I'm not the only one.'

'I can't leave, without explaining the situation to Stephen. That's the least I owe him.

'He'll only attempt to change your mind. Just bring what I suggest. If you don't arrive by midnight, I'll assume you've decided that prison is more desirable.'

Maria was faced with the sudden realisation that the war would no longer be a distant battle, but a far more personal day to day conflict, for which they were both ill-equipped.

'I have a couple of things I must do first,' said Maria.

'I'm hoping you'll prove me wrong,' said Yevgeny.

'What are you playing tonight?'

'Another number two, this time composed by someone famously opposed to yet another Russian psychopath.'

Yevgeny then asked Maria to pray for him, and all the others, fighting or not. She prayed that God would protect Yevgeny, and their fellow countryman, against the criminal invasion of the enemy, and the suffering being unleashed on the innocent.

For the people to remain resilient, and for the world to respond to Ukraine's plight, and receive the help it so badly needed. She then presented Yevgeny with the insignificant tin locket Popov had given to her on graduation.

'I'll wear it for both of us,' he declared.

Maria embraced him once more and added, 'Haven't you forgotten something?'

'Is it important?'

'You owe me a duet', she said.

The March winds blew across the common, and the ground was soaked. By early evening, only a few dog walkers trudged across its barren landscape. Suddenly, Maria was all too aware of the other life she had decided to escape. She didn't immediately enter the house, but instead, walked past several it times. She couldn't see Stephen's car on the drive, so walked slowly up to the front door and inserted the key into the lock. With the door half open, she listened for a few moments, but could hear nothing. She therefore quickly mounted the stairs, and entered her room at the back of the house. Her bright, red suitcase, packed for the honeymoon, had been placed on the bed, and her music still lined the shelves of the mahogany bookcase by the door. It didn't take long to re-pack. and include a small selection of her favourite music. She then descended the stairs, and placed the key on the hallway table, together with a letter addressed to Stephen. On reaching the front door, she turned to glance around at the house one final time.

No sooner had her fingers reached the latch than she was unable to move, and take the last few steps to freedom. It wasn't that his voice was aggressive or threatening, it wasn't. Instead, it was curiously supplicant, as he addressed her from the direction of the lounge.

Placing her case on the floor, she walked slowly back towards the room, and on entering found Stephen, seated on the sofa by the large bay window. His right arm was outstretched, and in his other hand, he held the sharp blade of a kitchen knife horizontally across the main artery on his wrist. He looked a pitiful sight, and his eyes followed her as she approached.

'Before you slip away, like you always do, I want you to see what a mess you've made of me. I want you to be here in person to witness my pain. I watched you walking up and down outside, and foolishly hoped you had decided to return. But just as before, you only want to torment me.'

Maria explained that she and Yevgeny were returning home to join the fight against Putin!

Stephen said nothing, and began pressing the knife into his flesh, whilst Maria pleaded with him to stop.

'War or not, I have no intention of you leaving here with clean hands,' he told her.

'Then I pray to God, one day, you will find it in your heart to forgive me,' said Maria.

'You talk to me about God!' Stephen said contemptuously. 'Yours is a God of pain and betrayal. A God of loss. Why would God place love so heavily on the heart, and then make it the subject of such derision? Tell me that?'

Stephen pressed the blade more firmly into his vein, and as a result, blood began to seep from the wound.

'See what you've done to my tedious air-brushed life? A spent-force between two compulsions. You and self-harm. In reality, they're both same thing, aren't they?'

Relaxing his grip, he slumped back on the sofa, whilst Maria rushed to the kitchen, and returned with a tea towel to bind his wrist. No sooner had she attended to the wound, than he pushed her away.

'If you wanted, you could save a life right now!' he insisted. 'But you would rather waste your life on someone who even refused to take responsibility for his own child. Why would you want to go back to a man like that? Why?'

'Sometimes, the future dictates its own terms, and sometimes, those terms are hard to accept, but it's better to face them, than run away. That is why before I go, I want you to do something for me. Something very special, and very hard for you to accept…I want you to forgive me!'

'Too late,' said Stephen…

'I know. And no salty tears will make up for it. No plea of mercy, clever argument, understanding of motive, personal sob story, nor misguided morality. The truth is…, the baby you paid to abort Stephen, wasn't Yevgeny's… it was yours! And do you want to know why I deceived you? Because I realised the real power that motivates you is not love, but control. You and I are both alike. We both mistrust love. Even now, you seek to exact revenge through guilt. But you're too late. The guilt is already mine. It was the price I paid for my independence. So, the blood flowing from your wound is wasted, and your crude bribe a failure. You could find a million reasons for me to live under your roof, except for the one my own guilty, foolish, and ill-judged existence is unable to provide…'

As the words departed from Maria's lips, Stephen sat in silence, trying to absorb the full implication of what she had said, unable to move, and lost for words. The knife remained firmly in his hand, and Maria looked down, and observed the blood slowly extending its wayward imprint. He then examined the crimson soaked tea-towel covering his wound, as the throbbing in his arm became more insistent, and the blood loss heavier. He now appeared utterly remote, as if on a distant island imprisoned by invisible walls, where hope was an inferior wisdom, and the unplanned journey within leaving a far deeper injury.

'I can't forgive you,' he said softly, 'Never…'

He didn't shout or demonstrate aggression, but remained perfectly still, as if absorbing a sentence for which there was no appeal, and hadn't yet come to terms with.

Maria took Stephens hand, and he released his grip. Taking the knife, she made her way to the kitchen, filled a bowl with warm water, then returned and cleansed his wound.

'I'll call for an ambulance,' she said.

'No,' said Stephen defiantly, and pulled his hand away. 'The wounds on the inside. Can you find a doctor skilled enough to heal that?'

Stephen sunk back into the sofa and looked at Maria, drained of purpose.

'I have no skill,' answered Maria. 'All I ever did was search for something I never succeeded in finding.'

'Revenge!' Stephen exclaimed, bitterly. 'You found that, and perfected it, in your very own cruel, twisted, and perverse way. But it isn't bloodless. Just like your convenient excuse of a war!'

Stephen ceased attempting to stem the blood seeping from his wound, and let his arm drape over the side of the sofa.

'I'm not the answer you've been looking for,' said Maria.

'That's because you refuse to accept it!'

'Just for once, I've found real purpose.'

'In lost causes!' Stephen said, contemptuously. 'One in particular!'

'Who knows how anything ends. What I do know is, you and I are both survivors, honourably wounded, but survivors You will start again. But not in the same way. Less trusting and more cynical, but also far wiser. My advice to you is to escape from the past. You're a far better person than you've ever given yourself credit for. All that needs to happen is for you to forgive yourself ....Can you do that?'

Stephen remained silent, and Maria kissed him gently on the forehead, as he continued to nurse his wrist, and looked at her helplessly.

'For now, it's the only hope open to either of us. Meanwhile, I've given my word to perform a duet in Kyiv.'

Without saying another word, Maria left the room. As she left the house, she glanced briefly behind, and felt a release from its airless capture. Then, as the landscape of the common receded, felt re-invigorated by new purpose.Revenge, she decided came in many guises, and closure was always waiting for a time and place in which to fulfil the destiny of some of life's ironies.

When Maria reached Paddington, she entered a cafe at the far side of the station concourse, and immediately recognised a woman wearing a nurse's uniform. Maria apologised for her late arrival.

'You gave us very short notice,' said the woman.

'It was unavoidable,' said Maria, 'Are you able to help?'

The woman who introduced herself as 'Jan' worked for an anti-trafficking action group that could offer victims a 'safe house', and weeks before Maria had sought their help. Now she was returning to Ukraine, she told them they needed to respond urgently.

'Normally, we carry out our own investigation to check out the facts, and work with the police. So far, there's been no reports of illegal activity, or police involvement, so we aren't able to enter the premises. We know it offers a massage service, through websites, but that isn't illegal. What we need is evidence. Something that will stand up in court.'

'I've already volunteered.'

'Except you weren't trafficked, and walked out the door a free woman.'

'So this is all a waste of time?'

'What we need is a whistleblower on the inside.'

'Jan' explained that all too often, the girls are afraid to talk, and remain loyal to their captors. Unless, of course, you could persuade some of the girls to defect?'

'If you do, we can't be responsible for your safety.'

'How long have I got?'

'I doubt if you'll have time for a long discussion. Choose your moment carefully. Once inside, we can't help. We're acting undercover as a private ambulance, and will park in the next street. You're familiar with the layout, and may be able to identify some of the girls. But remember, we can only aid voluntary escape.'

Maria nodded, and then followed 'Jan' out of the station to a side road close to the Bedfont Hotel, where a private ambulance was conveniently parked, its windows blacked out and inside, two rows of passenger seats. Once inside the ambulance, 'Jan' produced a dark blue 'hoodie', together with a wig, and handed them to Maria.

'Here, put these on, and when you enter don't hang around, and before making your way to the girls, if anybody asks, say you're looking for a friend.'

Maria entered the hotel, and quickly made her way up the stairs to the first floor. She then casually looked around, and then scouted the upper floors, pretending to be looking for someone, before climbing to the top floor. Fortunately, there was no sign of the gang, as she nervously approached the corner room that she and the other girls had previously occupied. Inside, she heard voices. As soon as she entered, the noise stopped, and the girls occupying the room looked startled. Quickly surveying the faces she recognised both Hong and Bao, then quickly removing her hood and wig she put her finger to her lips, and asked them not to raise the alarm, quickly reassuring them she was there to help.

The girls looked at each other puzzled, and started talking among themselves. Maria approached Hong.

'Don't you recognise me?' she asked.

'We were told you were working elsewhere!'

'Well, I'm not! I've come with some other people, who rescue trafficked women. Tell the others, and remind them who I am!'

Hong and Bao spoke to the other girls, and they began to talk amongst themselves.

'Hurry,' Maria urged, 'We don't have much time!'

'They're not sure who you are?' said Hong.

'Tell them. Quickly. I have very little time!'

One of the girls asked,

'Where do you want to take us?'

'To escape imprisonment. Don't you want that?'

Hong began talking to the girl, and then told Maria.

'The girls aren't sure. They don't know you, or your

organisation?'

'But you do!' said Maria. 'Look at me, I'm free!

A spokesman for the other girls approached Maria,

'Easier said than done. For all we know, this is a trap!'

Hong asked Maria to wait outside.

Maria left the room, and waited at the top of the stairs. Several minutes later, Hong joined her carrying a small make-up case, looking afraid.

'Where is everyone else?' asked Maria, alarmed.

'It's just me!' said Hong.

Maria put the wig back on, and covered her face with the hood, and hurried down the stairs followed by Hong. On reaching the ground floor, Maria took Hong by the arm and together they hurriedly left the hotel. On reaching the ambulance, the doors were flung open, and they were greeted by 'Jan' and a co-worker.

'Is that all?' enquired 'Jan'.

'It's a hundred per cent more than twenty minutes ago!' exclaimed Maria.

As the driver closed the rear doors of the ambulance, 'Jan' confirmed she was a nurse, and quickly examined Hong for signs of abuse, drug use and infection, and urged Maria to travel with Hong to a safe house, North of the river.

'I can't,' said Maria. 'I have a plane to catch. Besides, it's only a short walk to the station.'

Maria assured Hong she was in safe hands, and told her, the lives of other girls depended on her, before the ambulance departed,

It had now begun to rain, and Maria decided to take a short-cut through a nearby garden square. The air smelled fresh, and her feet rose several inches off the ground, as she hurried down a path that passed by trees and some small benches, intoxicated by the excitement of Hong's liberation, the anticipation of a new chapter in her life, and returning home. She then remembered Stephen, and his need for medical attention, the clothes she would need, and other items for the trip, and wondered whether

Yevgeny had booked her flight? So many issues now began to enter her head, that she felt overwhelmed, and decided to call Yevgeny…, when all of a sudden she bumped into someone. Her immediate response was to apologise, and move to one side, but couldn't, and looking up, faced the penetrating eyes of someone she knew well. Nothing was said, as she attempted to hold onto his shoulders, but as she did so, he pulled away, and she fell to the ground. As she lay on her chest gasping for air, an onlooker would have thought, such a silly thing had happened, as the burly figure of Luca disappeared into a waiting car. Maria attempted to stand up, but lacked the strength, so lay with her head to one side. It was quite possible she was unaware of the loss of blood that now mingled with the rain, and slowly extended its reach beyond the footpath like traces of foam, graphically pleading for assistance, or had heard someone summon help, as her heart pumped furiously, and the rain composed its own lament, by bathing her body in the fading light. The few people that gathered assumed the likely cause was robbery, and the phone in her hand suggested she tried calling for help, but no one was sure. Later on, someone thoughtfully laid some flowers in the place where she had fallen with her bright red suitcase, still unopened!

Maria herself was now free of all consciousness, and would anyway claim, an act of violence will return time and again, to haunt the aggressor, and destroy them from within, like cancer.

She also believed the spirit is the fingerprint of the soul. That whoever it touches is changed by the consequence of that encounter, along with the characteristics, traits, quirks, mishaps, pain, foolish mistakes, sacrificial acts and the treasured moments that claim our senses, and a thousand and one other things, on the journey, that defines who we are.

It was something that Hong finally had the courage to face, and in the event provided some essential clues, and despite initial doubts, proved a reliable witness, exposing Lily, Luca and Ivan as ring leaders of trafficking and slavery, additionally accusing them of murder. As a result, the hotel was raided, and the sex workers freed, although no evidence of 'Scrawn' was ever found, and despite their pleas of 'not guilty', all three received long sentences, including both Max and Pavel, although the members of the gang that had held Yevgeny captive were never traced.

However, the longest sentence was reserved for Luca, who received a life sentence for the murder of Maria, together with kidnapping, and false imprisonment, due to the testimony of both Hong and Yevgeny. There was also evidence the gang were a part of a far larger criminal network, but as Hong declared, when she gave her testimony.

'In the end, they condition you to believe becoming someone else's property is normal.'

It was also Hong who provided one of the shortest and most eloquent speeches at Maria's funeral. She told everyone she once asked Maria if God was just an idea?

'Not when you play Bach, Beethoven or Mozart!' replied Maria.

'How can he be?'

EPILOGUE

Fifteen years later.

A packed auditorium applauds Yevgeny at the end of a recital in Paris.

Following his performance, he is ushered into the foyer, where he is invited to sign autographs for a long line of audience members. People present him with the item they wish him to sign, and he smiles politely. Some include warm words of congratulation, while others remind him of a former concert they attended. He acknowledges each of them individually until the crowd disperse. He exits the foyer, and climbs into a waiting limousine that transports him to his hotel. He is now older, and more mature, his hair far shorter. No longer the young prodigy. He has just completed a series of concerts, and looks tired.

The following morning, a chauffeured limousine takes him to the airport, and he boards a plane bound for Avignon. On arrival he collects his car and drives forty-five kilometres from the city, arriving at an elegantly converted farmhouse. He enters as a children's party is in progress, and the sound of 'Iko Iko' is heard coming from the direction of the dining room.

It is his daughter's birthday. Today, she is eight years old. As he enters the room, she is dancing with a group of her friends, oblivious to his presence. He walks up behind her, and places his hands over her eyes, she quickly turns and embraces him joyfully. He produces a gift, wrapped in expensive gold paper and a bright red ribbon, from his pocket. She eagerly tears open the wrapping, to reveal a velvet box containing an expensive looking bracelet, with what appears to be precious stones from a leading Paris jeweller.

It has links in the design of a treble and bass clef, and its clasp is in the shape of a grand piano. Her eyes light up, and she looks delighted as he places it on her wrist, while the other party guests look on in admiration. He then produces from his other pocket a small tin locket in the shape of a heart, and holds it by the chain in front of her eyes. He explains that the locket is very special, and far more valuable than the bracelet, because it is a symbol of hope. His daughter looks at the locket curiously for a few moments, and then snatches it out of his hand and runs away. Yevgeny pursues her as she runs through the rooms on the ground floor of the house, and follows her, as she heads through the orchard, and into the surrounding farmland.

She wants to play a game and invites him to find her. He asks her to be careful, and not lose the locket. But she laughs, and runs further from him.

She is small, and can easily hide in the vast field, which is now abundant in early summer.

She giggles, and temporarily shows herself, inviting him to pursue her.

He calls to her and declares, 'J'abandonne. Je suis fatigué!'

She giggles, but still insists that he chase her.

He sets off in the direction she revealed herself, but she is an excellent runner, and eludes him.

Once again, he calls her, but this time she doesn't give away her position. As a result, he tells her that he is not going to chase her any more, and reminds her that her party guests are waiting for her to join them.

She doesn't answer.

He calls to her once more, before walking back towards the house. But she remains hidden.

No longer being pursued, she stands up, examines the locket and then opens it up. Inside are some old seeds, which she discards, and an inscription with her name, and some words written in Ukrainian. His daughter calls out, and asks him to translate what it means.

'I will never forget you,' he tells her.

She closes the locket, looking deep in thought, and her eyes then follow Yevgeny.

As he is about to enter the house, he calls out to her,

'Maria!'

She remains resolutely still for a few moments, and then runs towards him excitedly.

He leans forward, with his arms open wide, and picking her up, embraces her enthusiastically before announcing triumphantly,

'We're all waiting for the greatest pianist in Provence to play for us!'

'Am I, Papa?' she asks, 'Really? The best pianist in Provence?'

THE END

Printed in Great Britain
by Amazon

41193520R00162